HOPELESSLY ROMANTIC

OCEAN SHORES #1

BARBARA FREETHY

BARBARA
FREETHY
—BOOKS—

Fog City Publishing

PRAISE FOR BARBARA FREETHY

"A fabulous, page-turning combination of romance and intrigue. Fans of Nora Roberts and Elizabeth Lowell will love this book." — *NYT Bestselling Author Kristin Hannah on Golden Lies*

"Freethy has a gift for creating complex, appealing characters and emotionally involving, often suspenseful, sometimes magical stories." — *Library Journal on Suddenly One Summer*

"Barbara Freethy is a master storyteller with a gift for spinning tales about ordinary people in extraordinary situations and drawing readers into their lives." — *Romance Reviews Today*

"Freethy is at the top of her form. Fans of Nora Roberts will find a similar tone here, framed in Freethy's own spare, elegant style." — *Contra Costa Times on Summer Secrets*

"Freethy hits the ground running as she kicks off another winning romantic suspense series...Freethy is at her prime with a superb combo of engaging characters and gripping plot." — *Publishers' Weekly on Silent Run*

"PERILOUS TRUST is a non-stop thriller that seamlessly melds jaw-dropping suspense with sizzling romance. Readers will be breathless in anticipation as this fast-paced and enthralling love story evolves and goes in unforeseeable directions." — *USA Today HEA Blog*

"I love the Callaways! Heartwarming romance, intriguing suspense and sexy alpha heroes. What more could you want?" — NYT Bestselling Author Bella Andre

PRAISE FOR BARBARA FREETHY

"Gifted author Barbara Freethy creates an irresistible tale of family secrets, riveting adventure and heart-touching romance." NYT Bestselling Author Susan Wiggs on Summer Secrets

"Freethy skillfully keeps the reader on the hook , and her tantalizing and believable tale has it all -- romance, adventure and mystery." Booklist (Starred Review) on Summer Secrets

"A warm, moving story of the power of love." *NYT Bestselling Author Debbie Macomber on Daniel's Gift*

"Freethy's zesty storytelling will keep readers hooked, and the sisters' loving but prickly interactions will make anyone with a sibling smile." *Publishers Weekly on Summer Secrets*

"Freethy has a gift for creating complex, appealing characters and emotionally involving, often suspenseful, sometimes magical stories." — *Library Journal on Suddenly One Summer*

"Tragedy haunts her, regrets shadow him and passion lures them into a mystery as dangerous as their feelings for each other. Freethy captivates with a sensuous game of tainted hearts and tempting romance. My Wildest Dream is a hotbed of intriguing storytelling. Brodie and Chelsea are sure to get under your skin." Isha C – Goodreads

"I have just finished CAN'T FIGHT THE MOONLIGHT and WOW such an emotional story. Absolutely loved this book...and can't wait for the next one!" Booklovers Anonymous

HOPELESSLY ROMANTIC

CHAPTER ONE

"To your future...may it be everything you dreamed of." Ava Campbell lifted her champagne glass to the crowd gathered around the pool in the courtyard of the Ocean Shores apartment building in Oceanside, California. She smiled through teary eyes at her younger sister, Serena, who had married Brad Morrison several hours earlier, and was now ready to take off on her honeymoon.

Serena raised her glass in return as they exchanged a look filled with so many emotions it was impossible to define them all. It had just been the two of them for the last ten years. But now her sister had a husband, a man she loved. It was bittersweet. But this moment wasn't about her.

"To Brad and Serena," she finished.

"To Brad and Serena," the crowd echoed, clinking their glasses together and sending more happy wishes to the bride and groom.

It hadn't been the wedding reception Ava would have planned for her sister, but Serena had wanted to get married within two months of getting engaged, which had limited her options. Not that Serena had had any desire to have her reception anywhere but the courtyard where she and Brad had shared their first kiss seven months earlier.

Their love had happened so fast. Maybe too fast.

She worried that Serena had lost her mind in a dizzying spin of love and lust. She was only twenty-six years old. She didn't need to rush into marriage with a man she barely knew. But when she'd expressed her concern, Serena had only laughed and said everyone lost their mind when they were in love. That's what was so magical about it. And that she should try it sometime.

Magical was a word Serena had used a lot lately, ever since she'd left what she'd called her boring office job in Los Angeles and moved into this Oceanside building with a girlfriend. Within weeks, Serena was waiting tables at Maverick's Bar and Grill, which was only supposed to be a temporary gig while she looked for a more permanent job. But that plan went out the window when Serena had met Brad, who owned the bar with his brother, Tyler Morrison.

Ava should have come to Oceanside long before now to check up on her sister, but she'd never imagined her sister would fall in love so fast and change her entire life, a life that now didn't seem to include her. But as Serena walked over to her, a smile on her glowing face, Ava had to admit that her sister had never looked so happy.

Serena had changed out of her off-the-shoulder, gauzy wedding dress into skinny white jeans and a colorful crop top, her long brown hair flowing around her shoulders. She looked like the beautiful free spirit she'd always been. Not for the first time, Ava felt like the too-rigid, not-as-much-fun older sister, whose blonde hair and blue eyes were cool and off-putting, while Serena's dark looks were warm and friendly.

"Thank you for everything, Ava." Serena grabbed her hand and pulled her away from the crowd that had gotten louder as the margaritas and champagne had flowed.

The reception had been going on since five. It was now eight and time for Serena and Brad to head to the airport for their late-night flight to Paris, another dream coming true for her younger sister.

"I realize this was a lot of work for you," Serena continued. "But I knew if anyone could pull it off, it would be my big sister."

"I hope you won't regret not having something fancier."

Serena shook her head, not a trace of doubt in her brown eyes. "It was perfect. And it's not like I would have had that many people to invite to a bigger or more formal wedding."

She couldn't argue with that statement. Their parents had died when she was thirteen and Serena was ten. After that, they'd gone to live with their aunt and uncle who had been kind enough to give them a roof over their heads and food on the table. But she'd essentially been Serena's second mom, and they had always been incredibly close.

It would be difficult to let that closeness go, to make room for a husband. Just watching her sister move to Oceanside eight months ago had been hard, but she'd thought her sister would come back to Los Angeles, not get married and set up a life in a city two hours away from her.

"This was the perfect wedding," Serena continued. "I know you didn't understand why I wanted to have the wedding on the beach and the reception here by the pool, Ava, but Ocean Shores is home, and these people have become my family. Not like you, of course," she added hastily. "You're my first family; they're my second family. No one, and I mean no one, will ever replace you, Ava. You know that, right?"

"I wouldn't let Brad hear you say that." She blinked as moisture crept into her eyes and she tried to hold back the flood of emotion that was making her eyes water.

"Brad knows you're the first love of my life. I can't wait for the two of you to get to know each other better. I know you feel blindsided by our love and are worried about me, but it's right. I know it. I feel it."

The conviction in Serena's voice was unmistakable. "Then I'm happy for you. But I'm still going to worry because that's what I do best."

Serena laughed. "That's true. You are the best at worrying, but you don't have to be concerned. Brad is a good man."

"He does seem pretty great," she admitted. She'd only had a few conversations with Brad, but he'd assured her more than once that making her sister happy would be his top priority. She hoped that was true, but she thought they were both dazed by love.

"I guess it's time to say goodbye," Serena said. "Before I do, I want to thank you again for agreeing to stay in our apartment for the next ten days until we get back from Paris. Miss Daisy hates strangers, and if someone else was there, I'm not sure she'd ever come out of hiding long enough to eat. She barely tolerates Brad, and he's been sneaking her treats for months. But she loves you, and I'll be able to relax and not worry about her."

"I wouldn't say Miss Daisy loves me." The cat Serena had brought home five years ago had barely tolerated her for the time they'd lived together. Her sister's cat was finicky, snooty, and disdainful. She was much more likely to hiss than to purr at anyone who wasn't Serena.

"Of course she loves you. And I'm very grateful you can work remote. I know how impossible it is for you to take time off." Serena hesitated for a split second, as if she wanted to say something else, then shrugged and said, "I better make the rounds."

"Wait! Were you going to say something?" she asked, giving her sister a curious look. She'd always been able to tell when Serena was holding something back.

"No. Just goodbye."

Serena gave her a long, tight hug that reminded her of the key moments in their lives when they'd clung together, having only each other to hold onto. She had a feeling Serena was remembering, too.

"I love you, Ava," Serena said as they broke apart.

"I love you, too."

"And while you're here, don't be your usual standoffish self. Be friendly, talk to people, get to know my friends. You'll have a better time, I promise. And if you need anything, ask Josie."

"Don't worry about me. I'll be working most of the time."

"That's what I don't want you to do. You'll be living at the beach. Have some fun. And don't forget the hot guys in 12B. Max and Gabe are both very single."

She rolled her eyes. Serena had pointed out the two attractive men several times, but she wasn't interested in meeting anyone new, not when she would only be in town a short time. "The last thing I need is a man."

"Not if it's the right man," Serena said earnestly. "Love can change your life."

"I'll take your word for it. You should go. Don't worry about me or Miss Daisy. Just have fun."

"I will." Serena smiled again, and then moved away to join her new husband.

As she watched Serena and Brad say goodbye to their friends, she was reminded again of how far apart they'd grown. Serena had all these friends she didn't even know. She had somehow become the outsider in her sister's life, and that was a strange feeling. But life moved on, even if she didn't want it to. She'd learned that hard truth a long time ago.

She drained the rest of her champagne, thinking that maybe she'd get a little drunk tonight, which was not something she usually did, because she was the responsible one. But there was no one to be responsible for tonight. Serena was off, and she was alone.

Walking over to the table, she grabbed an open bottle of champagne and took it upstairs to the two-bedroom apartment she'd promised to house-sit for the next two weeks.

Miss Daisy immediately jumped off her perch on the back of the couch to skid into the larger of the two bedrooms and under the bed. She'd deal with her tomorrow. Her sister had already fed her and given her the medicine she had to take every night, so she didn't have to worry about the cat right now.

Drawing the blinds, she picked up the bottle of champagne she'd set on the coffee table and poured herself another glass. Then she sat down on the couch and kicked her feet up on the table. It had been a long day and an even longer couple of months since the beginning of Serena's whirlwind engagement. But all her duties were over now. She could relax and anything else could wait until morning.

Ava woke up with a start, not sure where she was for a moment, until she realized she'd fallen asleep on the couch in her sister's apartment. She didn't know what had woken her until she heard a thump outside the front door.

Jumping to her feet, she caught sight of the clock on the wall. It was after midnight, and someone was trying to get into the apartment. Her heart raced as she searched for a weapon, something to use to defend herself.

She ran toward the kitchen, but there wasn't time to find a knife. The front door was opening. She grabbed the broom and raised it as she ran back toward the man coming into the apartment.

It was too dark to see him clearly, but he was tall, with broad shoulders, and there was something glinting in his hand.

Oh, God! He had a gun!

She swung the broom at him as hard as she could, hoping to knock him down long enough for her to get out of the apartment.

He saw her at the last second and ducked. Her broom connected with the lamp by the couch, sending it against the wall so hard it shattered. As she attempted to take another swing at him, he caught the handle with one quick hand.

"What the hell are you doing?" he demanded.

She struggled to get the broom away from him, but he hung on to it.

"Get out of my apartment," she ordered, trying to sound as strong and forceful as she could, but he was much taller and stronger than she was.

"This isn't your apartment. It's Brad Morrison's apartment."

His words gave her pause. "You know Brad?"

"Yes. He gave me the keys so I could stay here while he was on his honeymoon."

"I'm staying here while Brad and Serena are away."

"That doesn't sound right. He said I could stay here and take care of his cat."

"Miss Daisy is Serena's cat, and Serena is my sister. I'm the one who's taking care of the cat and this apartment."

"Okay, it sounds like there's been a misunderstanding. If I let go of this broom, will you take another swing at me?"

Not one to trust easily, she thought about that for a second; then, she slowly nodded. He knew Brad, so he wasn't just a random burglar.

He let go of the broom. "How about I turn on a light? If I can find one you didn't break."

"There's a switch by the wall," she said.

He moved toward the door and flipped the switch, flooding the living room with the light from the ceiling, and she got her first real look at him. He was over six feet tall, with wavy brown hair and bright-green eyes that dazzled, along with the smile that slowly lifted his lips. He was probably in his early thirties and was tan and fit in worn jeans and a maroon T-shirt with the Maverick's Bar and Grill logo on it, the bar that Brad ran.

"Liam Nash," he said, holding out his hand.

"Ava Campbell." She moved the broom so she could shake his hand.

His warm fingers closed over hers, and she felt a tingle run down her spine.

"Nice to meet you, roomie," he said.

"We're not going to be roomies. I promised my sister I'd take care of her cat."

"And Brad promised me I could stay here until he got back. There are two bedrooms, right?"

"Yes," she said with a frown. "But I'm not going to share this apartment with you. You're a stranger."

"Think of me as a new friend," he said with an Australian accent that made her gaze narrow.

"I don't need a new friend," she muttered.

"Well, I don't have anywhere else to go tonight."

"How about a hotel?"

He turned around and walked out of the apartment.

For a moment, she thought she'd won the argument. Then he returned, pushing a large suitcase with a duffel bag resting on top into the apartment. Then he went back outside and brought in a long, thick case.

"Surfboards," he said at her confused look. He shut the door. "Since there are two bedrooms, I'm taking one. It really shouldn't be a problem for you." His smile dimmed, his accent thicker, as he added wearily, "And I have as much right to stay here as you do. I'm surprised your sister didn't tell you. I'm sure Serena knew."

She suddenly remembered the gleam in her sister's gaze, the way she'd hesitated as if she knew she should say something, but she didn't want to. She suspected Serena had known about Liam all along but knew she wouldn't like sharing the apartment with a stranger.

Serena probably hadn't wanted to say no to her new husband, so she'd let her be blindsided. Of course, looking at Liam, she was quite sure there was also the ulterior motive of forcing her to meet an attractive man.

"Where are you from?" she asked curiously.

"Sydney, originally."

"And tonight?"

"I just got off a plane from Hawaii that was delayed for seven hours, which is why I missed the wedding and got here so late."

"Do you live in Hawaii?"

"No. I was there for a surfing championship."

"You're a surfer." That wasn't surprising considering how tan he was, and she knew Brad liked to surf as well. "Did you win?"

"Came in second. Last wave took me down. But still a decent cash prize. How was the wedding?"

"It was beautiful."

"Good. I'm happy for Brad. He's crazy about your sister."

"The feeling is mutual. Look, I really think you'd be more comfortable in a hotel."

"I'm comfortable here, but you can leave." His glance moved toward the empty champagne bottle on the coffee table. "But maybe you shouldn't drive. Looks like you enjoyed the wedding."

"I am completely sober." Although she did have a headache threatening to rage. "And I can't leave; I have to take care of the cat. Miss Daisy needs medication every night."

"Then it looks like we're both staying. Which bedroom do you want? Never mind, I'll take this one," he said, heading toward the smaller room with the double bed. He gave her another wicked smile from the doorway. "See you in the morning. I'll make breakfast."

The door closed before she could sputter out an indignant answer. And then she heard the click of the lock.

He was locking her out! And there was not a damn thing she could do about it.

She walked over to the front door and made sure that the deadbolt was turned, which it would have been earlier if she hadn't fallen asleep on the couch after too many sips of champagne. Not that she had killed the entire bottle. It had been only half full when she'd grabbed it. But still, she should have locked up before falling asleep.

That would have been the smart, responsible thing to do, which was what she usually did, but this wasn't her usual life.

Maybe she'd made a mistake in agreeing to take care of Miss Daisy. Tomorrow she'd tell Serena that Brad's friend could handle the job, and she could go back to her nice, safe life, free of an incredibly good-looking surfer with a sexy Australian accent. He had trouble written all over him, and the last thing she needed was trouble.

CHAPTER TWO

LIAM WOKE UP WITH A GROAN, squinting at the bright sunlight flooding through the room. He should have closed the blinds last night, but he'd been exhausted. Rolling onto his side, he grabbed his phone off the side table. It was half past eight on Sunday morning. He rarely slept this late. Usually, he was on the ocean by seven, but he'd been overdue for sleep.

As he came completely awake, he heard sounds in the kitchen: clattering dishes and the whir of a coffee grinder. Maybe the noise was purposefully loud, he thought with a wince, a dull ache tightening in a band around his head. He'd banged his head pretty good on his last run. It still pissed him off that he'd blown his shot at the title. Not that he needed another trophy, but he needed to make as much money as possible, and first place was twice the amount of second. His days as a professional surfer were coming to an end. He was ready for more, but *more* required cash. Thankfully, he was close to having what he needed to take the last step.

As the grinder went off again, he got out of bed, pulling on jeans and a T-shirt before heading to the door. As he put his hand on the knob, he paused, knowing he couldn't storm into the kitchen and tell Ava to shut the hell up, even though that's exactly what he wanted to do.

She already didn't want him here and was probably trying to annoy him so he would leave. But he didn't want to waste money on a hotel room when he had more pressing things to do with his cash. He couldn't yell at Ava. He needed to work his charm. Women usually liked him. He didn't know why she'd had such a negative reaction. She'd probably just been scared by his arrival. She'd thought he was breaking in, and then her fear had turned to anger. He couldn't hold that against her.

On the other hand, the way she'd looked at him with cool, calculating blue eyes that had grown disdainful when she'd learned he was a surfer was hard to forget and something he could hold against her. She didn't know him at all, and she'd judged him within two seconds of meeting him.

He wouldn't have expected Serena's sister to be such a critical, snotty ice queen. She was nothing like her sister, that was for sure. Serena had brown hair and brown eyes, a free spirit, and a soft smile. Ava was a cold blonde, her eyes blue steel, and her body thin and hard, as if she put it through paces every day to make sure she was ready for whatever battle she was about to face.

He didn't want to be her next battle. He needed to make her a friend, even though that seemed like a monumental challenge at this point. But he needed to get on with it.

Turning the knob, he opened the door and headed across the living room into the kitchen, which was small and cluttered with Serena's collection of ceramic pig décor and Brad's penchant for leaving every box of cereal he might be interested in eating on the counter.

When Ava saw him, she started the grinder once more. He patiently waited, happy to get another look at her, to see if his first impression was wrong.

She'd changed out of her sophisticated silk cocktail dress from last night and wore shorts with a bright-orange tank top and running shoes on her feet. Her blonde hair was pulled into a ponytail, and it didn't appear she was wearing any makeup, not that she needed it. She was actually prettier than he remembered, in an edgy, I-might-kill-you-in-your-sleep kind of way. She would be a challenge to win over, but he liked challenges. Being faced with a tough obstacle was usually what excited him the most. It was certainly better than boring.

Finally, the grinder went off.

"Are you making coffee for the entire building?" he asked.

"Just for the next few days." She poured some ground coffee into the coffeemaker and pressed start. "I like to get organized on the weekends."

"What do you do during the week?"

"I work."

"At…"

"I'm a financial analyst for a venture capital company."

That sounded about right. He had a feeling she was more comfortable with numbers than with people—definitely nothing like her sister. "Do you like it?"

Her lips parted, but she didn't have an immediate response. Then she shrugged and said, "Of course I do. It's a good job."

"Doesn't sound like you love it."

"I like it. It pays well. And it can be interesting." She cleared her throat. "Anyway, I made some calls for you. There's a motel down the street. The available rooms look clean, and it has good reviews."

"Then you should go there. I'm not leaving."

"I can't leave. I have to take care of Miss Daisy."

His gaze swept the room. "Where is the cat anyway?"

"She's hiding under the couch now. I need you to leave so she'll come out and eat. She's afraid of strangers."

"I'm not exactly a stranger. I met her a few weeks ago when I was in town."

"You would still be a stranger. Trust me. Miss Daisy does not like many people. She barely tolerates Brad, from what Serena told me."

"I'm good with animals. I can take care of her if you want to go back to wherever you live." He paused. "Where do you live?"

"Los Angeles. But I promised Serena I would stay her and take care of the cat, and that's what I'm going to do. I never break my promises."

"What about your job?"

"I'll be working remotely for the next ten days." She paused, licking her lips. "Don't you have another surfing event to get to?"

"No. I'm actually looking into buying a business a few blocks from here."

Surprise ran through her blue eyes. He liked that he could challenge her view of him. Not that he should care what she thought.

"What kind of business?" she asked slowly, as if she wasn't sure she should express any interest in him.

"It's a retail store—the Beach Shack. It sells everything you need for a day at the beach, although it could offer more than it does. I have plans to grow the business. I just need to get the owner to sell. He said he was ready, but lately he seems slow to reply to me. It's probably nothing," he muttered, not sure why he'd told her that.

"Or it's something, and he's changed his mind. That could be a problem."

"I like to look at problems as challenges."

She rolled her eyes. "Oh, you're one of those."

"One of those?" he echoed.

"Always optimistic people, who think they can overcome everything with a positive attitude."

"Well, I'm not sure about everything. But a positive attitude usually goes further than a negative one." He paused, then added, "The owner of the store wants to move on. I've been talking to him for the past year. He's owned the store for more than thirty years and he's ready to retire. I think he's just feeling nostalgic, which is understandable. He wants to make sure I'll keep the store going so that his legacy lives on."

"Is that why you think he's stalling, because he's feeling nostalgic?"

He frowned. "I'm not sure. Brad mentioned to me that he thinks John, the owner, is having an issue with his wife, or his soon-to-be ex-wife, Maggie."

"What's the issue?"

"He wants to move back East. She wants to stay here."

"Sounds complicated." She reached for a coffee mug and filled it with coffee.

"Can I get in on that?" he asked hopefully.

She hesitated, then filled another mug and pushed it across the counter in his direction. "I hope you have a backup plan because the sale of this business seems fraught with problems, especially if there's a personal relationship involved. People can be incredibly stupid when it comes to love."

Her words dripped with cynicism. "You are nothing like your sister, are you?"

Her lips tightened. "Hopelessly romantic and always thinking Prince Charming is about to ride up on his white horse? No. I have never been attached to that fairy tale."

"Why not? Your sister found love. The fairytale came true for her."

"We'll see. Brad and Serena haven't known each other for even a year."

"It's not always about time."

"Maybe not, but I don't think the odds are in their favor."

"I'm guessing you always play the short odds."

"And you probably only play the long ones," she countered.

"Those bets are more exciting when they pay off." He sipped his coffee. "This is good."

"I brought the beans with me. I can't start the day without a good cup of coffee."

"Or a run?"

"Or a run," she agreed, pushing a sweaty strand of hair off her forehead. "I'm surprised you weren't on the ocean this morning. There were a lot of surfers out there."

"I'll get out tomorrow."

"Are you sure you can't just go to the motel?" she asked, sending a pleading look in her gaze.

He sighed. "I won't bother you, Ava. You do your thing, and I'll do mine. It's less than two weeks. We'll just be roomies."

She frowned. "Stop calling us that."

"Fine. How about coexisting apartment sitters? Brad can vouch for me. You can give him a call."

"I don't want to interrupt their honeymoon. They probably just got to Paris."

"Do you want something to eat?" he asked, opening the fridge. "There are eggs. I can whip something up. I did promise you breakfast, and I don't like to break my promises, either."

"I don't need any eggs."

"I won't hold it against you if you change your mind," he said, as she headed toward the door. "Or do you never change your mind, either?"

She ignored his question as she left the kitchen. A moment later, her bedroom door slammed. He smiled to himself. He really shouldn't enjoy getting under her skin so much, but there was something about her uptight, grumpy, cynical self that made him want to see if he could make her break free of all that rigidity. But that was probably one challenge he should walk away from.

———

Ava hoped a shower would clear her head and put her in a better mood. But as soon as she finished getting dressed and walked back into the living room and saw all of Liam's stuff, she got annoyed again. She couldn't believe she had to share the apartment with him, but he wasn't going to move, and she couldn't leave. They were at a stalemate.

Frowning, she returned to her bedroom. Despite not wanting to interrupt her sister's honeymoon, she couldn't resist sending her one specific question in a text—why hadn't she told her that Brad had given Liam a key and access to the apartment?

She was surprised when instead of getting a text back, her video app rang. She answered immediately, seeing her sister's happy face as she sat at a small table in some bustling Parisian square, a glass of wine in front of her.

"Paris is amazing," Serena gushed. "You would love it here, Ava. There's so much art and history. The clothes are amazing. The women are dressed so stylishly. The food is incredible, too. And being here with Brad is like the best dream I've ever had. I never imagined I could have a life like this."

"I'm glad you're having fun," she said, touched by her sister's heartfelt declaration. "But you should have told me about Liam. You knew he was going to stay here, didn't you?"

Serena flashed her a guilty look. "Yes. I'm sorry. It was a last-minute thing, and I didn't feel comfortable putting Liam in charge of Miss Daisy."

"You should have warned me. I almost knocked him out when he came into the apartment. I thought he was a burglar."

"Oops," Serena said with an apologetic smile. "But is it really a big deal? It's a two-bedroom apartment. He'll take the smaller room. You'll have the bigger bedroom with its own bath. You barely have to see him."

"That's not the point. He's a stranger."

"He's a great guy—and very attractive, don't you think?"

Her cheeks actually warmed at that question, which only made her frown again. "That doesn't matter."

"It could matter, if you'd open up your mind a little."

"He's a surfer. I'm a financial analyst. I don't think we have a lot in common, if anything."

"You never know. And surfing is what he does, but it's not all he is. You shouldn't be so quick to judge, Ava. Liam is smart. He's buying a business."

"Fine. I did judge him, but that's not important. I'm only going to be here for ten days. And then I'll be gone."

"Ten days is plenty of time for a fling. Seriously, you should consider it."

"I'm not interested in a fling."

"Why not? You could just have fun, not worry about anything long-term. Put your checklist away and live in the moment. Anyway, I have to go. Brad is waving to me that our table is ready. Please don't be mad at me. I won't be able to enjoy Paris if you're angry."

Seeing the plaintive plea in Serena's gaze, she did what she always did. She put her feelings aside to make her sister happy. "I'm not mad. It will work out. But you will owe me when you get back."

"Anything you want. How's Miss Daisy?"

"I'm trying to get her out for breakfast, but she's been hiding."

"I'm sure she'll be out soon. Don't forget to give her the medication tonight."

"I won't."

"Talk soon," her sister said. "Love you."

"Love you, too."

Her sister was so happy, she thought, as she hung up the phone. Serena deserved her fairy tale, so she would deal with the mess her sister had left behind, which was pretty typical. It was only for ten days. She could suffer Liam's presence for that long. She'd just stay out of his way, and hopefully he'd stay out of hers.

CHAPTER THREE

AFTER THE CALL with her sister, Ava walked over to the desk, which seemed to be more of a makeup table at the moment. She moved Serena's things to the side and then set up her computer so she could work. She was used to working weekends, and it seemed the best way to maintain her distance from Liam. But even with her door shut, she was distinctly aware of his presence.

For the next three hours, she heard him cooking breakfast, strumming Brad's guitar, groaning with every play made in some basketball game on TV, and talking on the phone to his friends. He seemed to have a lot of friends, all of whom wanted to meet up with him. While that fact suggested she might be able to get him out of her hair at some point, she grew more and more annoyed with his distracting presence. The walls in the apartment were paper-thin, and she was getting nothing done.

A glance out the window revealed that the pool area was quiet. Only one woman was sunbathing, with an e-reader in her hand. There were two empty tables under umbrellas. Maybe she'd work outside for a while. Grabbing her laptop, she left the bedroom and entered the living room just as Liam ended his latest call.

"You've been quiet. Did you fall asleep?" he asked.

"I've been working. And you have not been quiet. You have been very, very loud. Don't you and your friends believe in texting? Who talks so much on the phone anymore?" she grumbled.

"You don't talk to your friends?"

His cheerful smile irritated her even more. "We text, like normal people."

He shrugged. "I like to talk. And I thought I heard you on the phone earlier."

"That was Serena calling from Paris to tell me she was sorry she didn't tell me about you."

A smile lifted his lips. "Did you rip her a new one?"

"No. I didn't want to ruin her night. She's so happy." Pausing, she added, "Here's a thought… since you have so many friends around here, why don't you stay with one of them?"

"And give up this place with such a fun and flexible room-mate?" he joked. "Never."

"Fun and flexible has never been my thing."

"Really? Your sister is a lot of laughs."

"My sister has never had to worry about anything because I have always taken care of her. She got to have fun because I made sure that's all she had to do. Although, now I'm wondering if I should have forced her to be more responsible because she married someone she barely knows."

"Why did you have to take care of Serena? What about your parents?"

She stiffened, not wanting to talk about the past, but she'd opened herself up to that question. "They died when we were young."

"I'm sorry. Who took care of you after that?"

"We were raised by an aunt and uncle until we were old enough to be on our own. Or, I should say, until I was eighteen and old enough to take care of Serena."

"Eighteen isn't very old."

"I was legally an adult and my aunt and uncle wanted to move out of the country, so Serena moved into my off-campus apartment at my college, and we were on our own."

"That must have been difficult, going to college and taking care of a teenager. How old was Serena then?"

"Fifteen. She was in high school, and I had to make sure she got to school on time, did her homework, and didn't make too many stupid mistakes."

"That's a lot to handle. How old were you when your parents died?"

"I was thirteen and Serena was ten. It was a car accident," she said, suspecting that would be his next question.

"That must have been rough."

"I don't really want to talk about it anymore."

"Okay. By the way, Miss Daisy came out of hiding and ate the food you left her."

She was surprised to hear that. "Seriously? I thought she'd be hiding until you left."

"Apparently, she likes me better than you do," he said with a grin.

"Well, I'm glad she ate," she said, ignoring his comment. "She was probably starving. Anyway, I'm going to work outside."

"I can be quieter, Ava. I didn't realize I was bothering you."

"You didn't realize? I've been pretty clear that your presence is bothering me."

"True. But I can be quieter."

"Whatever. I could use some air." It wasn't really the noise he'd been making; it was just him. He was far too distracting with his great hair, sparkling green eyes, and sexy, lazy charm. He probably had a woman at every beach he'd ever surfed. Not that that mattered. She wasn't interested in him or in a fling, and she doubted she was even close to his type.

Stepping outside, she shut the door and forced her thoughts away from him. As she moved downstairs to the pool area, she realized how beautifully warm it was—seventy-five degrees and sunny in the middle of March, with the ocean less than a hundred yards away. She really should be happier about spending time here.

While she was used to warm LA weather, her downtown apartment was nowhere near the beach and her usual view was skyscrapers and parking garages, not palm trees, golden sand, and the deep blue of the not-so-distant sea.

As she walked into the pool area, the woman who had been reading by the pool was now stretched out on her back in a beautiful coral-colored bikini, her skin tan, her eyes closed. She'd met her briefly at the wedding reception. Her name was Kaia, and she was a paramedic.

Happy that Kaia was sleeping and she didn't have to engage in small talk, she settled in at the first table she came to and opened her computer. As a financial analyst, her job involved an extensive amount of research. She analyzed data for possible investments, looking at a company's history, the founder's experience, the capital investment already in play, and the company's product or service. It was somewhat interesting, but also could be frustrating when her reports weren't read, or her recommendations were ignored, she thought with a frown. But it was a good, stable job that paid well and gave her the security she craved.

She liked her paycheck, her retirement accounts, her ability to rent a decent apartment in a safe building—all things she had spent the past seven years, since her college graduation, trying to achieve. Having lost her parents so young and being dependent on the generosity of her aunt and uncle who had given them a roof over their heads but little else, she had wanted to make sure she could take care of herself and her sister. Although, it was no longer her job to take care of Serena, which was a fact she still hadn't fully come to terms with.

"Excuse me," a man said as he walked into the courtyard, wearing a delivery service uniform, a box in his hand. "I need a signature."

"Uh… For who?" she asked.

"Hunter Kane, Apartment 7A. No one answered the door. Can you sign?"

"I don't know him."

"I just need a signature, or it's going back to the sender," he said impatiently, handing her a pen and a clipboard.

"Okay, I guess so." She signed her name on the slip.

He dropped the box on the table in front of her and then jogged out of the courtyard. She stared at the package. She had no idea who Hunter Kane was. She didn't remember meeting him at the reception. All the residents had been invited because Serena had said that the Ocean Shores building had become her home and the tenants her extended family. But probably not everyone had been there.

She should just drop the box in front of his door, but the apartment was on the first floor and the courtyard was wide open. Anyone could come in and steal it.

Damn. She really shouldn't have signed for it. Now, she felt responsible. She'd have to hang on to it until Hunter returned home. She glanced over at Kaia again, who was still asleep. She hadn't woken up during her conversation with the delivery guy, or she just hadn't wanted to get involved, which was what she should have done—not gotten involved.

She returned her attention to her computer but several minutes later, a shadow crossed her screen, and she looked up at the annoyingly handsome face of her roommate. Liam had exchanged his jeans for a pair of swim trunks, and his tan, fit body sent an unwelcome thrill down her spine. He was hot as hell, and she was quite sure he knew that.

"Thought I'd go for a swim," he said, dropping his towel on the chair next to hers.

"Don't let me stop you."

He glanced at the package on the table. "What's that?"

"A delivery for someone who isn't home. The delivery guy needed a signature, and he was determined to get one from me. I probably should have said no because now I don't know what to do with it."

"Put it in front of the person's door."

"What if someone steals it before they come home? I feel responsible for it now."

He laughed. "I suspect you feel responsible for a lot of things."

"When I'm put in charge of something, I do. I just wish I wasn't the only one here or the only one who was awake," she added as his gaze moved to the sunbathing beauty. "Do you know Kaia?"

"No, but I'd like to."

"I'm sure," she muttered.

He laughed. "You're pretty, too, Ava."

Her lips tightened. "You don't have to say that, and I don't care who you ogle."

"I wasn't ogling," he denied. "Wait a second—what exactly is ogling?"

"Leering, staring…"

"I glanced in her direction for ten seconds. I've been looking at you longer than that."

At his words, she felt her cheeks warm. She might need a dip in the pool, too. "I should get back to work."

"How can you work on a beautiful Sunday like this?"

"I have a report due tomorrow. And you're keeping me from it."

"Got it." He stripped off his T-shirt, tossing it on the chair by his towel and giving her an up close and personal view of his broad chest and well-defined abs. "Now I know what you mean by ogling," he said with a knowing laugh. Then he took three steps and jumped into the pool, sending a spatter of drops in her direction.

At the splash, she saw Kaia stretch and open her eyes, coming into a sitting position as she saw Liam. A few minutes later, he was at the other side of the pool, and Kaia was introducing herself.

Well, that was just fine, she told herself. Now she didn't have to worry about him interrupting her.

She turned her gaze back to her computer, but the table of numbers barely held her interest. She was all too aware of what was going on across the pool.

At the sound of more voices, she lifted her gaze to see two older women walking toward the table. One of them was Josie Keller, the manager of the building. Josie was in her late sixties and was a vibrant, cheerful woman with dark-red hair and big brown eyes. She wore a colorful summer dress and platform sandals. According to Serena, Josie had been managing the building for thirty years and was the heart and soul of Ocean Shores.

She didn't recognize the second woman, who was of a similar age to Josie, but definitely a more conservative, paler shadow of Josie. She was dressed in a long skirt with a white knit shirt, with a big sun hat covering her white-blonde hair and very fair skin.

"Hello, Ava," Josie said, with a bright smile. "Are you enjoying your Sunday?"

"I am. How about you?"

"It's another beautiful day in paradise." Josie waved her hand toward the ocean waves crashing in the distance. From their vantage point, they could see the palm trees that surrounded this area of the beach as well as a sliver of sand and the shimmering ocean. "This is my friend, Maggie Peterman," she added. "She's staying with me for a few months. Maggie, this is Ava Campbell. Serena's sister."

"It's nice to meet you, Maggie."

"You, too," Maggie replied. "You're the financial wizard, aren't you? Your sister was raving about you the other day."

"I don't know about wizard, but I've always been good at math."

"I'm so sorry I missed the wedding," Maggie continued. "A

friend of mine's granddaughter had her first birthday yesterday, and I couldn't skip it."

"You missed quite a party," Josie said. "And while Serena is off to Paris, we're going to make sure that Ava has a good time." She gave Ava a pointed look. "Serena said you need to have more fun."

She frowned at the sparkle in Josie's eyes. "I have plenty of fun."

"Do you?" Josie challenged. "Looks to me like you're working. But don't you worry, you will have fun here, even if you're not looking for it."

"It's not that I don't want to have fun." She felt defensive and a little pissed off that her sister had set her up as some boring woman who worked all the time. Even though that was basically the truth.

"I have a gift waiting for your sister when she gets back," Maggie said, thankfully turning the conversation in a different direction. "I just love Serena and Brad together. They really complement each other. I have a good feeling about them." Maggie let out a small sigh. "But then, what do I know about love lasting forever?"

"It's never one person's fault," Josie said, giving Maggie a compassionate look.

"Sometimes, it feels like it is," Maggie replied with a heavy note in her voice, then turned to Ava. "I'm separated from my husband."

"I'm sorry."

"It's for the best." Maggie put on a forced, determined smile. "I spent years trying to please him. Now I'm going to start pleasing myself. Anyway, do you play bridge?"

"I don't."

"A smart girl like you will pick it up fast," Josie said. "And we need a fourth."

"But there are just two of you," she said, looking for an escape route from what felt like a longer break from her work than she wanted.

"Lexie will be here soon. Did you meet my niece yesterday? You're about the same age."

"I met her briefly. She was taking photos at the wedding."

"Yes. She's a former lawyer reinventing herself as a photographer, and I am cheering her on. She's only been here for three months, but she's already getting busy with parties and weddings," Lexie lives in the apartment next to mine, 2A.

"Event photography sounds fun," she said, although she actually thought it sounded like a nightmare, trying to wrangle kids and party people into the right shots.

"Lexie prefers nature and wildlife photography, but parties pay the bills. She's also helping me around here, although she thinks I need more help than I do. I've been managing this place for three decades."

"That's a long time."

"I've seen it all and done it all," Josie said, a twinkle in her eye. "I love newcomers. They keep things interesting. Now, let's play some cards. Lexie is a beginner, too, so it will be fun if you join us, Ava. What do you say?"

"I was actually working on a report."

Josie gave her comment a dismissive wave of her hand. "Oh, you can take a break. It's Sunday."

As Josie and Maggie settled in at the table, she had a feeling she didn't really have a choice, so she closed her computer.

"What's this?" Josie asked as she picked up the package.

"It's for someone in 7A. The delivery service insisted I sign for it. I guess the tenant wasn't home. Maybe you could give it to him."

"He's probably home and just didn't answer the door," Josie said, a somber look in her eyes. "Hunter Kane is a Marine helicopter pilot, recovering from an injury. He moved in three weeks ago, but no one has seen much of him, including me. When he moved in, he barely spoke. He looked angry, in pain, and completely unreachable. I'm hoping one day he'll open the door and see that he has support here if he needs it. But if it doesn't happen soon, I may have to give him a nudge."

"Let the man be," Maggie said. "He was in a helicopter crash. He lost some of his friends. He needs time."

"I know. But I've let him be for three weeks now. Sometimes people need a push."

Maggie sighed. "I know I can't stop you, but I'd give him more time."

Josie didn't answer as her phone chirped like a happy little bird. She looked down at it, then frowned. "Oh, no. Lexie is going to be late," she said with disappointment.

Ava was actually happy with that turn of events. Now, she wouldn't have to learn how to play Bridge.

Liam suddenly appeared at the table, his sculpted body dripping wet. He grabbed his towel off the chair, his green eyes glistening in the sunlight, making her stare far longer than she should have. But it wasn't his eyes she was looking at. The man had the tightest abs, the sexiest vee of dark brown hair running down his chest. And she was definitely not going to let her gaze go further.

"What's happening, ladies?" Liam drawled in an accent that made him impossibly sexier.

Josie perked up at his dazzling smile. "We want to play Bridge, and we need a fourth. What do you say?"

"I'm sure Liam does not know how to play bridge," she said hurriedly.

He dried off his body and then sat down at the table. "Actually, I do. Deal me in."

CHAPTER FOUR

LIAM KNEW Ava didn't want him to play cards with them, but she was no match for the excited persistence of Josie, who now had four for her card game.

While he didn't care at all about the upcoming game, he was more than happy to sit down at the table. He had been wanting to get to know Maggie Peterman better, and this was a great opportunity to do that. Maggie was John's soon-to-be ex-wife, and if she was holding up the sale of the store, he needed to figure out how to change her mind.

Maggie, however, looked even less thrilled than Ava to have him join their game, but Josie seemed oblivious to the tension as she dealt the cards.

"Maybe you can help Ava in this first round, Liam," Josie suggested. "You two will be partners, and Maggie and I will team up."

"Happy to," he replied, giving Ava a cheerful smile. He then explained that bridge was a trick-taking game, and the highest card wins the trick. As he gave her the basic strategy, she tried to pretend she was interested, but he could tell she hated having him explain anything to her.

"Let's just play a hand and see what happens," she interrupted. "And I can only play for a short time. I have work to finish."

He didn't want to tell her that bridge wasn't a game anyone played for a short time, but he'd let her discover that for herself.

The first three hands were rough, and they were solidly trounced by Josie and Maggie, but then Ava started to get a handle on the game, and her competitive drive kicked in. She was no longer just playing to make a couple of older ladies happy—she wanted to win. She wanted to prove she was as good as he was.

He liked how fast she caught on, how her sharp brain could calculate things quickly. She might not be great with people, but cards and numbers and wanting to win were clearly her forte.

When he was able to stop giving her so many instructions, he finally had a chance to talk to Maggie.

"I don't know if your husband told you, but I'm interested in buying the Beach Shack," he said.

"I'm aware," she said, not looking at all happy about it.

"That potential sale is a bit of a sore subject," Josie said, sending him a pointed look.

"I'm sorry. I didn't realize. John told me you were on board with him selling the Beach Shack."

"I don't care if he sells the store," Maggie replied. "John has worked hard for a long time, and he deserves time off. I just want him to retire in California, but he wants to move to Michigan, where his family is. He says the sales price won't bring us enough to live comfortably here. I suggested he re-evaluate."

His stomach dropped at that piece of information. John might be stalling because he wanted to see if he could get more money from another buyer so he could stay in Oceanside.

"I don't blame you, Liam," Maggie continued. "What John does after the sale isn't on you."

"Well, I would like it to work out for everyone," he murmured.

"I'm not sure that's possible," she replied. "But whatever business you have with John is between the two of you. I'm not a part of it."

"Who wants some cookies?" Josie interrupted with a bright smile. "I made some last night. I'll get them."

"I'll help you," Maggie said.

"Well, you definitely know how to clear a table," Ava said dryly. "So, let me get this straight. You're buying Maggie's husband's store, and Maggie and her husband have fought about that plan and their retirement options so much that she's moved into this apartment building after more than thirty years of marriage."

"But she just said she doesn't care about John selling the store to me."

"She does care about how much money John is going to make from the deal, because she wants to stay in Oceanside. You should be prepared to increase your offer."

"I can't do that. I'm at the limit. John and I have a verbal agreement. We've been discussing this for weeks. I'm giving him a deposit tomorrow."

"Sometimes it doesn't matter how long or how hard you work on something. It still may not happen. I've seen entrepreneurs practically kill themselves, bleed their bank accounts dry for a dream that just wasn't going to come true. And that's not my personal experience; it's my job."

"What exactly do you do again?"

"I research companies looking for financial investments from my firm. I evaluate their profit and loss potential, and I calculate the risk of investment."

"I don't suppose emotions come into play in your calculations," he said dryly.

"No. But sometimes…"

She ended her statement there, which was intriguing. "Sometimes what?"

"Sometimes, there's an intangible value I can't calculate, and that can be frustrating. I can see the owner's passion, hear the hunger in their voice, and I am touched by their desire, but the numbers don't add up. Or at least they don't add up enough to impress my bosses."

He was surprised she could see the intangible. He'd thought she would have only seen the numbers. "Do you ever suggest investments that don't get funded?"

"Yes. But not very often because I'd be fired if I brought them too many high-risk propositions. Sometimes even when I really believe in a company, I still can't make it happen. I don't have the power to make that decision."

"That must be frustrating."

"It is. I wish I had the money to do my own funding, but that will never happen."

"Never is a long time."

She shrugged, then cleared her throat, as if she regretted having said so much. "Anyway, you might want to have a backup plan. You should always have another option."

"Not if there's only one good option," he argued. "And I personally think having a safety net is what stops people from going after what they want. As long as they know they can't fall, they don't have to try as hard. But when everything is on the line…"

"You either succeed or come crashing down," she finished. "You would definitely not be someone my company would like as an owner."

"Why not? I'm bold."

"And probably reckless and driven by emotion. It's fine if you want to risk everything you have, but no investor will want to take the risk of crashing down with you. That's not how they make money."

"Thankfully, I don't need an investor."

"You might if John wants to drive the price up."

He frowned. "That's why I need to close the deal as fast as possible."

"Is it just the two of you involved? Are there lawyers? Financial advisors?"

"No advisors. John has a lawyer who will draw up the final papers, but he prefers to keep things between the two of us right now."

"What about you? You should have your own representation."

"John is a good man, and I'm smart enough to see if he's screwing me over. I'd rather save my money so that I have it available for refurbishing the store after I close the deal."

"Lawyers can be expensive but they can also save you money in the long run. You could get burned by a contract if you don't read it carefully, even if you are a smart guy."

"I'll read it carefully. I'm more worried about Maggie getting in the middle of this."

"She said she didn't want to be in the middle."

"I know, but I'm not sure I believe her."

Ava thought Liam had his work cut out for him. Despite his best efforts to charm Maggie during the second hour of their card game, Maggie maintained a cool distance. There was no further conversation about the store, but it felt like there was an undercurrent of tension that never went away.

She didn't know why she cared about his deal. She didn't know him. She wasn't his friend. And it sounded like he was willing to risk everything he had on the purchase of a retail business that might or might not be profitable. He could be headed for a big fall, and he was a man who didn't believe in a safety net.

That was stupid. Everyone needed a net or a backup plan. But she doubted Liam would listen to anyone's advice, especially hers. He had a vision, and he was going for it. There was a small part of her that admired his bold choice, but watching the way Maggie was interacting with him told her he had problems ahead.

She didn't need to be concerned about those problems. Unfortunately, she was prone to worry, even about people who meant nothing to her. That was a habit she needed to break.

As they were wrapping up the last hand, Josie's niece, Lexie Price appeared. Lexie wore a denim miniskirt with a yellow print top, her brown hair falling around her shoulders in a pretty cascade of waves. An apology ran through her brown-eyed gaze.

"Sorry, Aunt Josie," Lexie said. "The birthday party went on and on. I couldn't leave."

"Oh, it's fine," Josie said. "As you can see, we found players. Do you know Liam and Ava?"

"I met Liam the last time he was here," Josie said, sending Liam a smile, before turning to her. "And Ava and I met at the wedding yesterday. Although, we didn't get to chat. Hopefully, we can do that soon."

"Hopefully," she murmured.

"In fact," Lexie continued. "Why don't you come to Maverick's tonight? It's Tyler's birthday. Drinks and apps are on the house from six to eight, courtesy of Brad, who won't be there to help his brother celebrate, so we all promised to go."

"Uh, I don't know," she said hesitantly. A party at a bar with people she didn't know didn't sound appealing.

"You should definitely come, Ava," Lexie persisted. "You and Tyler are family now. In-laws."

"That's true, I guess." She hadn't really thought about it, but Brad was her brother-in-law, and Tyler was Brad's brother. That connected them in some way, not that she thought Tyler would care if she came to his birthday party or not.

"We could go together," Liam offered, a mischievous gleam in his eyes. "That way you won't have to go into the bar alone, Ava."

"That's perfect," Lexie said. "Because I have to stop and pick up some cupcakes on the way. I'll see you both there. And sorry again, Aunt Josie, but no cards for me today. I have to edit some photos."

"No worries. We've already played for a couple of hours," Josie replied.

As Lexie left, Ava got to her feet, eager to make her own exit. "I'm going to head upstairs. Thanks for the game. It was fun."

"We'll catch you another time," Josie promised. "You'll have even more fun the second time around."

She gave Josie and Maggie a smile, then grabbed her computer and walked away from the table. She wasn't completely surprised to find Liam catching up to her at the bottom of the stairs. She couldn't seem to shake him.

"You caught on quick today," he said approvingly. "Although, you did have a good teacher."

She ignored that as she moved up the stairs.

"So, will you come to Maverick's tonight?" he asked, staying right on her heels.

"I should work. I just blew off half the afternoon."

"Well, the day isn't over yet. Why not work for two hours, and then we'll go down to the bar?"

"I can go to the bar without you," she said as she reached the apartment door.

She was about to pull out her key when he said, "It's unlocked."

"You didn't lock it when you came down?"

"I was just going to the pool, and I didn't think I'd be gone this long."

"Great," she muttered, turning the knob. "You're annoying and irresponsible."

"It's not a big deal. I could see the door from where I was sitting. And it's the middle of the day. You worry too much, Ava."

"Clearly, you don't worry at all, but while you're staying here, I'd appreciate it if you'd lock the door when you leave."

"Yes, ma'am."

His cocky, amused response only irritated her more and made her feel like she was in the wrong, when she wasn't. She walked into her bedroom and shut the door.

But while she could keep him out of her room, keeping him out of her head was going to be a lot more difficult.

CHAPTER FIVE

IT WAS AROUND six on Sunday evening when Liam heard Ava moving around in the kitchen. She seemed to be talking to the cat, trying to tempt her out of a hiding spot. He smiled to himself. He could help her, but he'd see just how good she actually was with Miss Daisy.

He got up from the bed and stretched his arms over his head. He'd taken a nap and then worked on his business plan, giving Ava what she probably thought was much-needed space.

Despite her prickly attitude, playing cards with her had been more fun than he'd expected. She'd been quick to catch on, very strategic, and highly competitive. For a while she'd forgotten how irritated she was by him and had shown him a different side of herself. That side had disappeared as soon as they'd returned to the apartment. But he was hoping they could come to some sort of amicable truce so that the next ten days weren't tiringly uncomfortable.

As he picked up his notepad and set it on the dresser, his mind turned to his upcoming meeting with John. Hopefully, tomorrow he could hand John his deposit, and they could set up a time to meet with John's attorney and close the deal. But he suspected he was being too optimistic. Maggie's attitude toward the sale was troubling. She had been perfectly pleasant during the card game, but she'd also made it clear she thought John should sell the store for more money so they could stay in Oceanside. If John was out looking for other buyers, his deal could be in jeopardy.

A sudden crash sent him quickly to the door. He walked out of the bedroom and into the kitchen. A container of Cheerios was on the ground with cereal spread across the floor. Ava was on her knees, looking at the opening between the stove and the refrigerator. "It's okay, Miss Daisy," she said in a pleading voice. "We're friends, remember?"

"What's going on?" he asked.

She shot him a dark look, her face flushed. "I need to give Miss Daisy her medicine, and I thought I had her, but she jumped out of my arms and knocked over the cereal, and now she's managed to squeeze herself into this narrow space."

He moved across the kitchen and looked over her shoulder, seeing Miss Daisy giving them both a scoffing look as if they were crazy to think she was going to come out just because they asked nicely.

"Maybe you should give her time and space," he suggested. "She won't come out now, especially with you blocking her escape route. She'll be more determined to stay put."

She frowned, then got to her feet and backed away. "I was just checking to see if she was okay. I know she likes her space."

"Seems to run in your family," he said dryly. "Although Serena never seems to need to be alone."

"Serena loves people and noise," Ava agreed. "She could never do her homework when it was quiet. There had to be a TV on or music playing. She couldn't stand being the only one at home. She always wanted me to be there or to have friends over. She thrives on being in a group."

"It sounds like you two have very different personalities."

"In many ways," she admitted.

"But you're still close?"

"As two sisters could be. Unfortunately, that will change now."

"Why?"

"Because she's married. She has a husband; she needs to put him first. She'll probably have kids soon, a family of her own."

He could hear the uncertainty in her voice and realized that while Ava might like to present herself as a strong, independent woman, she still needed at least one person, and that was her sister. "I'm sure your relationship won't change that much."

"How would you know? Do you have a sibling who has recently gotten married?" she challenged.

"No. I'm an only child. So, my advice is probably worth nothing."

"Exactly. I'm sure Serena will try to stay in touch. We'll both do that. But we live two hours apart, and I saw what happened over the last eight months. She was having so much fun with Brad, she hardly ever answered her phone. Life changes, and I need to change with it. I'm just going to miss her."

He found himself wanting to comfort her, but he had no idea how to do that, especially since she was barely tolerating his presence. He certainly couldn't give her a hug, which he thought she desperately needed. She was obviously missing her sister and the close relationship they'd had, but she'd probably punch him in the face if he tried to put his arms around her.

If he couldn't cheer her up, maybe he could do something else that was helpful. He opened a few cupboard doors, looking for one specific item.

"What are you doing?" she asked. "I need to clean up the cereal before you step all over it."

"Hang on. There will be time for that." He pulled out a can of tuna. "This is what we need."

"Why? Are you going to make a sandwich?"

"I'm going to get Miss Daisy out of hiding." He opened the drawer and took out a can opener. When he got the lid off the can, he scooped a chunk of tuna out on his finger. Then he turned to Ava. "Do you mind backing up, maybe to the doorway? I want her to feel like she can come out."

Ava frowned. "Why don't I try to feed her the tuna? She knows me better than you. Although, I don't think it's going to work."

"It's worth a shot. Since I have a more positive attitude, let me try first."

"Fine. Go for it."

As she backed into the doorway, he slowly lowered himself to the floor and sat down so the cat could see him. He wasn't blocking her exit. She could easily come out since he was off to the side. He extended his hand at the opening, showing her the tuna. He remembered Serena doing this the last time he'd been in the apartment, and it had worked. Of course, he wasn't Serena, so Ava might turn out to be right about his plan, but he was hoping she'd be wrong.

Nothing happened for a long minute.

"It's not working," Ava said.

"Give her some time," he said softly. He didn't look at the cat, but he spoke in soothing tones. "You must be hungry, Miss Daisy, and you need to take your medicine so you can stay well. We have to get some food into you before we do that. Just come out and get the tuna." He waited another minute before trying again, keeping his voice soft and reassuring. He could see Ava impatiently shifting her feet, ready to call it all a failure.

And then, somewhat surprisingly, the cat moved forward.

As Miss Daisy slid toward him, he moved his hand just out of reach so she would have to leave her hiding spot if she wanted the tuna.

A few more stops and starts that seemed to go on for almost ten minutes, and then she was all the way out. She gave him another wary look before licking the chunk of tuna off his finger.

When pieces of it fell to the floor, she went after that next, and that's when he put his arms around her and pulled her into his body. She squirmed a bit, but she didn't try to bite or scratch him.

"That's a good girl," he said, gently stroking her. "I bet you want more food now, don't you?"

Ava brought the rest of the can of tuna over and he put it on his thigh so he could hold on to the cat while she ate.

"Do you have the medicine?" he asked Ava.

"I'll get it." She moved to the fridge and pulled out a bottle, then measured some medicine into an eyedropper.

As Miss Daisy finished eating, Ava moved quietly toward them and slowly sat down next to him. He stroked the cat a few more times as she cleaned the can, and then he grabbed her scruff with one hand, holding onto her body with the other.

"Give it your best shot," he told Ava.

"My sister put the dropper in the corner of her mouth," Ava said as she attempted to duplicate that action.

The cat started to squirm, but Ava got the dropper into her mouth with stubborn determination and managed to get most of the medicine down her throat.

When she was done, the cat charged away, running from the room as fast as she could.

Ava blew out a breath. "Thank goodness that's done. I feel like I could use a drink."

He smiled at her. "Then come to Maverick's with me." He could see the instant refusal charge into her eyes. Before the words left her lips, he added, "There will be food there. And there's not much to eat here. You don't want to shop and then cook, do you?"

"Not really," she admitted.

"You can have a drink, some food, meet your sister's friends, and then come back and work until midnight."

"I met some of her friends yesterday at the wedding."

"I'm guessing you didn't get to know them well. I'm sure you were running around with Serena."

"I was," she admitted. "Okay. I'll go for one drink. It's not far, is it?"

"Three blocks away. It's a nice walk."

They got up, and he dumped the empty can of tuna in the trash bin.

"I hope feeding Miss Daisy the tuna was okay," she said. "My sister wanted me to only give her cat food."

"Well, I saw Serena give her tuna when I was here a few months ago. She said Miss Daisy couldn't resist it, and it worked great when they had to give her medicine."

A frown crossed Ava's face. "You could have said that earlier, Liam."

"I told you the plan."

"But not where you got your information," she said pointedly.

"So, if Serena had told you it would work, you would have believed her?"

"Yes," she said quickly, then shrugged. "Okay, maybe not. My sister has as many bad ideas as she has good ones. But I would have been more amenable to trying it." She paused. "I have to say, you were good with Miss Daisy. She somehow trusted you. I've never seen her sit on anyone's lap besides Serena's, and that cat lived with me for five years."

"I don't know if it was trust or hunger," he said dryly. "But the important thing is she got her medicine and her food. Time for us to do the same. And by medicine, I'm thinking an icy-cold beer."

"That sounds perfect."

He raised his brow. "It does? Are you seriously going to tell me you're a beer drinker?"

"Yes. You really shouldn't judge people so quickly," she said, giving him a smart-ass look that he actually found rather endearing.

"Look who's talking," he said dryly.

"I need to clean up the cereal before we go," she said, grabbing the broom.

She was definitely a responsible person." I'll help," he said, getting the dustpan. "Then we can get out of here."

CHAPTER SIX

MAVERICK'S BAR and Grill was a one-story, large, rustic wood building situated on a bluff overlooking the ocean. There was a parking lot next to Maverick's where a food truck was cooking up something that smelled delicious. In fact, there was a line of ten people waiting to order.

"Maybe we should stop there first," she said, her stomach rumbling. She hadn't eaten lunch, and she was starving.

"Gabe fulfills taco orders from inside the bar, too. He's friends with Tyler and Brad. He lives at Ocean Shores with Max."

"Right. He's one of the hot guys in 12B."

He laughed. "I can't speak to their hotness, but I can tell you that Gabe is an aspiring restaurateur with a food truck, and Max is a bartender by night and a screenwriter by day."

"I'm sure Max has a tremendous amount of competition in the world of screenwriting. And restaurants are often the most likely business to fail in the first year. They both have their work cut out for them."

"I'm sure, but they're very determined. They're also both single, if you're interested."

"I'm not," she said quickly. "I just referred to them as the hot guys in 12B because that's what Serena called them."

She actually thought any man was going to seem a little cool when compared with Liam. He was very attractive, with a sexy accent and a tempting smile. She had a feeling he didn't have to do more than flash that smile to get a woman to fall at his feet. But she certainly wasn't going to do that. She was looking for more than physical attraction. She wanted to feel an emotional and intellectual connection, although that seemed impossible to find. Not that she'd spent much time looking lately.

She forced those thoughts out of her head as they neared the entrance to Maverick's. The front door was framed by colorful surfboards with autographs scrawled all over them. "Are these signed by famous surfers?" she asked Liam as she paused by the boards. "Hey, wait, is that your name?"

"Yes. I'm one of the famous surfers."

She gave him a questioning look. "Are you really famous?"

"In the surfing world, not so much outside of it."

"Can you make a lot of money as a surfer or is just something you do for fun?"

"It can be both fun and profitable if you're at the top of the game."

"Should I assume you are?"

He shrugged. "You don't care, do you? Let's go inside and get those beers."

He was right; she didn't really care. But as she followed him into the bar and grill, she wondered if he was being modest, or if it didn't take much to be famous enough to sign a surfboard outside of a bar.

Maverick's seemed loud and busy for a Sunday night. All the tables were full and there was a line at the bar. Two big-screen televisions on either end of the room were on, one playing a surfing competition, the other a basketball game. There was a definite beach vibe to the bar with surfboards hanging on the walls, as well as photos of surfers and banners from surfing competitions all over the world.

"This must feel like your mother ship," she said to Liam.

He grinned at her comment. "I never thought of it that way, but you're right. It's definitely a bar for surfing enthusiasts."

"If the business you want to buy is nearby, you could probably do joint promotions with this bar, like discount coupons to be used here if they buy merchandise from you or vice versa. Since you know Brad, I'm sure you could work something out. Maybe you could sponsor some local surfing competitions, too."

"I am interested in doing all those things. I just have to make the deal happen." He urged her toward a hallway. "I think our group is on the smaller private patio."

She hadn't realized there were two patios but as they walked down the hall, she saw one door leading to a crowded patio filled with tables and heaters and another more private area that overlooked the ocean.

The smaller patio was lined on two sides with a white lattice fence for privacy and an overhang to protect the area from the wind. There were six people sitting at one of two long tables. She quickly recognized Tyler Morrison, Brad's younger brother. Tyler had blond hair and blue eyes, a square frame and a stocky build. Next to Tyler was Kaia Mercer, the beautiful redhead from the pool. She was laughing at something Tyler had just said to her. Next to Kaia was a petite blonde with a lightly freckled, fair complexion and hazel eyes.

Across from the blonde was one of the hot guys from 12B who Serena had pointed out to her yesterday—Max Donovan. He had hair so brown it looked almost black, and he had striking light-blue eyes. He was engaged in conversation with the woman next to him, Lexie Price.

When Tyler saw her, he jumped to his feet to offer her a welcoming smile and a chair next to Max.

"Ava," he said. "I'm glad you came."

"Happy birthday, Tyler."

"Thanks." Tyler grabbed Liam's hand and gave it a shake. "Good to see you, Liam. Missed you yesterday. How did the competition end up?"

"First loser," Liam replied.

"I think they call that second," Tyler said with a knowing smile.

"Same thing."

"You're too hard on yourself."

"I could have won. I just messed up the last run."

"You can't be perfect all the time. I thought you were done competing."

"The possibility for cash was too tempting to pass up while I'm waiting for John Peterman to close our deal."

"How's that going?" Tyler asked.

"I'll know more tomorrow." Liam turned to her. "Do you know everyone, Ava?"

It was thoughtful of him to ask. "Not everyone," she murmured, feeling a little awkward as Liam's question turned all gazes on her.

"Sorry, let me introduce you," Tyler said. He waved his hand toward the redhead. "This is Kaia Mercer. She's a paramedic and can tell you some truly gruesome stories."

"But I won't," Kaia said, giving her a friendly smile. "Not until we know each other better. I saw you at the pool earlier. You made a rookie mistake."

"What was that?" she asked, surprised by her words.

"Getting suckered into one of Josie's bridge games. You always need a ready excuse."

"I'll keep that in mind."

"Josie stopped asking me," the woman next to Kaia said. "She finally realized how bad I was."

Kaia laughed. "But then you made another rookie mistake, Emmalyn. You expressed interest in yoga, and now you have to learn the downward dog."

"Well, it's better than cards," Emmalyn said. "I'm Emmalyn McGuire from 15B. I'm a kindergarten teacher at Ravenswood Elementary."

"It's nice to meet you," she said. "I saw you both at the reception, but we didn't have a chance to speak."

"You were busy with Serena." Emmalyn tipped her head to the man across from her. "Max—did you meet Ava yesterday?"

"For a split second," Max said, his eyes warm and friendly. "Have you heard from Serena and Brad?"

"Yes. They are loving Paris."

"I would have expected nothing less."

"And I already met Ava. In fact, I told her to come," Lexie interjected with a happy smile. "I'm so glad you did."

"I appreciate the invitation."

"What can I get you both to drink?" Tyler asked. "I've got a new IPA, Liam, if you're interested."

"Sounds good. Whatever you recommend."

"Ava?" Tyler asked.

"Whatever you're getting for Liam is fine with me."

"That's easy."

As Tyler headed into the bar, she and Liam sat down across from Emmalyn and Kaia. Kaia immediately engaged Liam in conversation, which was fine with Ava. She was happy to talk to Emmalyn, who Serena had described as a real sweetheart.

"Serena told me you have a very important job," Emmalyn said.

She had to smile at that. "Not really. I'm a financial analyst for a venture capital firm."

"What does that entail?"

"I research companies, mostly start-ups, and then write reports on whether my financial group should invest in them."

"That sounds interesting."

"It can be. But probably not as exciting as kindergarten."

Emmalyn grinned. "Five-year-olds can be very dramatic. Sometimes it's more babysitting than teaching, but I love my students. They're so innocent and open to ideas. It's fun to watch them learn and experience new things, to nurture their interests, give them support and build their confidence. Children really need adults in their lives who can give them that." A dark note entered her voice that made Ava wonder if Emmalyn was talking about more than just her students—maybe herself.

"It sounds like you are a great teacher," she said.

"I'm still learning. I got my credentials only two years ago. I'm not super experienced, but every year I hope to get better. I'm grateful to have a job that I care about. And I just love kids, even with their tantrums and meltdowns."

"I've run into tantrums and meltdowns at my job," she said dryly. "And not from five-year-olds."

Emmalyn laughed. "Well, you know that old saying—everything you need to know, you should have learned in kindergarten."

"I don't think that's true," Lexie said, interrupting their conversation. "I learn new things all the time. And I'm sure Max does, too. Weren't you researching poisons the other day?"

"I was," Max replied. "But you didn't need to tell Ava that. She'll think I'm up to no good." He gave her a mischievous smile.

"I heard you were a screenwriter," she said. "I'm betting that was research."

"Which is exactly what you should tell the cops if they ever come asking."

"Unless you're planning to poison someone in the next ten days, I don't think I have to worry about that."

"You would be the last person anyone would suspect of poisoning someone, Max," Lexie said. "Now, Gabe…"

Max laughed. "Don't let Gabe hear you say that. He prides himself on not poisoning anyone."

Lexie grinned back at him.

The two were in such sync, Ava wondered if there was something going on between them, although they weren't touching in any way. They could just be friends.

"I love how both you and Gabe are going after your dreams," Lexie said. "I'm a little late to that party, but I feel inspired by the two of you." Her gaze moved to Ava's. "I used to be an attorney, but after three years of law school and three years of working eighty-hour weeks at something I didn't even like, I finally found the courage to quit a few months ago."

"So, now you're going after your dream, too, as an event photographer?"

"The events pay my bills, but what I really want to photograph is nature and wildlife, as well as humanity around the world. I'd like to travel and go to places that are hard to reach and bring back photographs that people have never seen before. There are still places in the world that are almost completely untouched by civilization. I just have to get myself there."

"You will," Max said. "It's one step at a time. I have to write the beginning before I can attack the middle. So do you, Lexie."

"But you could write out of order," Lexie said.

"I could, but it wouldn't make sense, and I'd have to rewrite it anyway."

"I suppose. I've never been a patient person," Lexie continued. "But I am learning patience, especially when I have to get a two-year-old to smile along with her parents and siblings. That can take a good hour and sometimes it doesn't even happen."

She laughed at Lexie's disgruntled expression, appreciating how very down-to-earth she was. Lexie had big dreams, but she was still working it all out.

She sat back in her seat as Tyler dropped off beers for her and Liam. She took a long sip from the frosty glass, pleased with the taste of the IPA. She had been needing this drink for a while, and it hit the spot.

As the conversation flowed around her, she got a better feel for the individual personalities. Kaia was sharp and sarcastic. Emmalyn was sweet and a bit naïve. Max was funny and self-deprecating but also creative and outgoing. Lexie liked to talk and was quick to join in every conversation. She was extremely smart and well-read, able to articulate discussions about current events more than any of the others. Tyler was still an enigma to her. He and Liam spent a lot of time talking about surfing and the bar, but she couldn't quite get a read on Tyler. He seemed to be the kind of man who kept a lot of things inside.

One thing that resonated with her was how passionate they all were. They each seemed to be chasing a dream or living their dream, which made her wonder what the hell she was doing.

She had a good job, but it wasn't a dream. It wasn't a nightmare, either. It was just okay. But it paid well, and security was important to her. Dreams were fine, but being able to support herself was worth more than some pie-in-the-sky vision. Not that she'd ever really allowed herself to dream. Instead, she'd worked hard and set attainable goals. Now all that hard work and moving slowly up the career ladder seemed boring, certainly not awe-inspiring.

Max was creating stories from nothing. Lexie wanted to capture the whole wide world on film. Kaia was saving lives, and Emmalyn was educating the next generation. Even Liam, the hot surfer guy, wanted to own something that was his, create a business for himself.

Frowning, she told herself not to get carried away. She had a good life. And maybe there weren't the extreme highs, but there also weren't the despairing lows. There was something to be said for that.

When a couple of waiters dropped off plates of nachos, she dug in, happy to eat, and she wasn't the only one suddenly starving. The plates were emptied in a matter of minutes, with Tyler signaling the waiter to bring another round.

While they were waiting for more food, Kaia suddenly turned an assessing gaze in her direction. "So, what do you think of Ocean Shores, Ava?"

"It's great. Everything my sister told me and more."

"What did she tell you?" Kaia asked curiously.

"Serena said she'd never lived any place that was as friendly and welcoming as Ocean Shores. She didn't just find a wonderful place to live, she found friends, a second family." She was still a little bitter that Serena had felt the need to have a second family, but she was beginning to see where her connections had come from.

"It is amazing how well we all get along," Kaia said. "Well, most of us anyway. There are some holdouts, people who have moved in that we don't know at all."

"Like who?" she asked.

"There's a new guy named Hunter Kane in 7A," Emmalyn interjected. "Josie told me he's a Marine who was injured in a helicopter crash. I caught a glimpse of him when he moved in. He's probably early thirties, but he was hobbling on a cane, and he had an expression that screamed don't talk to me. Kind of a scary-looking guy."

"Who is probably in pain," Kaia said. "We can give him some time. But there's also a woman on the first floor in 6A, next to Hunter Kane, who no one has ever seen. All we know is that her name is Elisa Navarro."

"And her apartment is always dark during the day," Emmalyn continued. "But once when I got up in the middle of the night, I saw lights moving through the apartment like someone had a flashlight on."

"That's weird," Lexie said. "Did you tell my aunt about that?"

"Well, no. What would I say? Do you know anything about that woman, Lexie?" Emmalyn asked.

"Aunt Josie said a corporation pays her rent. I think she met Elisa when she moved in but hasn't had any contact with her since. She's left her notes a few times about cocktail parties and barbecues, but she never responds."

"Maybe she just wants to live in peace without being gossiped about," Tyler suggested dryly. "You three are bad."

"Or maybe she's up to something nefarious," Max put in. "The moving lights in the middle of the night is very interesting. You almost make me want to stay up just to check them out, Emmalyn."

"I don't know if it was just that one night," Emmalyn said.

"I'm glad I don't live in the building," Tyler interjected. "Or you'd all be talking about me."

"Only if you were doing something interesting," Kaia said with a laugh. "Does that ever happen, Tyler?"

Tyler smiled in return, but he didn't seem that amused by her comment. "No. I'm boring as hell, and grateful not to be in your gossip mill."

"It's not just gossip," Emmalyn defended. "We genuinely care about the people living in the building, Tyler. We want to be good neighbors."

"That's what Ocean Shores is about," Lexie agreed. "Aunt Josie has told me lots of stories about how the apartment building has literally saved people, starting with herself."

"What do you mean?" Ava asked.

"My aunt was a film star in the seventies and had a turbulent romantic life," Lexie said. "I don't know all the details, but after a scandalous divorce that also sabotaged her acting career, Josie moved to Ocean Shores. She started over and fell in love. She even got engaged, but the man she was seeing suddenly disappeared one night, and she was alone again. However, her friends at Ocean Shores rallied around her. A year later, she was feeling better and taking over as the building manager. That was thirty years ago. She still loves running things."

"Managing an apartment building must have been a big step down after being a movie star," Ava said.

"I think she was burned out. Josie said she wanted a real life." Lexie paused. "I also believe she originally stayed because her fiancé disappeared, and she thought he might come back. But then, she was happy to have stayed and built a family around her. I can't tell you the number of former tenants who keep in touch with her. She's a godmother to more than eight kids and has officiated a bunch of weddings, including Serena's. She was touched that Serena asked her, Ava."

"Josie did a good job," she said. "Josie made the wedding feel personal, which was what Serena wanted."

Lexie nodded. "Aunt Josie loves to bring people together. She says that Ocean Shores is a place for people to find themselves, get a new start in life, or discover a family they never expected. That's why she likes to put on so many good neighbor events, so we all get to know each other."

"Which I love," Emmalyn said. "When I first moved in last year, I didn't know a soul, and now I feel like I have so many friends."

Emmalyn's words echoed the ones that Serena had said to her. There definitely was something about the building that made people love living there.

It would be strange to go back to her apartment in LA, where she'd only spoken to one of her neighbors in five years of living there, and the other tenants she'd barely seen in passing.

On the flip side, no one was gossiping about her.

Or maybe she wouldn't know if they were talking about her.

She doubted the mysterious woman or the injured soldier had any idea they were the subject of discussion. On the other hand, she was nowhere near as gossip-worthy as either of them.

"Do you want another beer?" Liam asked, tipping his head toward her empty glass.

"Yes," she said.

He gave her a knowing smile. "Feeling overwhelmed?"

"A little. But everyone is nice. I'm just not used to people caring so much about their neighbors."

"Me, either," he said, surprising her with his words.

"Really?"

"I've moved around a lot in my life. And while I like making friends, I don't always stay long enough in one place to keep them."

"You like making friends?" she asked. "It always seems difficult and exhausting to me."

"Why?"

"So many questions. So much time spent trying to find something in common. So much judgment."

"I suspect you judge yourself more harshly than anyone else, Ava, and that I can relate to."

"I bet you can—first loser," she said pointedly. "You don't really think of second place like that, do you?"

"If I don't win, then I've lost."

"But you came close."

"Doesn't matter. Close isn't good enough. I want the win."

"So do all your competitors."

"Which makes the victory all the sweeter when I come out on top," he said. "I want to go against everyone when they're at their best. There's no point in competing otherwise." He paused. "You like to compete, too. I saw it when we were playing cards."

"Maybe a little."

"More than a little. And you also like to win. It's part of the control thing you have going on."

She frowned at his comment but could hardly deny that she liked to be in control. When she was in charge, she could get exactly what she wanted, but when she wasn't, she was at the mercy of other people's ideas, some of which were terrible.

"I do like to win," she admitted. "But sometimes it's not up to me. I compete in a professional world where I have to be part of a team. I'm not a solo performer. I don't ride a wave by myself. And sometimes my coworkers get in my way."

"Then you have to move them out of your way."

"Easier said than done."

"Maybe you need to change jobs."

"I'm not going to give up my ground just because someone else wants it," she said. "I've worked too hard for too long. I just wish I was better at playing the social game, but that is not my strength, and it might cost me."

"The social game isn't difficult. Just smile, ask questions, and pretend to be interested in the answers. I'm sure you've done that on a few dates," he said dryly. "I know I have."

"I have as well. But do I have to do that at work, too?" she asked with a sigh.

He smiled. "You already know the answer to that question. And you might be better at the social game than you think. I like talking to you, Ava. You're very quick and articulate."

She actually enjoyed talking to him, too, for the same reason. Sometimes her brain moved so fast, it was hard for others to keep up with her. But Liam never seemed to fall behind or get too far ahead. They were oddly in sync. That thought sent something else down her spine—a shiver of attraction.

Fortunately, they were interrupted by Tyler, who set down two more beers in front them.

"I was just about to get up and get another round," Liam told him. "You read our minds."

"I just saw your empty glasses."

Tyler slid into the chair on the other side of her that had been recently vacated by Max, who had to start his shift in the bar. "What do you think of our siblings getting married to each other, Ava?"

"It's fast," she said. "I wish they would have gone a little slower."

"I thought it was quick, too," Tyler admitted. "Not that I don't love Serena. She's a great girl. But they went out once and were basically never apart after that. As soon as Serena's roommate moved out, Brad moved in. He's always been an impulsive person, but that was a lot, even for him."

She felt a little vindication that Tyler shared her worry. "I'm glad I'm not the only one who had some concern."

"Well, my concern has faded the more I've seen them together. They click. They look at each other and there's this weird silent love language going on. It's like they can read each other's minds."

She'd thought she had an ally, but clearly Tyler had already moved past his initial worries. "Well, I hope it works."

"My brother is a good man."

"I'm sure he is. I just don't know him."

"I get that. I've had a front row seat to their love affair the past several months, so it's different for me. Do you think you might move down here now that Serena will be staying permanently in Oceanside?"

"My job is in LA, so, no."

"Too bad. Serena would love to have you around. She talks about you all the time. You're her smart, responsible older sister who always took care of her."

"I tried." She felt a sting of sadness at his words because her sister's admiration felt very much in the past now. She took a sip of her beer. "I really do want Serena and Brad to be happy."

"So do I. I just hope…" Tyler paused, then shook his head. "It doesn't matter."

"What were you going to say? What are you hoping for?"

"I want Brad to take more interest in this business again. This bar was his obsession before he met your sister. I came in to support him, not to take over the business, and I'd like to get my partner back."

She heard an edge of bitterness in his voice and thought there was probably more to that story than he'd shared.

"But speaking of business," he continued. "I need to check on things out front. We'll talk more later, Ava."

"Sure. Although, it seems like you should be able to take a night off on your birthday."

"You'd think so, wouldn't you," he said dryly as he got up and left.

As Tyler headed out of the patio, he was waylaid by a new group of men and women just entering, some with birthday presents and bow-embossed wine bottles. Lexie and the others also seemed to know the newcomers. Realizing there weren't nearly enough seats for everyone at the table, she decided to make her exit.

Liam was talking to Kaia, so she slipped out without a goodbye, not wanting to make her departure anyone's focus.

After leaving the bar, she paused in the parking lot. There were only a few people in line at the food truck now, and all she'd had to eat were nachos. She might as well stay with the Mexican theme and get some tacos to take home.

She walked quickly across the parking lot, stopping to peruse the menu on the truck while Gabe took care of the customers in front of her.

It was almost her turn when her shoulder was suddenly nudged, and she found Liam at her side.

"Thought you could sneak away without me, huh?" he joked.

"I wasn't sneaking away. The patio was getting crowded, so I decided to get some food and take it back to the apartment."

"I had the exact same thought. What are you getting to eat?"

"I was thinking about the taco trio."

"Excellent choice. I'll do the same. And we can walk back together."

She sighed. "I really can't shake you, can I?"

"Not tonight."

CHAPTER SEVEN

THE TACOS SMELLED DELICIOUS, and the three-block walk back to their apartment seemed to take far too long, but eventually they sat down together in the kitchen to eat.

Two bites in, and she realized that Gabe definitely knew how to make a taco. The fish was grilled to perfection with a spicy slaw on top. "This is delicious," she said. "Way above my expectations."

"Which one are you eating?" Liam asked.

"The fish taco."

"I'm on the steak. The meat is tender, with a peppery flavor, and the salsa is hot, which I like."

"I'll go for that one next."

They ate in happy silence for the next several minutes. The steak taco was as good as the fish taco, and when she finished the chicken taco, she realized she couldn't pick a winner. "They were all great," she said, wiping her mouth with a napkin. "Each one was good in a different way. No wonder Gabe's food truck is so popular. I'm surprised anyone orders food at Maverick's after tasting these tacos."

"That's why they sell his tacos inside the restaurant, too. But

Maverick's also has a good chef. Their burgers and fish and chips are top of the line."

"How often do you come to Oceanside?" she asked. "You seem to know a lot about Maverick's and the people who live in this building."

"A few times a year. I love this town."

"Because of the surfing or the people?"

"Both," he replied. "Brad and I met years ago in San Diego at a surfing competition. After that, we'd run into each other every couple of months. We took some trips together as well and became good friends. When Brad opened Maverick's two years ago, I came out to visit, and that's when I really started to appreciate Oceanside. Last summer when I was at the Beach Shack getting supplies, John told me about how he started the business after wrapping up his surfing career. That was more than thirty years ago. Now, he wanted to sell the store and retire, but he hated to see the business die out. The more we talked, the more I realized an opportunity was staring me in the face, and I needed to grab it."

"It seems like such a huge change to go from traveling the world, competing in adrenaline-charged surfing competitions to staying in one place, owning a store, stocking inventory, and dealing with customers."

He smiled. "You're not the first person to say I'm crazy."

"I didn't say crazy, you did."

"I knew I wanted to move onto something else a while ago; I just wasn't sure what I wanted to do. But I like the idea of owning a business, an actual building, a place that I can develop as I want. Oceanside is a great town, and I want to be part of the business community. Aside from selling surfboards and apparel and shovels and pails, I want to run a surfing school, sponsor local events, and share my love of the sport with a new generation."

"You don't think you'll miss the traveling?"

"I've been traveling my entire life."

She gave him a thoughtful look. "Even when you were a kid? What did your parents do?"

"My father was a professional surfer, too. I followed in the family business. When he grew too old to compete, he worked on the tour, setting up events in various locations. After that, he moved on to being a sales rep for a surfboard manufacturer, which also meant traveling to competitions and to trade shows. We were nomads."

"What about your mom? Was she around? Did she work?"

"Yes. She was very supportive of my father's career. She waited tables and tended bars in restaurants around the world. She never complained. She loved the life we led. Neither one of them was ever interested in working an office job."

"Did your mom also surf?" she asked, intrigued by his family dynamics.

"She could surf, but it was never her passion. She was happier with a book and a chair on the beach. And she didn't care what beach it was. She liked the constantly changing scenery. My parents were adventurous in surfing, eating, and experiencing life."

"They sound very cool. And what a fun way to grow up. Where are your parents now?"

"They live in Honolulu."

"Are they settled there?"

"They've been there a year, but when I visited them last week, my mom told me my father was getting itchy feet, and so was she. My father is semi-retired now, but he's been promoting a couple of events on Oahu this past year. They're actually thinking about visiting California in the near future."

She smiled. "They must miss you."

"We keep in touch."

"What do they think about you wanting to settle down and become a business owner?"

"They think I'll be bored in fifteen minutes," he said dryly. "But they have trouble imagining why anyone would want to buy anything. They've always been renters. No permanent address for them."

She wondered if his parents might be right about Liam getting bored quickly. It was one thing to have a dream and another to live it. "Do you worry they might know you too well?" she asked.

He smiled at her question. "I know myself. That's what matters. I've done everything I wanted to do on the tour. And to be honest, I'm outgrowing it. I'm thirty-one years old. Most of my friends have already retired from surfing. They've gotten married, had kids, bought houses, and become responsible nine-to-fivers. I can't go that far. I definitely cannot see myself in an office job or tied to a computer like you are. But I think I can merge my current interests with my past life when I purchase the Beach Shack. I just have to seal the deal."

"What if it doesn't go through? What will you do?"

"No idea. I'm just focused on it working out."

In other words, he was going to bury his head in the sand and hope for the best. She'd never seen that strategy work.

His gaze narrowed as he studied her. "You don't think much of my approach, do you, Ava?"

"It's what I said before, Liam. I believe everyone should have a backup plan. But we are very different people."

"We are, and I can see why you'd want a backup plan. Losing your parents when you were a teenager had to feel like hitting the ground without a safety net. You would never want to feel that way again. I can understand that."

She appreciated his insight. "That's exactly how it felt. To you, losing everything is theoretical, but I know what it feels like to have my entire life end in a second. That's why I like to control everything that happens now. I'm not stupid. I know where some of my compulsions come from. I just can't always fight them."

"You must also know that no backup plan will ever make up

for the kind of loss you experienced. You can't prepare for a tragedy like that."

"I agree. But there are ways to protect myself, and what I can protect, I do. Why wouldn't I? Why put myself in a position to get hurt when I don't have to?"

"Because no risk means no reward."

She rolled her eyes. "Oh, please. Spare me the clichés. You can get plenty of rewards with minimal risks."

"But how big can those rewards be?"

"Big enough for me," she replied.

"That's kind of sad, Ava."

She bristled at his words. "I do not need you to feel sorry for me. I have a great life, a good job, and money in the bank. I am not sad." Even as she finished speaking, she wished the last sentence had come out as strongly as the first two. But her voice had caught in her throat as an image of Serena saying goodbye to her had suddenly popped into her head. Clearing her throat, she added, "You don't have to agree with me. You have your way of doing things, I have mine."

"It's interesting that Serena didn't go in the same direction as you. She doesn't seem like someone who thinks about being careful or needs to control things."

"She doesn't think that way. She never had to. I took care of things for her. She didn't have to worry because I did. I'm glad she didn't have to feel that way because it wasn't fun to be constantly filled with anxiety." She paused. "All I ever wanted was for Serena to be happy. I knew my parents would want that, too. They loved her so much. Serena was always the brightest light in our family. She could make everyone laugh. She had our parents wrapped around her finger, and me, too. I didn't want to see the light go out of her eyes, so I tried to make sure that didn't happen."

"You succeeded. Serena has a bright personality. Brad told me he fell in love with her light on first sight."

"A lot of people have loved Serena at first sight. And I have to admit she's always fallen pretty fast, too. But I never thought she'd marry a man she'd only known for eight months. I know you like Brad, and everyone seems to as well, but I don't know him. And I don't think I'll completely trust him until I do."

"That's fair. You should get to know him. For what it's worth, he's an honest and genuine person. Brad doesn't lie, doesn't cheat. And he's in love with your sister."

"I hope you're right. But everyone is different at the beginning of a relationship. They're putting their best foot forward."

"I can't disagree. Not everyone shows their true colors right away," he said, a harder note in his voice.

"Are you speaking from personal experience?" she asked.

"Yes," he said, but he didn't elaborate. Instead, he changed the subject. "Have you ever fallen in love at first sight, Ava?"

"Never."

"How long does it usually take?"

"To fall in love?" She had to think about that question. "I don't know. It hasn't happened yet."

"You've never been in love?" he asked with surprise.

"I've had relationships where I really liked someone, but, no, I never thought I was in love." She paused, giving him a thoughtful look. "I suppose you have."

"A couple of times. The first time was when I was nine. I got to sit next to Genevieve, the prettiest girl in my class. She had long blonde hair that hung down to her waist and the bluest eyes. When she smiled at me, I couldn't look away. Although her blue eyes weren't as pretty as yours."

She stiffened at the surprising compliment, not sure what to say to that.

He smiled, a knowing gleam in his gaze. "Surely I'm not the first person who said your eyes were like the sea, changing with the light. One minute they're a steel blue and then they're a shadowy turquoise, or they have a deep blue shimmer. You show more emotions in your eyes than you realize."

She had never in her life had anyone rhapsodize about her

eye color, and she found herself falling a little under the spell of his words until she reminded herself that this flirty, good-looking surfer guy probably knew exactly what to say to a woman. She needed to end whatever was happening right now because she didn't like the tingle running down her spine, or the sudden moisture on her palms.

"I think we should stop talking about my eyes," she said so abruptly, he laughed. "What?"

"You hate me even when I'm giving you a compliment," he said.

"I don't hate you. You're just making me uncomfortable. Maybe you made Genevieve uncomfortable, too. Or did she return your love?"

"Sadly, she did not. She said I was too tall, and I always smelled like seaweed." He shrugged. "My love was unrequited."

She couldn't help but smile at his dramatic words. "I doubt you were heartbroken."

"I was definitely heartbroken. But I got over it when I met Melody Harper. She was my thirteen-year-old crush."

She pointedly glanced at her watch. "I don't think I have time for your entire romantic timeline."

"There weren't that many."

"Why don't I believe you? You're a surfer, and you're relatively good-looking. Plus, you have an accent."

"It's only an accent when I'm not in Australia."

"True."

"Anyway, Melody and I went out for a good two months."

"Practically a lifetime at thirteen," she said dryly.

"Exactly."

"And after Melody?" She wondered why she was encouraging this story when she had work to do before tomorrow. But she couldn't seem to end the conversation. She was having fun talking to him, more than she would have expected.

"A bunch of different girls," he said. "No one serious for a long time. Since I moved a lot, it was hard to have anything last for too long."

"Did you even want a long-term relationship? I bet there were a lot of cute bikini-clad girls at every beach you hit."

His green eyes sparkled. "There were a lot of those," he admitted.

"Was there another important relationship in your life after you became an adult?"

"Yes."

"What happened?"

"It ended," he said with a shrug.

"So, no one now?" she pressed, not sure why he suddenly seemed less interested in talking about his life. There was a story there, but he didn't seem to want to tell it.

"No one now," he agreed.

"Then you've proved my earlier point," she said. "Love doesn't necessarily last even if you think it will. I wonder if Serena would have married Brad if she'd given their relationship more time."

"Who knows? But she took a chance. If she hadn't said yes, she might have missed out on something fantastic."

"Or saved herself some heartbreak."

Liam frowned. "You are far too pessimistic, Ava."

"I'm a realist," she corrected. "And that's enough sharing for tonight. I have work to do."

"You've been saying that all day."

"Because I keep getting distracted," she said. "Mostly by you."

He smiled. "Okay, roomie, I'll let you get to work. But there's just one more thing I want to say."

"What's that?" she asked as she got to her feet.

"It's going to be okay, Ava. I know you miss your sister, and you think your relationship is forever changed, but she loves you, and you love her. That's not going away just because Brad is in the mix. You haven't lost her. And she hasn't lost you."

His simple, reassuring words touched her heart. She couldn't remember anyone telling her she would be okay since her parents had died. Not even her aunt and uncle had wanted to make that promise. They'd left it to her to comfort herself and her sister. But this man, who she'd only known for a day, wanted to make her feel better. She didn't understand it. She didn't know why he would even care. Or why she felt moisture gathering in what most people described as her cold blue eyes, but Liam had seen a lot more in her gaze than she'd wanted to show him, and that was a little scary. So, she did what she always did when she was scared, she took herself out of the situation.

"Goodnight, Liam," she said as she left the kitchen. But she was still thinking about him when she got to her room and for a long time after that.

CHAPTER EIGHT

Monday morning Ava woke up to a stream of bright sunshine flowing through the part in the curtains in her bedroom. A glance at the clock told her it was eight fifteen, which shocked her into a sitting position. She was usually at her office by eight, not just waking up. Thankfully, she didn't have any meetings until one, and while she had plenty of work to do, she could push it back. She needed a run this morning, and that's what she was going to do before anything else.

After dressing in shorts and a tank top, she put on her running shoes and headed out of the bedroom. Liam's door was closed, and his surfboard case was still propped against the living room wall, so he was probably asleep. That was fine with her. He'd cluttered up her thoughts all night, and she needed to get him out of her head even if she couldn't get him out of her apartment. Running was the best way to do that.

As she left the building, she headed for a path along the water. She'd only gone a hundred yards before she saw a group of teenage boys with surfboards running across the sand. Her mind immediately flashed back on the stories Liam had told her about his life growing up in the surfing world. He'd probably been one of those boys eager to jump into the water a million times.

He wasn't like anyone she'd ever met before. His upbringing had sounded exciting and a little wild. She couldn't imagine growing up like that. Her parents had been wonderful, and her childhood had been filled with love and happiness, but they'd never traveled anywhere. In fact, her mom used to brag about making their staycations more fun than an amusement park. Of course, later she'd realized they'd never gone to an amusement park because her parents had been living close to the edge financially. But she hadn't missed what she hadn't known.

But now that Serena was in Paris with her handsome husband, she was starting to wonder about the limitations of her tunnel vision. Because she didn't always want to be the anxious worrier, the pessimist, the narrow-minded thinker. She just didn't really know how to change, and the side of her brain that was hyperfocused on caution always seemed to win out.

Liam's brain certainly didn't work that way. His mind dared him to look for challenges, to have adventures, and to take risks. He must think she was the most boring person alive. She certainly felt a little dull and dark next to his sunny personality. She wondered if he ever got down.

He had seemed annoyed by his second place—or first loser— finish at his last surfing competition. So, apparently, he could be disappointed and feel down. But she doubted he stayed down long. He'd no doubt he'd be back up on a board very soon, chasing after another title.

His refusal to be happy with anything less than first place had also made her think about herself, and her goals. She had a competitive drive, too, but she was coming in second a lot at work these days. Her reports and analyses were damn good, but they didn't get the respect they should from her manager, Dave, who seemed to be finding a bromance with her coworker, Jeff.

She knew that Jeff portrayed some of her insights as his own, but he so sly about what he was doing, it was difficult to bring it up, but she was starting to feel like Jeff was getting ahead of her when she should be ahead of him. She'd been at the company for seven years; he'd been there for less than two.

She'd always told herself to play the long game, that she would be rewarded in the end, but she was starting to wonder if that was true. On the flip side, if she pushed too hard, her impatience might cost her the hard work she'd already put in. She just had to be patient and keep doing the best possible job she could do. It would pay off in the end.

Unfortunately, her mental pep talk didn't work as well today as it usually did. Since she'd come to Oceanside three days ago, she'd watched her sister marry her crazy dream of a boyfriend and jet off to Paris and then heard about Liam and his grand plans to own a business, not to mention Max's screenwriting dreams, and Gabe's hopes of opening a restaurant. So many people were going after what they wanted. Was she selling herself short? Was she being too patient?

That question burned through her brain over the next mile, and she was still thinking about it when she ran out of beach path and paused to take a breath before turning around. As she looked out at the ocean, she felt a deepening rumble that seemed to shake the ground beneath her feet. And then the sound grew louder as three military jets flew into view, probably on their way to the Camp Pendleton, a marine corps base adjacent to Oceanside.

As the air stilled once more, her phone vibrated in the pocket of her running shorts. As she pulled it out, she saw that Lisa Ray, one of her coworkers, was calling. "Hi, Lisa."

"You may have a problem, Ava."

"What's happened?"

"I just ran into Jeff, and he asked me if I had your notes for the Calyx pitch."

"Why would Jeff be asking you for my notes? He's not in that pitch, and it isn't for three weeks."

"He said Dave asked him for the information, and he didn't want to bother you on vacation."

"I'm not on vacation; I'm working remote," she said with annoyance.

"I reminded him of that."

"I wonder why Dave didn't just ask me. He knows I'm still working," she murmured.

"That's why I said you might have a problem," Lisa replied. "Dave and Jeff have been huddled together since they came into the office this morning. I think Jeff is going to use the fact that you're working remote to get ahead of you."

"This is only my first day remote. Even Jeff couldn't work that fast."

"I wouldn't put it past him. He's the fastest-moving analyst at this company, and he and Dave apparently played golf together over the weekend. I had to hear them talk about their strokes and shots when I was getting coffee in the lounge. Anyway, I told him I didn't have your notes; he'd have to get them from you."

"I appreciate that."

"You might want to reconsider how long you'll be out of the office."

"It's just ten days, and I'm still working."

"I agree. Maybe I shouldn't have bothered you. I just wanted to give you a heads-up."

"I appreciate that."

"Are you enjoying Oceanside? On Friday, you said you were dreading having to watch Serena's cat and apartment for so long."

"I was, and I don't know why, because it is beautiful here. I'm standing by the ocean right now. The weather is warm, the sun is bright, and the ocean is shimmering like diamonds in the light."

"Wow, that's poetic for you, Ava. And I'm super jealous. All I'm looking at is the parking garage."

"It is a nice change," she admitted.

"And the wedding was beautiful?"

"It was everything my sister wanted, so it was perfect for her."

"Are you feeling better about the groom?"

"I don't know Brad any better now than I knew him before the wedding, but he looked at Serena with love in his eyes, so I hope it works out."

"Me, too. Serena is such a lovely person. She deserves the best. So do you, Ava. Has all this wedding action made you at least want to get into the dating pool again?"

"I wouldn't go that far," she said, feeling unsettled when her mind immediately flashed on Liam's handsome face. She was definitely not going to date him. She was only in town for short time, and he was not her type at all. Although, he was really attractive.

"I hate to see you give up," Lisa continued. "A friend of mine has a brother you should meet."

"No setups," she protested. "I hate those. And if this guy can't get his own date, he can't have much going for him."

"He's a lawyer, so he works a lot. But he's very well-read and has a great job, and he just bought one of those penthouse condos in the Harper Building on Eighth Street, so he's not hurting for money."

She felt a little unsettled that all the things Lisa had brought up as selling points felt superficial and boring. But how could she blame her friend when she'd put those items on her own checklist a long time ago? "I don't want to meet anyone right now," she said. "Or at least I don't want to be set up."

"If you change your mind, let me know. I better get back to work."

"Thanks again for the warning."

"You're more than welcome, Ava. I've got your back."

"And I've got yours."

After ending the call, she did a few stretches since she'd gotten cold while she'd been talking to Lisa. Then she ran back the way she'd come. She was only a few blocks away from Ocean Shores when she saw the colorful, hand-painted sign for the Beach Shack, a weathered, wood- paneled building with a large display window featuring surfboards and boogie boards.

In front of the store was a pathway leading from the parking lot, lined with nautical ropes, and a table with a colorful beach umbrella that sat on a grassy patch next to a large water dish with puppy paws on the outside.

But it wasn't only the building that drew her attention; it was the man pacing back and forth on the sidewalk in front of it. Liam was dressed more conservatively than she'd seen him to date, wearing charcoal slacks and a button-down shirt.

"Hey," she said as she jogged up to him. "Are you getting ready for your meeting?"

"John isn't here," he bit out, his gaze tense, his green eyes unusually worried. "We were supposed to meet at nine thirty before he opened the store at ten. It's ten fifteen now, and there's no sign of him. I tried his phone, but it went to voicemail."

"I'm sure he's just running late. Maybe he overslept."

"I don't have a good feeling about this."

She was surprised to see the perpetually lighthearted Liam with concern in his gaze. "John wouldn't just blow you off, would he?"

"I sure as hell hope not."

"Maybe you should reach out to Maggie."

"His soon-to-be ex-wife? I don't think so. I'll just wait. He has to show up sometime, right?"

"Right." It didn't seem like a good sign that John hadn't shown up to their meeting. On the other hand, the store was called the Beach Shack. Maybe John was lax about when he opened up the store.

None of this had anything to do with her, but she felt like she couldn't just run on by, not with Liam looking so worried. As she was debating what to do, her phone vibrated again. She pulled it out and saw a message from Jeff asking her to give him a call. She wasn't going to do that anytime soon.

"Everything okay?" Liam asked.

"I think my coworker is trying to steal one of my accounts while I'm working remote."

He raised an eyebrow. "Sounds like you work for a cutthroat company."

"It seems to be getting that way more and more every day."

"You could go back to LA. I can take care of Miss Daisy."

After he'd managed to charm Miss Daisy into taking her medicine the night before, she knew that might be true. On the other hand, Liam had needed her help to do that. Getting the medicine into Miss Daisy still felt like a two-person job. "I told Serena I'd stay, and I'm going to do that." As she finished speaking, she was distracted by the sight of an older man staggering down the sidewalk. "Who's that?"

"That's John," Liam said, following her gaze.

"He looks sick."

"Or drunk," Liam said tersely.

"So early in the morning?"

Liam didn't have to reply because as John drew close to them, she could see his bloodshot eyes and smell the liquor on his breath.

"You're late," John said to Liam. "I told you not to be late."

"I've been waiting for you since nine thirty," Liam said evenly. "It's after ten."

"It can't be. I open the store at ten every single day, rain or shine." John squinted as he lifted his watch up. His frown deepened. "It is after ten. What the hell?"

"Why don't we go inside?" Liam suggested.

John's gaze moved to her. "Who are you?"

"Ava," she said, not bothering to explain because he wouldn't remember or care.

"You his girlfriend?"

"No. I'm his…roommate."

John put a hand to his head. "I feel dizzy."

"Let's get you into the store," Liam said, taking the keys out of John's shaky hand. "I'll make you coffee."

"Coffeemaker is broken."

Liam frowned. "Then I'll go get you a coffee. But let me get you inside first."

Seeing that he had his hands full, she decided to help. "I'll get you both coffee from Tidal Brews," she said. "What do you want?"

"Anything strong," Liam said, sending her a grateful smile as he steered John toward the store.

She jogged to the coffeehouse three blocks away, happy to see there wasn't a long line at the counter. She ordered three coffees as well as some pastries, thinking John might need some food to soak up the alcohol in his system.

After paying on her phone, she moved down to the pick-up area, where she saw Kaia talking to a tall, good-looking guy she didn't recognize.

"Ava," Kaia said with a smile. "Good morning. Looks like you're a runner."

"I am. It keeps the stress level down."

"You took off early from Maverick's last night."

"It was getting crowded, and I had work to do."

The attractive man next to Kaia cleared his throat. Kaia smiled at him. "Sorry, Ben. Ava, this is my older brother, Ben Mercer. This is Ava Campbell. She's apartment sitting for her sister, Serena, who lives at Ocean Shores."

"I met Serena last time I was here," Ben said, extending his hand as he gave her a friendly smile.

Ben was as attractive as his sister, with brown hair and eyes.

"Ben is moving into Ocean Shores next month," Kaia said. "He's transferring from Los Angeles."

"That's nice. What do you do?"

"I'm a police officer," he replied. "I'm looking forward to working by the ocean."

"I can relate to that. I also live in LA and nowhere near the beach. I'm going to miss the views when I go home."

"Maybe you'll change your mind and decide to stay, Ava," Kaia said. "It happens to a lot of people who think they'll just be here for a few days or weeks."

"Well, my job is there, so I can't change my mind."

Ben's phone buzzed, and he gave her an apologetic smile. "Sorry, I have to get this."

As he walked away, she couldn't help but notice the worried look that entered Kaia's eyes. "Is everything okay?" she asked.

"I hope so. My brother has had a rough couple of months. I can't wait for him to move here so I can make sure he's okay. Anyway…" She forced a brighter smile onto her face. "How are you and Liam getting along? He's a charmer, isn't he?"

She shrugged, not wanting to even try to respond to that question since her thoughts about Liam were all over the place. "I suppose."

Kaia gave her a curious look. "You suppose? You might need to get your eyes checked."

"I'm good," she said with a smile. "You two seemed to be getting along well yesterday."

Now it was Kaia's turn to shrug. "I'm not looking for anything right now." Kaia paused as her name was called. "I better grab these and go. My shift starts in an hour." She picked up two coffees, then paused. "We're having a girls' night in my apartment Thursday night. You should come. Seven o'clock."

"Uh, I don't know."

"Don't say no. It will be fun, and we can get to know each other better. I'll see you then."

Kaia was gone before she could find a more definitive way to say no. That was becoming a pattern. But it was just a girls' night. Maybe it would be fun. She hadn't spent a lot of time with women her age in a while. A lot of her friends from college had either moved away from LA, gotten engaged, married, or had children. It might be nice to have a few glasses of wine, and it wasn't like she was starting any friendships. She'd be gone in a little more than a week. If she didn't like them or they didn't like her, it would all be over soon anyway.

Liam couldn't believe John Peterman was drunk—not just buzzed, but falling down drunk. Apparently, he'd started drinking last night and continued on until dawn, although John didn't really remember when he'd had his last drink.

It seemed so out of character. He'd met John several times over the years, and he'd always seemed like a sharp, practical, dedicated business owner and member of the community. He sponsored local surf competitions and youth sports teams. He went to church every Sunday. He'd always thought John had it all together. But he didn't have it together now.

After getting John's keys so he could open the store, he steered John into the employee lounge, a small room with a loveseat, refrigerator, hot plate, and a microwave, as well as a table with two chairs. It was also kind of a mess, which seemed to be the state of everything in John's life right now.

John sank down on the couch and said, "I'm tired."

He set his proposal folder on the table, grabbed a chair, and pulled it over to the couch. "What's going on, John? You don't drink like this."

"She left me," John replied, anger and defeat in his red-rimmed eyes. "Thirty-eight years of marriage, and she's gone. Living with her girlfriend, flirting with that jackass Frank, who just moved into the building. I knew he was going to be trouble. He's a lawyer, a widower, and a player. He's looking for a new woman, and Maggie is the perfect target."

"Have you spoken to Maggie?" he asked.

"She won't talk to me. She says I know what I have to do, and I just have to do it. Like it's all her decision." He waved his hand in the air in bewilderment. "This store has been my life. I've worked tirelessly to support Maggie and our daughter, to give them both the lives they deserved. My daughter is now grown with a husband and children of her own. And Maggie has always had everything she wanted. It's my turn."

"And you want to…"

"Move to Michigan, where my brother, his wife and kids and grandkids are. It's cheaper there. Our money will last longer and go further."

"But your daughter is here, right? Is that part of the problem?"

"No. Tori is in Santa Barbara. That's a four-hour drive. We couldn't get there much faster driving from here than we could flying from Michigan. It's Maggie's friends that are the problem. That damn Josie has been filling her head about how they can have so much fun going places together."

"Got it." He should be happy that John was digging in his heels on his plan to sell the store and move to Michigan, but judging by his current condition, he was more conflicted than he was letting on.

"I have coffee," Ava declared as she entered the room. "And there's a customer in the store looking for help."

"I better get out there," John said as he started to stand up, then immediately swayed.

"I'll do it." He pushed John back onto the couch. "You drink some coffee and sober up."

Ava gave him a brief smile as she set the coffees and a box of pastries on the table. "I also got donuts and a strawberry tart."

"Well, aren't you as sweet as you are pretty," John said.

Ava smiled. "And you would be more charming if you weren't so drunk." She handed John a coffee, then turned to Liam. "Go help the customer. I'll watch him."

He was both surprised and appreciative of her offer. She didn't seem like the type of person who got involved in problems that weren't her own. But he wasn't going to question her assistance; he would just take it.

When he entered the showroom, he found a father and his teenaged son looking for a surfboard. As he talked to them about exactly what they wanted, he felt completely at home. This wasn't his store, but these were his people, and he knew the products exceptionally well.

Within ten minutes, he was ringing up an expensive purchase and feeling much more certain that this was exactly what he wanted to be doing.

Although, he definitely had changes in mind. The store was too cluttered. The apparel was jumbled together. The beach supplies felt incomplete. The store was showing the same signs of weary exhaustion as the owner. He just needed to get John to make a deal with him so he could put his ideas into motion.

He decided to lock the front door and put up the Closed sign until he could get John in better condition. After doing that, he returned to the back room to find Ava sitting on the sofa next to John, listening to his sorrowful tale about his ungrateful wife.

"You need to talk to Maggie," Ava said when John paused to take a breath. "And not just talk. You need to listen, too. Hear what she's saying."

"She's saying that I have to sell the store for some astronomical amount of money so we can stay in Oceanside instead of moving somewhere cheaper. It doesn't make financial sense."

He frowned as he sat down in the chair across from John. "We have a good deal, John. The business needs improvements. There's a leak in the roof, and the inventory is down. Sales have been slower than usual. I don't think you'll find another buyer as enthusiastic as I am."

"Maybe someone with deeper pockets," John said. "I know you want to own this place, Liam, and I want to sell it to you, but Maggie says I need to make more money. I need you to prove to Maggie that you're giving me the best deal I can get."

"You can show her the proposal, the agreement we made."

"She said it's not detailed enough," John muttered.

"I gave you exactly what you asked for," he argued.

"Maggie wants to go on a cruise," John said, abruptly changing the subject. "I think if I could get a little more money, and I could take her on that cruise to Alaska she's been wanting to go on, she'd see it doesn't matter where we live, we can still travel together."

A cruise sounded expensive, and he could see numbers getting added to his deal. Everything he'd spent the last year working toward was slipping away along with John's marriage. But he couldn't give up.

"I can give you more details," he said. "To do that, I'll need to look more closely at your financial records and not just the summary report you gave me."

"I gave them to you before. You said you couldn't read them."

"Well, I need to try again. If I can see a way to improve my offer, I will, but you have to promise me you won't sell to anyone else until I have a chance to do that."

"I can give you time, but not too much," John said. "And I need dollars and cents, Liam. Not just your big ideas about changing up the displays. I also need to find a way to get Maggie on a cruise, so she'll fall in love with me again and go to Michigan."

He had no idea how he would get John and Maggie on a cruise, or get Maggie to fall in love with John again and move to Michigan. But he'd always liked a challenge.

"Okay, then," John said with a nod. "You get the books. They're in the office. I'm going to take a little nap." He rested his head on the back of the couch, his lids closing.

"I'll lock up the store, John," he said. "And then drop the keys in the mailbox."

John's answer was a snore.

He let out a sigh as he looked at Ava, who had a guarded expression on her face. He had a feeling she wasn't too impressed with his deal after hearing their conversation. But that was the least of his problems. "Are you going home now, Ava?"

"Yes. I need to get ready for my work calls."

"Let me grab his financial records, and I'll go with you."

"All right." She picked up the third coffee cup from the table. "I think you're going to need this."

"Would you mind holding on to that while I get his books and lock up?"

"Sure."

He headed into the office and located the financial records in several hardbound ledgers labeled by year. He selected the last three years, but judging by the overflowing stack of paper on John's desk, he wasn't entirely sure the books would reflect the correct information. But he had to start somewhere.

After he locked up and dropped the keys in the mailbox, Ava handed him the coffee she'd bought for him, and he took a long, welcome sip, needing the hit of caffeine to pump him up for his latest challenge.

"So, what do you think?" Ava asked as they started walking back to Ocean Shores.

"It doesn't seem difficult," he said dryly. "I just have to make Maggie fall back in love with John, figure out how to pay for an Alaskan cruise, and pump up my offer. Piece of cake."

She gave him a small smile. "You said you like challenges, the bigger the better. I'd focus on your offer, because you don't know what went on in their marriage. Maggie might have left John for a lot of reasons that have nothing to do with the sale of the business or going on a cruise. Have you looked through his records before? Is there a way to improve your offer?"

"I tried to look at his books, but they were a mess, so he gave me a profit and loss statement for the last two years that summarized everything."

She raised an eyebrow. "That's it? Was the P&L verified by an accountant?"

"No. I didn't think John was trying to screw me over."

"You still should have had someone look at the books if you couldn't decipher them."

He ran a frustrated hand through his hair. "You're right. But all I can do is look through them now. The real problem is that no matter what I discover, I can't raise my bid. Every last cent I have is going into buying the business."

A frown spread across her face. "That doesn't make sense, Liam. You need operating capital. You can't invest everything you have. If you do, how will you maintain the business?"

"I'll make money on the store, and I'll continue participating in surfing competitions to bring in extra cash. I'll pick up shifts at Maverick's. I'll work there at night and in the store during the day."

"That's a lot, Liam."

"I'm willing to do whatever it takes. But putting the money issues aside, I don't know how to make John and Maggie fall in love again."

"You might want to talk to Maggie. Find out what her attitude is about all this."

"She won't want to talk to me. You heard her yesterday when we were playing cards. Whenever I tried to bring up the sale, she shut me down."

"That's true."

"Maybe you could talk to her," he suggested. "Woman to woman. You could find out what her bottom line is—if a cruise will make her happy enough to let John sell the store and move her to Michigan." He took a breath as he considered what he'd just said. "That sounds ridiculous, doesn't it?"

"Yes. And I don't even know her, Liam. She's not going to tell me anything. You might have better luck with Josie."

"That's true." He blew out a breath of frustration. "I anticipated roadblocks, but I didn't think they would be about love."

"It is a tricky situation," she said. "You won't want to hear this, but you should consider whether this is still a good deal for you. Maybe you should open a store in another location, something cheaper with a more straightforward deal."

"The Beach Shack has the perfect location. I can run surfing classes right across the street. I'll get all the beach walk-in traffic. And it has a reputation, a brand. People trust it."

She shrugged. "Then you have to find a way to make John sell. Maybe there's something in his financial records that you didn't know about before that would actually decrease the value of the business. If you point that out to him, he might realize he won't be able to find another buyer with more cash."

"I don't know that I could lower my offer even if I did find something," he said slowly. "We'd have to start all over."

"But it might tell you whether or not John can find a better deal for his business."

"That's true. Maybe these ledgers will have an answer for me, if I can figure out his record keeping."

"I could take a look at his books if you want."

"Really?" he asked in surprise. "You'd do that?"

"It's what I do every day, but it will have to be later."

"Whenever would be great. I'll find a way to pay you back."

"I wasn't asking you to pay me for my time."

He smiled. "Good, because I can't pay you, but I can barter. You're giving me your expertise, so I'll give you mine. I'll give you a surfing lesson."

She immediately shook her head. "No. I don't like the ocean."

"Why not?"

"I don't trust it."

"Of course you don't," he said with a nod. "You don't trust anything you can't control."

"No one can trust or control the ocean, not even you, the master wave conqueror."

"You're right."

Surprise flashed in her blue eyes. "I am?"

"Yes. The ocean can be treacherous, but it can also be exhilarating to be a part of it. Just think about it."

"Maybe," she said. "But right now I need to think about work."

CHAPTER NINE

AFTER SPENDING the rest of Monday on video calls and research, Ava left her bedroom around five and found the apartment empty. She hadn't seen Liam during her lunch break, but she had heard him moving around during the afternoon. She was a little curious as to where he'd gone now, but that thought just reminded her she was getting too caught up in his life.

She probably shouldn't have offered to take a look at the Beach Shack books, either, but she'd made a promise, and she wouldn't go back on it.

When she entered the kitchen to get a drink, she saw his business plan on the table. She poured herself a glass of lemonade and sat down to take a look.

It wasn't anything like the reports she was used to writing or reading, but she was surprised at the depth of the proposal. There were some problems. He was underfunded, which made the investment high risk. He didn't have a lot of experience running a store, although he had mentioned in the section on his background that he had worked at a similar store in Sydney for several years. He knew the surfing world and the equipment because of his father's experience working for a manufacturer, so Liam had connections, and he definitely had passion.

His plans for the shack included keeping John Peterman's legacy alive. That would make John happy. But his legacy wasn't at the top of John's mind; his wife was. That was a problem beyond her financial expertise. She closed the proposal and decided she'd go through the ledgers next, but maybe after she found something to eat.

As she stood up to check the contents of the fridge, she heard the front door open and close. Liam entered the kitchen a moment later with two large grocery bags.

His smile sent a tingle down her spine. She was starting to like him more than she'd expected. And his smile was hard to resist.

"I hope you're hungry," he said. "I'm going to make you a great dinner."

"Really? Why?" she asked in surprise.

"Because you're helping me out. And while you're still thinking about a surf lesson, I thought I'd make you a meal."

"You don't want to just order takeout?"

"No. I'm a fantastic cook."

In the face of such charming cockiness, she could do nothing but laugh. "You certainly have a lot of confidence. Is there anything you don't do well?"

He thought for a moment and then said, "I can't think of anything off the top of my head."

She rolled her eyes at that comment. "What's on the menu?"

"I hope you like steak. I thought I'd grill downstairs. There's a large barbecue on the patio. If you're not into red meat, I also bought a chicken breast I could barbecue."

She smiled at that. "Wait a second. You had a backup plan? I thought you didn't believe in that."

He laughed. "Point taken. I did have a backup plan. You must be rubbing off on me. So, chicken or steak?"

"I like steak," she said, thinking that sounded absolutely perfect.

"Good. I'm also going to do a salad, baked potatoes, and I'll throw some vegetables on the grill."

Her stomach rumbled at the thought. "How can I help?"

"You can't. You're not helping with dinner. You're going to look at John's books. Or did you do that already?"

"No. I just read through your proposal."

He set the bags on the counter and gave her a questioning look. "What did you think? And be gentle."

She hated that he thought he needed to add that warning. She really wasn't as big of a hard ass as he seemed to think. "I thought it was well-done."

"Seriously?"

"You could have added more detail, but it was good, especially for someone who probably hasn't written one before."

"It is my first, but I've rewritten it half a dozen times."

"Well, now that I've read your proposal, I'll take a look at John's ledgers and see how I think everything matches up."

"I really appreciate this, Ava. And I'm probably pushing my luck, but I do have one more favor to ask."

"Seriously?" she asked.

"Maggie, Josie, and Frank are having drinks by the pool. I was thinking you might want to chat with them while I grill the steaks."

"Can't you do that? You'll be right there."

"I think Maggie would find you easier to talk to. You could get some insight into her attitude toward John."

She hesitated. "I'm better with numbers than with people."

"I suspect you're better than you think. And just to add a little more incentive, I am going to make you dessert, too."

"You're pulling out all the stops, aren't you? Do you really think I'm that easy?"

"Let's see. What do you think about hot fudge sundaes with all the toppings?"

She stared at him in surprise. Hot fudge sundaes were her

absolute favorite dessert. Her gaze narrowed at the gleam in his eyes. "What made you think about making me a sundae?"

"A conversation I had with your sister last time I was in town. We all made dinner, and she wanted sundaes for dessert. She said you used to make them for her all the time after your parents died, and that they're your favorite dessert as well."

"I'm surprised you'd remember that," she said, thinking how often Liam was surprising her.

"What do you say?"

"Fine. I'll see if I can crash cocktail hour with Maggie, Josie, and Frank, but don't expect a lot."

"Whatever you can get is fine."

"Who is Frank anyway?" she asked. "I haven't met him yet. Does he live in the building? Based on what John said earlier, it sounds like John thinks Frank and Maggie have something going on."

"That's what John implied. Frank is a widower and a retired attorney. He moved in sometime in the last year. Seems like a decent man. Has kids and grandkids. That's all I know about him."

"Is he interested in Maggie?" she asked.

"No idea."

She thought about the possible emerging love triangle. "You could play this situation two different ways. Try to get Maggie and John back together so they move to Michigan and live happily ever after. Or you could encourage Maggie to move on with Frank, leaving John with no other option than to sell the store and move away. Sometimes it's easier to tear people apart than put them back together."

Liam frowned. "I don't want to tear Maggie and John apart."

"Even if it gets you what you want?"

"Even then."

"Interesting." She suddenly realized another truth about Liam. Despite his desire to own the store, he was not ruthless. He had boundaries.

"Why is that interesting?" he asked.

"I thought you were willing to do whatever it took to get what you want."

"Anything that doesn't break the law or someone else's heart."

"Got it. But it may not be your choice. Maggie is having cocktails with Frank, so something could be brewing between them. And how do you know that Maggie and Frank wouldn't be happier than Maggie and John? I can't believe the sale of the store is the only thing that split them apart. There has to be more."

"Well, we need to get down there and find out what's going on."

"Okay. But before we do anything else, we need to give Miss Daisy her medicine. Since you think you're the cat whisperer, I'll let you take the lead on that."

———

Thirty minutes later, the cat was medicated and fed. They had vegetables and meat ready to grill. The baked potatoes were in the oven and the salad was done. While Liam had wanted to do everything on his own, she'd convinced him it would be quicker if she helped, and she was once again surprised at how natural and comfortable it had felt to be cooking with him.

She couldn't remember preparing a meal with a man. She'd made a few men dinner and had been a recipient of some meals herself, but this had felt different. They were more in sync than they should be. But she wasn't going to think about that too long. It was time to figure out what was going on with Maggie and Frank.

As they reached the courtyard patio, Josie immediately waved them over. She pointed to the blender on the table. "Frank just made another batch of margaritas. Why don't you join us?"

"Well, I've got to start the grill, but I'm sure Ava wouldn't mind a drink," Liam said.

She sat down at the table. "I would love a margarita, if you have plenty?"

"We do," Josie said. "Have you met Frank Wickham?"

"No, I haven't," she said, giving him a smile. Frank was quite a handsome man with pepper- gray hair and light-blue eyes. He also had an easy, warm smile. "It's nice to meet you. I'm Ava Campbell."

"You're Serena's sister, right?"

"I am."

"Lovely girl. So fun," he added as he poured her a margarita. "Serena reminds me of my daughter, Kim. She never met a person who wasn't a friend in the first five minutes of meeting her."

"That's my sister," she said as she took a sip of her drink. "How long have you lived here, Frank?"

"About six months," he replied. "But Josie and I go way back."

"Frank was an entertainment lawyer at the first talent agency I worked with when I was twenty-two years old," Josie said.

"I heard you were a very successful actress," she said, more intrigued by Josie than by Frank.

Josie beamed at her words. "I was very good. I had my time in the sun. But that brightness was followed by darker days."

"I'm sorry to hear that." She wanted to hear more, but she didn't want to be too nosey.

"We all have our trials," Josie said. "Fortunately, I found my way here, and my life got better again. The sun always comes back out, even if we think it never will, especially here at Ocean Shores, where there's always a little magic at play." She sent Frank a pointed look. "Even if you're not a believer, the magic can find you."

She had no idea what Josie was talking about, but Frank gave Josie a nod of acknowledgment, so he clearly knew. Maybe Josie was referring to Frank being a widower and needing to find some joy in his life again.

"What is this magic you speak of?" she asked. Even though, magic was the last thing she would ever believe in.

"There's something about Ocean Shores that's healing. I don't know exactly what it is," Josie said. "I think it's the connections with the people who live here, the sea being so close, the warm breezes. It all adds up and creates this beautiful healing haze."

"It's not any of that," Maggie interjected. "It's you, Josie. You're the one who makes everyone happy. It's not some breeze. You're the magic."

"I might play a small part, but this place helped me heal, so there's more at play than just me."

"What if someone moves in here just to live, and they don't need healing?" she asked, unable to resist playing devil's advocate.

"That can happen," Josie admitted. "But we tend to get more singles than couples, and singles often have a hole in their lives, something they're missing, or running away from. Or they're trying to find something or someone to run to. Serena said she found a new version of herself here."

"I thought her old version was pretty good."

"I'm sure it was. But Serena wouldn't have left LA if she wasn't looking for something," Josie said.

She didn't want to believe that was true, because she'd always thought she'd given her sister everything she needed.

"Did I say something wrong, Ava?" Josie asked with a frown. "Sometimes I talk too much."

"You didn't say anything wrong. I was just thinking I didn't realize my sister was looking for something that she didn't have in LA, but you're right; she was. I only wish I'd known she was unhappy."

"She might not have been unhappy, just restless," Josie said. "Serena told me you were always there for her. But she also said she was excited to have you stay here for a few weeks." Josie gave her a sly smile. "Maybe Serena thinks you might be looking for something, too."

"I'm not," she said quickly. "I've worked very hard to build a life for myself in LA, a good job, a nice place to live. I'm happy. I'm just here to cat-sit." Josie didn't say anything, but there was an unconvinced look on her face as she sipped her margarita. Wanting to get the focus off herself, she turned to Maggie. "You mentioned you moved in here a few months ago. Will you be staying permanently?"

"That's to be determined," Maggie replied, her gaze straying to Liam. "I'm sure you know my husband and I are separated because we each see the next chapter of our lives in a very different way."

"How do you see your life?" she asked.

"I'm not entirely sure, but I love this area. It's home. It's where I've lived for the past forty years. I have friends here, and I don't want to leave. But John, my husband, does. He's become fixated on money and retirement, and he wants to live somewhere cheaper. I think we'd be giving up the best part of our lives if we left." She gave a helpless shake of her head. "It doesn't seem like we can both be happy."

"Maybe you need to spend more time together instead of apart," she suggested, feeling very bold for offering her opinion, but she hadn't missed the pointed looks Liam kept sending in her direction. "Like a vacation," she added. "What about a cruise? That would give you time for you to reconnect."

"I would love to take a cruise to Alaska," Maggie said with a wistful sigh. "It's been on my bucket list for years, but John has never had time to go. Now that he's about to have time, all he wants to do is move across the country. I couldn't get him to take a vacation with me, much less go on a cruise. He'd be bored, and I'd be annoyed."

"You could go on your own," Frank suggested. "I've been on several cruises since Diane died. The first one was booked before she passed away, and I wasn't going to go, but then I thought what the hell, I might as well be sad somewhere else. It turned out to be a great experience. Everyone was friendly. I didn't have to eat alone. There was always someone at my table." He paused. "I've always wanted to do that Alaskan cruise. The scenery is supposed to be magnificent. We should see when the next one is."

"I already looked. There's one in May," Maggie said.

"We could go together," Frank said. "Just so you'd have someone you know on board."

"That would be nice—to know someone," Maggie added hastily.

She watched their exchange with dismay. Frank offering to go with Maggie on her bucket list cruise would not get Maggie and John back together. She probably shouldn't have spoken about the cruise in front of all of them, but it was too late to take it back.

"What about you, Josie?" she asked, wanting to break up the intimacy building between Frank and Maggie. "Would you want to go on a cruise to Alaska, too?"

"No. I'm not a cruise person. I like to look at the ocean, but I don't want to be on it or in it."

"You're missing out," Liam interrupted as he came over to the table. "Being in the ocean is one of the best experiences in life."

"I've been in the ocean. It's cold, and there's seaweed and jellyfish. The waves are also too rough for me," Josie said. "I like the view from here."

Liam gave Josie a disappointed look. "For someone who is interested in healing, I would think you'd have more appreciation for the sea. It's where I've found the most peace."

"You must be a water sign," Josie said, her eyes lighting up with her words. "When is your birthday?"

"October twenty-fifth."

"There you go. You're a Scorpio, which makes perfect sense. You're a water sign. Scorpios are driven to succeed and are fiercely competitive."

"Sounds like you," Ava commented. "First loser."

He made a face at her. "Fine. I accept the fiercely competitive part. But I don't think my birth month decides who I am."

"Another sign of a Scorpio," Josie put in with a knowing nod. "They're determined to live their truth." She turned to Ava. "When's your birthday?"

She really didn't want to say because she had a feeling she was about to be analyzed and she doubted it would be helpful or positive. "I don't believe in astrology, Josie."

"I'm still curious," Josie persisted. "Come on, tell me."

Since she didn't want to make a big deal out of it, she said, "January eighth."

"Oh, you're a Capricorn and an earth sign. Capricorns are practical overachievers and very independent. Seems like that fits you, Ava."

She could handle being an independent overachiever.

"Aren't they also stubborn and pessimistic?" Liam asked.

"They can be," Josie said.

"Well, that fits Ava," he said with a laugh.

She frowned at him. "Aren't Scorpios also manipulative and secretive?"

"I thought you didn't know anything about astrology?" he challenged.

"I said I didn't believe in it, but Serena was a fan. I learned a few things. What about you, Liam? How do you know anything about my sign?"

He shrugged. "I don't. I was just taking a guess. Turns out I was right. Maybe there is something to this astrology stuff."

"Your signs actually complement each other," Josie said, her eyes gleaming with mischief.

"I seriously doubt that," she said dryly, taking another sip of her margarita. "And aren't you supposed to be grilling, Liam?"

He moved back to the barbecue to check on their steaks. As he did so, she caught a smile pass between Josie and Maggie.

"What are you two smiling about?" she asked.

"I was just thinking you and Liam remind me a little of me and John," Maggie said. "When we first met, we didn't like each other at all. I thought he was a flirt and a playboy."

She was surprised to hear John Peterman had ever been a playboy or a flirt.

"He had so many girls around him all the time," Maggie continued. "He was a surfer, just like Liam, and it annoyed me when girls would swarm all around him. But he kept coming over to me and wanting to take me out. Eventually, I said yes. That was how it all started." She paused. "I never thought it would end the way it did, that we would grow so far apart. John says it's my fault. He might not be wrong." She held up her empty glass. "I need another drink, Frank."

"Happy to take care of that," Frank said. "And don't blame everything on yourself, Maggie. It's rarely one person's fault."

"How did you make your marriage last so long?" Maggie asked Frank.

"A lot of talking, often more than I wanted. But Diane refused to let things fester. She always had to get everything out in the open. No silent treatment. Just endless discussions. They worked. We'd either get tired of complaining or figure out how to solve the problem."

"John doesn't talk or listen very well," Maggie said. "Lord knows I've tried to get him to hear me."

"Maybe you should try again," she put in. She rarely gave advice to anyone who wasn't her younger sister. She preferred to keep her distance in friendships and relationships. But here she was trying to give marital advice to a woman who'd been married longer than she'd been alive.

"I'm not sure it's worth it," Maggie said. "I don't want to hear any more about how great our lives would be in a cheaper state. And John hurt me with his callous disregard for my feelings. " Her gaze drifted to Liam, then back to her. "I know Liam thinks I'm the enemy. I don't want to be that person."

"He doesn't think you're the enemy. He just wants to buy the store."

"It's not that I don't want him to have it; I just wish John could make a better deal so he'd feel comfortable staying here."

"Is it really about the money?" she asked, feeling again like she was getting too deep into Maggie's life. But she seemed to be on a roll.

"John says it is." Maggie took a sip. "I don't know if he's telling the truth, lying to himself, or lying to both of us. Anyway, that's enough about me. Frank, why don't you tell us what new hobbies you're going to pick up now that you're retired?"

"I'm interested in reviving my golf game," Frank said, happy to go along with the change in subject. "I wasn't half bad when I used to play, and now I have time to go to the range."

"I used to golf, too," Maggie said. "I wouldn't mind picking up a club again, but it's been a long time."

Ava let out a small sigh as Maggie and Frank once again found something in common and were eager to talk to each other about their shared appreciation for golf. She glanced over at the grill and saw that Liam was putting their steaks on a platter.

She pushed back her chair, temporarily pausing the conversation at the table. "Looks like our steaks are ready. Thanks for the drink."

"Have a nice dinner," Josie said.

She could feel Josie's speculative gaze on her back as she helped Liam gather their food platters. The rumor mill would probably be swirling about her and Liam, if it wasn't already. But she wasn't going to worry about that. She'd be gone in less than two weeks. Nothing was going to happen between them.

CHAPTER TEN

"DID YOU LEARN ANYTHING HELPFUL?" Liam asked as he sat down at the kitchen table with Ava, whose cheeks were slightly flushed. He didn't know if that was from the margarita she'd had or the heat of the kitchen, but he liked the color in her cheeks and the sparkle in her blue eyes. In fact, he was starting to like a lot of things about her, and he hadn't expected that.

"Not much," she said as she cut into her steak. "This looks good, Liam."

"I hope I got the temp right."

"It's perfect. Everything is. You threw together a first-class meal."

He had to admit he was proud of the crisp on the grilled vegetables, the sear on the meat, and the abundance of vegetables in the salad. He'd even added sour cream, green onions, and bacon bits to the baked potatoes. He'd wanted to give her a good dinner as a thank-you for her help, and he'd delivered. "I hope you're hungry."

She didn't have to reply because she was digging into the meal with enthusiasm, and he liked that, too. He'd dated a lot of women who picked at their food or talked endlessly about the calorie count. But Ava didn't seem worried about that. Maybe because she ran her calories off every morning or was genetically blessed with a beautiful body. Either way, she was fun to have a meal with.

After their bad start, they'd gotten surprisingly comfortable with each other. Ava was starting to relax, to lower her guard walls, and he was enjoying getting to know her better. He wondered what it would take to get her to really let loose, give up control, throw caution to the wind… That would probably be a sight to see.

Clearing his throat, he told himself to think less about Ava and more about Maggie. "Did I hear you talking to Maggie about an Alaskan cruise?"

"Yes. Maggie wants to do that, but she is convinced John would never go with her, because she's been asking him to go for years. Frank, on the other hand, loves to cruise and would like to go with her if she ever decides to go and wants some company."

"Whoa," he said with a frown. "Frank needs to slow down. He's moving fast."

"He was being very friendly and helpful. And they have a lot in common. They want to be active. They like cruises. They both used to play golf. Neither one of them wants to spend their retirement years sitting around."

He sighed. "I never imagined I was going to run into this kind of problem. I thought it was all about money and a good business plan."

"That's what it's supposed to be. But the reality is that it's not, so what do you do?"

"What do you think?"

She looked surprised at his question. "What do I think?" she echoed.

"You have experience analyzing financial situations. What's your opinion?"

"I need to look at the books first."

"Fair enough."

"I'll do that after we eat."

"No rush. I want you to enjoy your dinner."

"I am enjoying it. You did a great job. When did you learn to cook?"

"When I was a kid. My mom often worked nights as a waitress, so Dad and I would grill. He liked to call himself a barbecue master. Occasionally, he let me take over when I got older, but I didn't like him telling me what to do, so I usually just let him grill while I did everything else."

"Did he teach you how to surf, too?"

"He was my first instructor. He had me on his board when I was three. My mother didn't like that he got me going so early, but I loved it, and I honestly don't remember a time when I wasn't surfing."

"I wonder what he would have done if you hadn't liked the water."

"Thankfully, he never had to find out," he said with a smile. "We spent so many hours on the water, and my father taught me as much about life when we were out there as he did about the sport."

"Like what?"

"Like living in the moment, not worrying about the future or the past, believing that things will work out even if it seems like they won't."

"Things don't always work out," she said quietly.

He knew she was thinking about her parents. "You're right. But the point was to appreciate what I had, not what I was missing. If I had a problem, he would ask me three questions: Are you healthy? Are you safe? Do you have people you love and who love you? If the answer was yes to all three, then I didn't have any problems."

"That's a good way to look at things, I guess. A little simplistic, though. It doesn't set the bar very high."

"I agree. And sometimes I just really wanted to complain about something. But my parents believed complaining was a waste of time. If I didn't like something, I should do something about it. I should take action, make a change. Even if the action I took was wrong, it would teach me something. My dad used to say you either win or you learn."

She cocked her head to the right, giving him a thoughtful look. "How did that advice work with your desire to always end up in first?"

"It didn't work very well. I didn't want to learn; I just wanted to win. But he wasn't wrong. I have learned from my losses." He watched a series of emotions play through her eyes that he couldn't begin to decipher. "What did I say?" he asked.

"Nothing," she replied.

"I can see the wheels turning in your head. You might think you have a poker face, but you don't."

"I was just thinking I don't remember any lessons my parents taught me. How is that possible? They didn't die until I was thirteen. They obviously taught me something before that. Why don't I remember?" she questioned.

He felt bad, seeing the pain in her eyes. He'd gone on and on talking about his parents when she'd lost hers. "I'm sure you remember something," he said. "Or their lessons are just ingrained in you, and you don't think about where you learned them."

"Maybe. Sometimes I think I've blocked out the good memories because I don't want to think about the bad ones."

"That makes sense. You had to do what you needed to do to protect your mental health."

"I guess. Anyway, it sounds like you had a good childhood with very wise parents who didn't worry about a lot."

"They probably should have worried a little more than they did. We didn't always end up in the best situations, at least in my opinion. I didn't find sleeping under the stars on a sandy beach to be the best option when there wasn't enough money for a hotel room or an apartment."

"The flip side of not planning ahead."

"Exactly. I had a good childhood because I had love, but

sometimes there were other things missing. Did you travel with your parents before they passed away?"

"No. My mom always said they wanted to take us to Europe when we were older, but that didn't happen. My aunt and uncle were always on the go with their travel company, but that was business, and we were not invited to participate."

"Never? That seems strange."

"Well, once they took us to Hawaii. That was lovely. I really liked the beaches on Maui. And the water was warm."

"I've surfed off every one of the Hawaiian Islands."

"I'll bet. We grew up very differently, Liam."

"But we both turned out good," he said with a smile.

She gave him a reluctant smile in return. "Well, I'm not as good a cook as you are, and I should be. My aunt and uncle worked long hours and I was often responsible for dinner. But I usually made sandwiches or heated up leftovers. I never wanted to spend time doing more. I was too busy trying to get my homework done and convince Serena to do hers. She was a huge procrastinator."

"I'm guessing you were not."

"No. I was determined to get good grades. I loved school and getting an A made me feel good. For Serena, the social scene was what made her happy."

"Were your parents focused on good grades?"

"Not really. They wanted us to do our work, but also have time for fun."

"What were they like?" he asked.

She hesitated. "Do you really want to know?"

"I wouldn't have asked if I didn't."

"My mom worked for an interior designer, and she would often take us to antique stores or thrift shops to look for hidden treasures in all the junk. I thought it was rather boring, but Serena loved it. My dad was an accountant. I get my love of numbers from him. He liked when things added up, and so do I."

"Did they have a good marriage?"

"I think so. They were always laughing and teasing each other. They were super affectionate, too. Sometimes, it was embarrassing to see them kissing all the time. But when I remember it now, I think it was sweet. We had a lot of love in our house." She drew in a breath, as her eyes grew watery. "Anyway, that was a long time ago."

"I'm sorry I made you sad."

"It's okay. It's been so long since they died that most people don't ask, and it's nice to talk about them. One of my favorite memories is of my parents dancing. Neither one liked television, but they both loved music. At night, after dinner, they'd put music on, and they'd dance in the living room. Serena and I would giggle and dance next to them or with them. It was so much fun. Of course, as we got older, we didn't want to do it as much."

"That's a nice memory."

"It is." She paused. "Thanks for pushing me to remember something good."

"They're a part of your life. They're in your blood and your heart; they always will be. You'll never forget them."

She blinked really quickly, then said, "You're right. I should never doubt that."

"You shouldn't."

She cleared her throat. "Anyway, this was an excellent meal."

"You haven't had dessert yet."

"I'm stuffed. Can I take a raincheck on the sundaes?"

"Of course. Later tonight, tomorrow, whenever..."

"Probably tomorrow. I want to start looking through John's ledgers now."

"Do you want me to do that with you?"

"I think it's best if I do it on my own."

"Okay. But don't forget, I still want to trade you a surfing lesson for your time. I think you'd enjoy it."

She gave him a doubtful look. "I can't imagine why you'd think that. Surely you've figured out I am not a daredevil."

"Maybe there's more dare and devil inside of you than you realize," he suggested.

"There's not, trust me. What do you like so much about surfing anyway?"

"So many things. Picking the right wave, challenging my mind and my body to perform in sync with the roll of the ocean, battling fear and other forces, getting the perfect ride, feeling one with the sea."

"You can feel like one with the ocean? I would think it would be a constant battle."

"It can be. I respect the ocean. I can't control it. But I can ride it, and that's when it feels like we're in sync."

"Have you ever been hurt?"

"A couple of times," he said, downplaying that answer. "But it never made me want to stop. It's exhilarating to surf, Ava. I want to show you how it can feel. And I know the perfect spot to take you. It's a cove a few miles away where the waves are gentle."

"I don't know. I'll think about it." She got to her feet. "This was…surprisingly fun."

"Surprisingly?" he asked as he stood up.

"We got along better than I thought we would," she admitted.

"You just needed to give me a chance, roomie. I knew we could be…friends." He didn't know why he'd paused before the word friends. Maybe because he liked the way the pink rose in her cheeks at his words and her eyes sparkled with uncertainty as their gazes clung together.

He found himself fighting an impulsive urge to take a step forward and see if her mouth tasted as good as it looked. But she'd probably slap him in the face if he did that, and while it might be worth it, they still had to live together.

Instead of reaching for her, he reached for her plate.

But his step forward made her jump backward, and he heard the catch of her breath as desire flared in her eyes. She was feeling it, too, this odd pull of attraction between them. He picked up her plate, and she flushed again, as if realizing she'd given too much away.

Then she abruptly turned and walked to the door. "I'm going to get to work."

"Okay," he said, but she was already gone.

He stared at the empty doorway for far longer than he should have.

Then he told himself what she was probably telling herself— that anything happening between them was a very bad idea. But it still might be worth it.

CHAPTER ELEVEN

TUESDAY MORNING AVA left her bedroom just before eight, prepared to face Liam with a neutral expression that would not give away the fact she'd been thinking about him all night. But he was gone. The door to his room was open, and there was no sign of him. Maybe he was surfing.

She blew out a breath as she went into the kitchen and started the coffeemaker. She hadn't seen Liam after dinner last night because she'd taken John's financial ledgers into her bedroom. She couldn't avoid him forever, and it was silly to even want to try. There was nothing between them. They'd had an odd little moment last night where she'd had the crazy idea he was going to kiss her, but he hadn't. And he wasn't going to. And she wasn't going to kiss him. That was the end of that.

She pulled out a coffee mug and wondered how she could be attracted to someone who was completely the opposite to her. Liam was not even close to anything she was looking for in a partner or even a date. He was too…everything, she thought.

Then she felt annoyed with herself for not being able to define exactly why he was so wrong. So, she'd make a list in her head, like she always did.

Leaning against the counter as she waited for her coffee to brew, she thought about all the reasons why Liam was wrong for her. Number one, he wasn't a serious person. He made his living surfing. He didn't have roots. He didn't even have a place to live right now. His finances were all going into the purchase of a store that had a good chance of losing money in the first year. What would happen then? Would he take off for a new adventure? It seemed likely. That's how he'd grown up.

His parents had taught him to live in the moment, and that was fine, but planning was a way to avoid future problems. And she was a person who was always worrying about the future. She'd saved every penny she'd ever made so she would never have to wonder if she had enough money to take care of herself and her sister. She was twenty-nine years old, and she'd already put retirement plans in motion. She was planning on buying a condo or a house in the next five years. And she'd been at the same job since she'd graduated from college. She hadn't jumped around like most of her friends. She'd put her head down, worked hard, and stayed the course.

God, she was so boring!

She frowned as she suddenly felt more disappointed in herself than in Liam. She didn't make waves, much less ride them. She'd built a safe, controlled life, with few surprises— good or bad. She had friends, although she wasn't close to very many people anymore. Her best friends had all moved away from LA and were with significant others now. Since she worked a lot, it was difficult to make friends, except the few she had at work.

But she had the life she wanted, the one she'd painstakingly built so that she would never have to feel scared again. The fear that had overwhelmed her after her parents' death was something she never wanted to relive.

It had been nice of Liam to ask her about her parents. He was a good listener, which wasn't something she encountered all that often. That was a point in his favor. He had also gone out of his way to make her dinner as a thank-you for something she would have done for nothing. Another point for him. He was very easy to talk to, and he was a curious person. He was interested in other people. He was interested in her.

Damn! She was adding a lot more pros than cons to her list. And she hadn't even allowed herself to think about the physical attraction that was starting to simmer between them.

Thankfully her coffee was ready. She filled her mug and then went back into the bedroom to get on a work call. After that, she'd go through the notes she'd made while reviewing John's books the night before so she could give Liam some advice.

She had already seen some problems in the books that could decrease the value of the business. That might help convince John he wouldn't get a better offer, but she didn't know if John's reluctance to make the deal was really about money. At any rate, she wanted Liam to have all the facts, and then he could make his decision.

Liam spent over an hour in the water, but his mind wasn't really on catching a wave. He'd always found the ocean a good place to think. Being offshore gave him a different perspective, one he needed. He'd been so focused on buying the Beach Shack that he'd rushed past some red flags. He knew that. He just hadn't been able to stop himself. He suspected Ava would find more red flags in John's financial records. And then what?

Did he withdraw his offer? Did he give up on that store in that location?

If he did, what then?

He couldn't think of an answer. He'd always believed that single-minded focus on a goal was the best way to achieve that goal. Having a backup plan was the easiest way to fail. But maybe Ava was right, and having another option in mind would have been the smart thing to do.

He hadn't had a chance to talk to her after dinner. He had a feeling her relocation to her bedroom had more to do with the small moment they'd shared in the kitchen than with her not wanting to work in the living room. Maybe that was just as well, because in getting to know her better, he'd started to like her more. But she was also like a thorny rose. One minute she was soft and pretty and another minute, she was drawing blood.

Not that he disliked unpredictability. It was the spice of life. But Ava was also Brad's sister-in-law, and he didn't want to mess with her and complicate things with his friend. Ava would also be gone in a week, and during that time he had to concentrate on getting his business deal back on track.

But he had to admit she was one of the most interesting women he'd met in a long time. She was very smart, driven, and sharp-edged, but she also seemed to have a softer side. He'd seen that when she'd spoken kindly to John. And she'd certainly been generous in offering her help to him when she clearly did not have to. She was a mix of contradictions, a tangle he wouldn't mind unraveling in ordinary circumstances. But she would be a huge distraction, and one that he did not need.

"Liam!"

The shout turned his head, and he saw Tyler and Gabe paddling toward him. Tyler was just the man he wanted to see.

"How's it going?" Tyler asked as he drew next to him.

"Good. You?"

"Can't complain. I thought you'd be out at the point. Bigger waves there."

He shrugged. "I know. I'm just enjoying the water." He turned to Gabe. "How's the food truck business going?"

"Getting busier every night," Gabe replied, running a hand through his dark hair as he sat up on his board. "But I need to change up my locations and see if I can find a wider audience. I have my eye on the corner by the park, near where Escalito's used to be."

He raised a brow. "I thought you were trying to get a group of investors together to rent that space and open your own place."

"Yeah. That's didn't happen. I couldn't find the investment. I need a bigger reputation, and I don't have it yet. There is a new restaurant moving into the space. It's supposed to open in a month or two. I heard it's going to be formal, fine dining." He shook his head. "I don't think it fits there at all."

"So you're going to put your food truck across the street." He could see the eager light in Gabe's eyes. "You're going to cause trouble, aren't you?"

Gabe grinned and gave an unrepentant shrug. "I say, let people have a choice, fine dining or fantastic tacos and burritos. I do have to get a permit, but it shouldn't be an issue. There's plenty of space on that block."

"Sounds like a plan. But the Maverick's customers will miss you."

"I'll split the week between the two locations. That will also make Dan happy," Gabe said referring to the long time cook at Maverick's. "He doesn't like it when people order my tacos and not his burgers."

"It might make it easier if you're not in the parking lot every night," Tyler conceded. "I can't lose Dan. He's rough around the edges, and complains a lot, but he's a damn good cook."

"Hopefully, my move works out for all of us. Eventually, I want to get out of the food truck business, but for now, it's my best option."

"Your food is damn good," he said. "Wherever you want to go, you'll get there."

"I agree. What about you, Liam?" Gabe asked. "How's your deal with the Beach Shack going?"

"Still going. John is having second thoughts about selling to me."

"John has been spending a lot of time at Maverick's," Tyler said. "Moaning about his wife, or maybe his soon-to-be ex-wife. I guess they're having problems."

"Problems that might derail my deal or significantly slow it down, which is why I wanted to talk to you about getting some shifts at Maverick's. I need to improve my cash flow while I'm working everything out. You need any help?"

"Actually, I do," Tyler replied. "One of my bartenders is on vacation for the next two weeks."

"Great. I'm available."

"Can you start tonight? We've got trivia at seven, which always brings in a big crowd."

"I'm there."

"Perfect. By the way, how's it going with Serena's sister? Ava seems very different from Serena, and I don't think she likes Brad at all."

"Ava doesn't know Brad, and she's worried they jumped into marriage too fast."

"Well, it was fast," Tyler agreed. "I can't blame her for thinking that."

"Love is fast," Gabe put in. "When it's right, you know it. Brad and Serena are great together."

"I'm glad Brad found his woman," Tyler said. "But he's really neglected the bar the last couple of months, and Maverick's was his idea. I was just going to help him out for a while, but a year turned into two years, and now I'm running it by myself."

He was surprised by the level of frustration in Tyler's voice. "You don't want to run the bar?"

"Honestly? No. It wasn't my dream, but Brad has always been there for me since our parents divorced and I wanted to support him."

"I'm sure Brad will get back to the bar as soon as he's home from his honeymoon. He loves Maverick's. He tells me that all the time."

"I think he's more in love with Serena than with the bar. I'm happy for him, but there comes a point where he has to get back to the business or we need to make some changes."

"It sounds like you two need to talk."

"At some point," Tyler agreed.

"What is Serena's sister like?" Gabe asked curiously.

"Ava is…" He couldn't quite find the right word. "Complicated."

Gabe laughed. "Interesting complicated or run-for-your-life complicated?"

He grinned. "Maybe both."

"So her hotness has not gone unnoticed by you," Gabe said, a knowing gleam in his gaze. "I personally have always been a sucker for a blue-eyed blonde."

He didn't really like the fact that Gabe was expressing interest in Ava, and that was an odd feeling. He'd never been a jealous person, and it wasn't like he and Ava were together. They weren't even friends, just slightly more than enemies.

"Should I be a friendly neighbor?" Gabe asked.

"You can be whatever you want," he said with an uncaring shrug, although judging by Gabe's sharp gaze, he wasn't coming across as disinterested as he should be. "But she's only here until Serena and Brad get back."

"A lot can happen in a short amount of time."

"I don't think Ava moves fast when it comes to men," he said. "She's not impulsive or a risk-taker. Everything is calculated in her head before she does it."

"Okay. That doesn't sound fun," Gabe said.

"I think she can be fun, if she'd let herself go a little," he muttered. "But she has a lot of walls up. She lost her parents when she was young, and that changed her. She became her sister's protector, and to do that, she had to make sure she could protect herself, too."

Gabe gave him a thoughtful look. "You like her. Why didn't you just say that?"

"We're roommates. There's nothing going on."

"Maybe not yet. But you still have time."

"I don't think so. I am only thinking about the Beach Shack right now."

Gabe gave him a doubtful look. "Okay."

"So, are we going to surf or what?" Tyler asked. "I don't know about you two, but I didn't come here to talk about women."

"Do you have a woman to talk about?" Gabe asked.

Tyler frowned. "No. Because I work all the time, and I'm not going to waste the next hour sitting out here, so…"

"Let's do it," he said, stretching on his board.

He paddled away from them to get in the right position. The sea hadn't brought him a lot of clarity this morning, not when it came to the Beach Shack, or his surprising attraction to Ava, but at least he'd gotten a part-time gig at the bar. That was something actionable, and he always felt better taking action. He'd put the future out of his head for a while and enjoy the moment, because it was really all he could count on at this point.

_____

When Liam got back to the beach around ten, he changed out of his wetsuit, threw on some dry clothes, and headed to the Beach Shack to talk to what he hoped was a more sober John Peterman. The store was quiet when he entered. John was rearranging a display of snorkeling gear on a shelf and muttering to himself as several items fell to the floor.

The displays definitely needed decluttering, and some of the products were starting to look dated. John wouldn't want to hear any criticism, so he kept his thoughts to himself. Clearing his throat, he said, "Morning, John. How are you doing today?"

"I'm fine," John said, giving him a wary look. "I have a vague idea of what happened yesterday morning, but I don't completely recall our meeting."

"That's why I'm here. I thought we should talk again."

"I don't know what I want to do, Liam," John blurted out. "I thought I did, but now I don't. And it's all because of that damn woman. All these years, I gave Maggie everything she wanted, and now she's not willing to give me what I want. Staying in Oceanside doesn't make sense from a financial standpoint. She needs to realize that I know what's best. I don't know why she doesn't trust me anymore."

"It feels like you need to be telling her all this," he said.

"I've tried. She doesn't listen."

"Maybe you need to try again. You've invested a lot of time and years in your relationship."

John stared back at him. "I don't know if I can handle her actually saying it's over."

He felt a wave of compassion for John, who was showing his age and his fear in every line on his weathered face.

"I also don't know," John continued, "if we still want the same kind of life. Maybe I should just go to Michigan and see if she wakes up, realizes she's alone, and changes her mind."

That would be the best plan for his personal interests, but he couldn't bring himself to agree with John. "Talk to Maggie, John. At least one more time."

"I thought you'd be telling me to sign the papers and go."

"I'm not against that, but you owe it to yourself, to Maggie, and to your marriage to have another conversation."

John slowly nodded. "I'll think about it. You take a look at my books yet?"

"I'm doing that today with help from Ava. You met her yesterday. I don't know if you remember her. She works in finance. In fact, she spends most days going through financial records of companies her firm might want to invest in."

John didn't look happy to hear that. "Well, I'm just a small business owner. And you know what I need to make this sale go through, Liam. Don't start thinking you can squeeze me for more money."

He wanted to say the same thing back to John, but he refrained. "I'd like to finalize our deal in the next day or two. I'll look at the books, and we'll meet tomorrow and see if we can move forward. In the meantime, I really think you should talk to Maggie and do it soon."

"Because Frank is swooping in, isn't he?"

He met John's gaze. "I don't know that anything is going on there, but I wouldn't wait."

CHAPTER TWELVE

Ava heard Liam come back around lunchtime, but she was caught up in calls for most of the day, so she stayed hunkered down in the bedroom, trying not to think about what he was doing and how long it had been since she'd seen him. By the time she was done with work, it was almost five. And she was more than tired of the four walls surrounding her.

When she entered the living room, she found Liam sitting on the couch in jeans and a T-shirt, strumming Brad's guitar, and her breath caught in her chest. With his messy brown hair, sparkling green eyes, and incredibly sexy smile, he was quite possibly the most attractive man she'd ever seen. He also seemed to be the most relaxed.

Maybe too relaxed, she told herself. Shouldn't he be more stressed out about his deal possibly falling apart? Didn't he have anything better to do with his time than play a guitar? She'd spent hours looking at John's books. Shouldn't that have been his job?

Although, she had offered, so she couldn't really judge him for that.

But she wanted to judge him for everything else. She wanted to start putting more checkmarks against him because she didn't like the way he made her feel—nervous and edgy, restless, yearning... She didn't know what she was yearning for, but she had a feeling it had something to do with his very full lips and the fact that she could see him strumming her body the way he was working the guitar.

She drew in a very tight breath at that errant thought.

Liam set down his guitar and got to his feet, his gaze fixed on hers.

As he took a step forward, she licked her lips. He could not be coming to her. He could not be feeling what she was feeling. He could not be wanting to kiss her the way she wanted to kiss him.

But he kept moving, and as he got closer, her anticipation and her anxiety clashed together. Her brain screamed at her to get herself out of this situation. It might be good for a while, but it wouldn't last, and then where would she be?

"Ava?" Her name on his lips sounded like a caress.

"What?" she asked breathlessly.

"It doesn't have to mean anything."

"What doesn't?" She barely got the two words out before he cupped her face with his hands and pressed his lips against hers.

The kiss set off a firestorm inside of her. His mouth was tender and demanding, and she wasn't at all in control, which was both amazing and terrifying at the same time.

When he lifted his head, a question in his eyes, her only answer was to pull him back in for another kiss and then another. She couldn't stop, even though she knew she should. But she kept telling herself that once she ended it, it would be over, completely over.

She wouldn't do this again. She wouldn't go crazy kissing him. That wasn't who she was.

But she didn't end it, and neither did he. And who knew where they might have ended up if Miss Daisy hadn't suddenly started meowing extremely loudly?

It took a minute for the sound to register, but when the cat slipped between their legs, they broke apart.

Her breath was coming fast, and so was Liam's. They stared at each other for a long minute before looking down at Miss Daisy, who was meowing loudly, clearly pissed off about not getting her dinner yet. Since she'd barely come out of hiding the last two days, Ava didn't know why the cat was suddenly right between them.

"Is she that hungry? It's early," she said.

"She's a cat. She doesn't know what time it is." He suddenly smiled. "Or maybe she's jealous. She didn't like you kissing me."

"You kissed me."

"The first time," he said pointedly.

She flushed at that comment, unable to deny it wasn't true.

"And I'm not complaining," he added. "Nor am I regretting what just happened. Are you?"

"No," she admitted.

He let out a breath. "Good. I was thinking you might say something else."

"There's nothing to say. You already said it."

"What did I say?" he asked in confusion.

"That it doesn't have to mean anything."

"Right."

"Exactly," she said, still flustered. "Just a kiss."

"Or twenty," he murmured.

"And they're over. We won't do this again."

"Why not?" he asked. "We did it very well."

"Because…" She saw the teasing light in his eyes. "You know the answer. I'm not someone who has flings, and that's all this would be, and that's why I don't want to start something."

"I think we already did that, Ava."

"Then we're ending it now." She licked her lips again, bringing his gaze to her mouth, which was not what she wanted to do. Clearing her throat, she said, "We might as well feed Miss

Daisy, since she's out. And we can give her the medicine at the same time."

"Good idea. I have to leave in about twenty minutes."

She was surprised by his words and both relieved and disappointed that he was leaving. "Where are you going?"

"I'm bartending at Maverick's tonight."

"Why?"

"To make extra cash. It appears I may need some." He picked up the whining Miss Daisy, who was surprisingly docile in his arms.

"You really have a way with her," she said in amazement.

"Maybe she was jealous."

"Can you blame her?" he teased.

His words brought a helpless smile to her lips. "You don't lack confidence; I'll say that, Liam."

"I'd like you to say more than that."

"Let's get Miss Daisy her medicine." That was a much safer reply than any other words she could utter.

She headed into the kitchen and busied herself preparing the cat's dose of medication. Liam sat down at the table, still holding a purring Miss Daisy in her arms. The man certainly could charm the ladies, she thought. He had just the right touch. A touch she really should not be wanting to feel as much as she did.

She waited until Liam caught Miss Daisy by the scruff so she could wedge the dropper into the side of her mouth and shoot the medication down her throat. As usual, when it was over, the cat flew out of Liam's arms, leaving a scratch on his arm.

"Oh, no," she said. "Sorry about that."

"It's fine. I'll live. One minute they love you, the next minute they don't," he said dryly.

She wondered if he was trying to make a point with those words but decided that was a treacherous path to go down, so she grabbed the cat food out of the cupboard and prepared Miss

Daisy's evening meal. She set it on the floor by the kitchen counter, knowing the cat would be back soon.

"I've been wanting to ask you if you had a chance to go over John's books," Liam said.

"I did. I've made some notes. We probably don't have time to go through them now, if you're leaving soon."

"I am. How does your morning look?"

"Pretty good. I don't have meetings until eleven."

"Great. Why don't we meet here at seven thirty?"

"That sounds awfully early and a very precise time," she said warily.

"It's the perfect time to hit the water. I'll give you a short surfing lesson before work. The weather is perfect, and I know just the place to go where the waves are very small. I promise that nothing will happen to you."

She didn't believe he could make that promise, because something was happening to her, and it had a lot to do with him.

He leaned forward, pressing his hands together, his gaze earnest and pleading. "I really want you to have this experience, Ava. You won't regret it."

She hadn't had anyone want anything for her in a very long time, and her heart squeezed at his words. "Okay," she said. Because how could she refuse his desire to make her happy, to show her something new? If she didn't like it, she could always quit.

"Really?" he asked in surprise.

"Don't make me say it again, or I might change my mind."

"All right. Then we're on for seven thirty. By the way, it's trivia night at Maverick's tonight. It's a great time, very fun. Maybe you should drop by."

"I don't know."

"That's always your go-to answer, isn't it?" he said as he got to his feet.

"I already said I was going surfing with you. Don't push it."

"Point taken. By the way, I spoke to John today, and I told

him he should talk to Maggie. Put his cards on the table and see what happens."

"That's risky—for both of you."

"I know, but after hearing him talk about her, I just couldn't push him to let her go so easily. They've been together a long time. I don't want to be the person who tears them apart."

"Even if you lose your dream?"

"I've never liked winning when I wasn't going up against someone at their best. And this feels a little like that. Anyway, I told John what I thought he should do. It's on him if he actually does it."

She nodded, wishing that everything he said didn't make her like him more.

———

After Liam left for work, Ava decided to do laundry. She gathered her dirty clothes into a basket and went downstairs to the communal laundry room. That was one thing she didn't like about Ocean Shores: no washer and dryer in each unit. On the other hand, she'd been inside all day, so it was nice to get out of the apartment.

The laundry room was located on the first floor across from Josie's apartment. There were four washers and four dryers, and two were already in use. She loaded her laundry into one of the empty ones and was happy to see there was no charge for their use. As she closed the washer door, Emmalyn came into the room.

"Hi, Ava," she said with a cheerful smile.

Emmalyn wore leggings and a T-shirt, her blonde hair pulled up in a loose knot. "Looks like it's laundry day for more than just me."

"It is. I like your shirt," she said, tipping her head to the bright Taylor Swift graphic on Emmalyn's T-shirt.

She smiled. "Thanks. I'm a new fan," Emmalyn replied. "Kaia

got me into listening to her music this year, and I was impressed. I know she's been around for a long time, but I'm still catching up on the music scene."

"What do you mean—catching up?" she asked as Emmalyn loaded the remaining washer.

"I didn't listen to music when I was a kid. It wasn't allowed. What about you?"

"Music was a big part of my childhood. My parents loved taking us to concerts, even ones I thought were kind of boring, like classical music. Not that I don't appreciate it now, but as a kid, I was more interested in songs about love, school, and friends, all that kind of stuff."

Shadows appeared in Emmalyn's eyes. "I'd like to go to a concert some time. I've never been to one."

"Never?" she asked in surprise.

"No." Emmalyn looked like she wanted to say more, then just shook her head and repeated the word, "No. So, what are you doing tonight? A bunch of us are going to play trivia at Maverick's if you want to join."

She started to say she didn't know when Liam's words rang through her head. She did answer a lot of questions with those three words.

Before she could think of another reply, Maggie came into the laundry room, followed by Frank.

"It's a crowd in here," Maggie said.

"We picked a popular time," Frank added with a cheerful smile.

"I've always done laundry on Tuesdays and Saturdays," Maggie said. "John set up that schedule a long time ago, and I guess I haven't broken the habit."

"Well, you can go a little crazy and not do your laundry again until Sunday," Frank said with a laugh that Maggie immediately returned.

Ava was beginning to think Frank was good for Maggie. He certainly seemed to lighten her mood.

"What's everyone doing tonight?" Frank asked, directing the question at her and Emmalyn. "Did I hear something is happening at Maverick's?"

"Trivia night," Emmalyn replied. "You should both come. I bet you would clean up in some of the categories."

"The old age categories?" he asked with another grin.

"Oh, no, I didn't mean it like that," Emmalyn said hastily, looking embarrassed. "But you were a lawyer and worked in entertainment, so you probably know history and movie stuff."

"I was just teasing you," Frank said. "What do you think, Maggie? Want to go with me and kick some young butt?"

Maggie smiled back at him. "I actually love trivia. But I don't know how good I am. I might bring you down."

"It's for fun. Doesn't matter how well we do. We'll see you there," he said.

As Maggie and Frank took their laundry and left, Emmalyn said, "I wonder if something is going on with them. They seem very friendly."

"I know Maggie isn't completely divorced, so…"

"But she's separated from her husband, and if she left him, she must have had a good reason. It's hard for anyone to walk away from a long relationship, even if they're unhappy. They can get stuck. They stop thinking about the future and what they originally wanted, and they give up. It's kind of impressive when someone is willing to make a change later in life."

She'd thought Emmalyn was just a sweet kindergarten teacher with an innocent vibe, but she seemed to have some darker thoughts in her head, too. And what she'd said about her past had also been a little unusual, not listening to music or going to concerts. There was a story there.

"Anyway, what about you, Ava? Will you come to Maverick's for trivia night?"

She decided to forego her usual answer of 'I don't know' and said, "Yes. I will."

"Great. We can walk over together. I'll meet you by the front door at six forty-five," Emmalyn said.

"Okay." She was about to follow Emmalyn out of the laundry room when her phone rang. Jeff's name ran across the screen. She hesitated. She'd been in meetings all day with him, but they hadn't had any private conversations, and she didn't want to have one now. Whatever he wanted would probably take up her night or piss her off, so she did something she never did—she let the call go to voicemail.

A text immediately followed his unanswered call: *Crisis with Woodward. Need your help tonight. Call me.*

Woodward Enterprises was Jeff's account. She had never been involved with them. He'd wanted the high-profile software company on his résumé alone. Usually, she'd be quick to offer assistance. She was the ultimate team player, but Lisa's warning yesterday had made her wary of giving Jeff too much help when she didn't know what he was doing behind her back. It was after five. He could wait. Or better yet, he could try to solve his own problem and prove he was as valuable as he thought he was.

She slipped her phone into her pocket and headed to the door. As she walked outside, she ran into John Peterman.

"John," she said in surprise. "Do you remember me? We met yesterday. I'm Ava Campbell."

"You're Liam's friend," he said with a nod and a troubled expression on his face. But at least his eyes were clear, and he appeared to be sober.

"I want to apologize for my behavior yesterday," he added. "I'm not usually like that."

"I didn't expect you were."

"I'm looking for my wife—Maggie. Josie said she was doing laundry. Is she in there?"

"She was, but she left."

"Do you know where she went? She's not at Josie's."

"I'm sorry, I don't know." She was glad she didn't know

because she didn't want to lie to him. She also didn't want to tell him she'd last seen Maggie with Frank.

"Well, I guess I'll keep looking for her." He paused. "Liam said you're reviewing my financial records."

"He asked me to take a look. I have a lot of experience in company financials."

"He mentioned that. I'm sure you must think I'm living in the dark ages, doing everything by hand. But I'm not good on the computer. And I like to write everything down."

She thought his records were a mess, but she wasn't going to tell him that. Her standards were higher than the average person. "I'm not judging. I'm just trying to help Liam get a better idea of the financials so that he can give you a more detailed proposal, as you requested yesterday. Liam really wants this deal to work out. I'm sure you know that."

"He's a good guy. He reminds me of myself when I first opened the Beach Shack. I had the same look in my eyes, the same sense of excitement."

"Which should make you feel good about passing the business on to someone who will treasure what you built," she said. "Liam has a lot of respect for your business."

"I do appreciate that. I thought I knew exactly what I wanted to do. I could finally sell the store and retire, have time to do what I wanted, but now...I don't know what's going on. My wife of thirty-eight years is living somewhere else. It doesn't make sense to me. I don't know how I got here."

His bewildered look made her feel sorry for him. "It sounds like you need to talk to your wife."

"That's why I came here. But she's like a different person now, and I'm looking at being alone for the rest of my days. I haven't been alone since I was thirty years old."

She wondered if it was the loss of Maggie or the being alone part that bothered him most. Maybe Maggie wondered that, too.

"I called Maggie hours ago, and she never called me back," he continued. "Now no one seems to know where she is, or they don't want to tell me."

She wanted to tell John he could probably find Maggie at Maverick's tonight, but she didn't think seeing Maggie and Frank together would be good for mending their relationship, so she stayed silent.

"I guess I'll go," John said.

"Good luck," she said, watching him wander away, looking as lost and aimless as he'd sounded.

As she walked toward the stairs, she heard a woman laughing from a downstairs apartment—Frank's apartment. She had a feeling John had his work cut out for him.

CHAPTER THIRTEEN

KAIA MERCER and a brown-haired man Liam didn't recognize slid onto stools at his end of the bar at Maverick's.

"Well, I didn't expect to see you serving drinks, Liam," Kaia said with a smile.

"Just picking up some shifts until I get my store going. What can I get you?"

"Vodka tonic for me. This is my brother, Ben Mercer. He's visiting from LA, soon to be moving here permanently."

"Nice to meet you. Liam Nash."

"You, too," Ben replied. "My sister seems to know everyone in this town."

"Not everyone, just the right people," Kaia said with a laugh. "Like bartenders who will give us a nice pour."

He smiled. "You got it. What are you drinking, Ben?"

"I'll take a Jameson neat."

"Got it." As he prepared their drinks, he said, "So you're moving here, Ben?"

"I'm working on a transfer. I'm a police officer."

He handed Ben his whiskey. "I'm moving here, too. It's a great city."

"I think it will be a nice change of pace," Ben said. "Although, I will be living very close to my sister, so there's that."

Kaia jabbed her brother in the side. "Not funny, Ben. You'd be lucky to live close to me."

"That hurt," Ben complained with a mock grimace.

"You're the one who taught me how to give it back to someone," she said with a laugh.

"Are you older or younger?" Liam asked Ben as he handed Kaia her drink.

"Oh, my God," Kaia said in mock horror. "How can you even ask that? Isn't it clear he's older?"

"Sorry," he said with a smile. "I didn't want to assume anything."

"I'm older by two years," Ben said. "Although sometimes it feels more like a hundred." He slid off the stool. "I'm going to find the restroom."

"Down the hall to your right," Liam said, surprised to see a gleam of worry in Kaia's gaze as it followed her brother through the bar. "You okay?" he asked.

"Oh, yes," she said, turning back to him. "I'm just hoping my brother makes the move here. He's had a rough year. I want him to be happy. Anyway…are you going to live at Ocean Shores after Brad and Serena come back? There are at least two empty apartments right now. It would be great to have you in the building."

"I'm strongly considering it. I can't make any final decisions until I close this deal."

"Is there a chance that won't happen?"

"There are a few complications, but I'm working on it."

"Good." She gave him a curious look. "I know it's none of my business, but is there something going on with you and Ava?"

"You're right; it's none of your business," he said pointedly, knowing that Kaia was the kind of person he could be direct with.

"I'm going to take that as a yes," she said with a gleam in her eyes.

"That's not what I said."

"Well, I kind of picked up on a vibe between the two of you the other night. But she's not staying in Oceanside, is she?"

"That's not her plan."

"Plans can change."

"I don't think Ava changes her plans once she makes them."

"She seems very different from Serena, but I don't know her that well. I'm hoping she'll come to our girls' night on Thursday." She paused as her gaze moved toward the entrance. "Oh, look— there's Maggie, Frank, and Josie."

He was surprised to see the trio grabbing a table in the bar. He didn't love seeing Frank pull out Maggie's chair in a thoughtful, gentlemanly kind of way. He'd hoped that John might have tried to talk to Maggie, that maybe they would be spending time together. But either John hadn't acted, or Maggie hadn't been interested in talking to John.

"I have a feeling those three are going to kick our butts in trivia," Kaia continued. "But Ben might be my secret weapon, at least when it comes to music categories. He used to be in a band, and he loves music from all genres and all generations."

"A musician turned cop, that's an interesting path."

"Sometimes I wish he'd stayed in the band. But he likes to protect people. He's driven to it."

"Seems like you are, too. You're both first responders."

"That's true. We're alike in some ways, but very different in others."

"I'll have to hear more about that later. I better get back to work."

"No problem. I'm going to find a table."

For the next fifteen minutes, he was kept busy making drinks. While he tried to keep an eye on what was going on with Maggie and Frank, he was too busy to pay much attention to them.

But his attention was definitely drawn to the sight of one pretty, hard-edged blonde who entered the bar a few minutes before seven. He was surprised to see Ava with Emmalyn but also extremely happy she'd left the apartment.

As soon as her gaze met his, he felt an unexpected jolt. Everyone in the bar fell away. All he could see was her. All he could hear was the beat of his heart. It shocked him how connected he felt to a woman he'd known only a few days and a woman who often seemed to hate him.

But she hadn't been hating him when she'd kissed him earlier.

Although, she might have hated herself for giving in to the impulsive and spontaneous make- out session. She'd told him it wouldn't happen again. But he didn't see how it couldn't happen again. There was a strong attraction between them, even though neither of them had been looking for that.

"Hello?" A woman's annoyed voice broke through his reverie. "Are you getting my wine, or what?" an irritated brunette asked.

"Sorry." He turned around, grabbed a wine glass and filled it with chardonnay, adding extra as an apology.

Her irritation quickly faded. "Thanks."

As the woman moved away from the bar, Emmalyn and Ava took her place.

"Hi, Liam," Emmalyn said. "I didn't know you were working here."

"Temporarily. What are you two drinking?"

"I just want a sparkling water," she replied.

"Sure. Ava?" he asked.

"I'll take a glass of pinot grigio."

"Going with wine tonight?"

"I like to mix it up," she replied.

"I'm glad you decided to come."

"Emmalyn talked me into it," she said, her gaze meeting his with a gleam of remembered intimacy that made his muscles tighten.

"I'm going to get us a table," Emmalyn said as he handed her a glass of sparkling water. "I see Kaia and her brother. Maybe we can team up with them."

"Okay," Ava said, but her gaze was still connected to his.

He filled her glass, then slid it across the bar.

"Thanks. Did you see Maggie and Frank?" she asked.

"Yes. I was hoping John had managed to get in touch with Maggie. But it doesn't look like that happened."

"John came to Ocean Shores. I was leaving the laundry room, and I ran into him in the courtyard. He was looking for Maggie, but she wasn't at Josie's. I knew where she was or at least I suspected, but I didn't tell him because she was with Frank when I saw her. I don't know if John has a chance of getting her back. She really seems to like Frank."

"Well, maybe it's too late then," he said heavily.

"It could work in your favor," she pointed out. "If John abandons all hope of a reunion, he might just take your offer and move to Michigan on his own."

"That's true. I just feel like they were together so long…it seems wrong for him not to fight for her."

"I think they have been fighting. That's the problem."

"Against each other, not for each other."

A thoughtful gleam entered her eyes. "It's nice that you care so much about them, even though it goes against your own self-interest."

"I just don't want my happiness to be at the expense of someone else's," he said heavily.

"You're not responsible for what's happening to them."

"I know. And there's nothing I can do about it anyway. I'll just have to see what happens. We can talk more later. I better keep working."

"That's fine. I'll join the others."

"It's good to see you here, Ava. You didn't sound interested when I asked you."

"Well, what you said kind of resonated with me."

"What I said?" he queried.

"About how my first answer is always 'I don't know.' I started to say the same thing when Emmalyn asked me, and I stopped myself. It's a habit that I probably will have a hard time breaking."

He smiled. "I'm glad you broke the habit tonight. Have fun."

"I'm going to try." She took her glass and walked across the room, settling into a table with Emmalyn, Kaia, and Kaia's brother, Ben.

There was no more time to think about Ava, Maggie or Frank as the line at the bar was constantly three deep for the next two hours. Maverick's was raking in the money for trivia night, and he was making good tips. It wasn't what he wanted to be doing, but it was cash, and a job he knew how to do. Hopefully by the end of the week, he would finalize his deal and be on his way to being his own boss at his own business.

***

"You are killing it, Ava," Emmalyn said, admiration in her gaze as Ava nailed another answer in the trivia game, putting their team of four into the finals of the event.

"You are," Kaia agreed. "Between you and Ben, Emmalyn and I are getting a lot of free drinks."

Since every winning round brought more drinks to their table, she was feeling both heady with her achievement and also a little drunk. But the finals were on, and she needed to get her head together.

Fortunately, Ben knew the categories she didn't—music and sports. But she was extremely good at history, geography, television, and film. Reading, studying, and watching old movies had sustained her after her parents died, and she'd retained a lot of that knowledge.

But there was another team that was damn good, and that

team included Maggie, Frank, and Josie. She couldn't help but notice that Maggie and Frank were sitting very close together, and occasionally, he had an arm around the back of Maggie's chair.

She really shouldn't be that interested in the love life of two people in their early seventies, and as she was thinking about that, her momentary distraction cost her as she missed answering a question she knew. That couldn't happen again. She wouldn't end up the first loser, as Liam liked to call second place. She was going all in. Her newly found concentration paid off, as she nailed the last three answers to win the game for her team. There were high fives and fist bumps all around as they were named Maverick's Trivia Champions, and the recipients of free drinks for the rest of the week.

"I feel like I don't deserve this," Emmalyn said as the crowd began to disperse. "I answered like two questions. Plus, I don't drink."

She had noticed that Emmalyn wasn't drinking alcohol but hadn't questioned why.

"You answered one more than me, Emmalyn," Kaia said. "And I'm not complaining."

"My sister never complains about free drinks," Ben said with a grin. "And you can have my coupon since I'm leaving tomorrow, and I won't be back for the rest of the week. I'm going to take off, Kaia. I'm meeting Bryce for a drink, or maybe I'll make it coffee," he added with a laugh. He turned his gaze to her and Emmalyn. "Ladies, nice teamwork. I hope to see you again soon."

"I'll probably be back in LA when you return," she said. "It was nice to meet you."

"You, too. Maybe we'll see each other again when you come to visit your sister."

"Sounds good."

As Ben left, Kaia said, "So, Ava, how did you get to be so smart?"

"I don't think knowing the names of kids on old sitcoms counts as smart," she said dryly.

"You're selling yourself short. You clearly have a vast amount of knowledge in your head."

"About a lot of trivial things. Your brother was good, too."

"Oh, yeah. Ben is super smart. Definitely more intelligent than me and my younger brother, Jason. Jason says Ben got the brains, I got the looks, and he got the athletic ability. He's in the minor leagues of baseball right now."

"Where does he live?" she asked.

"He's in South Carolina. The experience is not what he was hoping for, but he still believes he can make it to the majors, or whatever they call it these days. I hope he does. My brothers get a lot of pressure from my dad to excel. Me, not so much."

"But you are excelling," Emmalyn said. "You're a paramedic. You save lives."

"It's not always that dramatic, but sometimes," she said with a shrug.

"How do you stay so calm in the middle of a horrible situation?" Emmalyn asked.

"I rely on my training. Whatever the problem is, I look at that and only that. I don't let emotions get in the way."

"That doesn't sound easy," she commented.

"It's the way I was taught. I answer the call and then I let the call go."

"Isn't it difficult to let some of them go? Do you ever follow up?" she asked. "Go down to the hospital to see if someone made it?"

"I can't say I've never done that, but I try not to," Kaia replied. "Getting too involved is never good. It's not what my job is about. I don't have the skills to help anyone beyond what I already did when I treated them during their emergency."

"I don't think I could stop thinking about every call," Emmalyn said. "I could never do what you do."

"I couldn't either," she muttered.

"Really, Ava?" Kaia challenged. "I have the feeling you don't let a lot of people get too close. You've barely told us anything about yourself."

"There's not much to tell. And we've been busy," she added, feeling a little wary under Kaia's sharp gaze.

"Well, we know you're good at trivia, but what else are you into?" Kaia asked.

It was an easy question, one that should have an easy answer, but she couldn't seem to come up with one. "I just work a lot," she said finally. "And, clearly, I watch too much television. I also read a fair amount. That's about it."

"Speaking of reading," Kaia said. "Are you coming to book club Thursday night?"

"I thought it was a girls' night."

"Well, that's really what it is. Sometimes we also discuss a book, but reading the book is not a requirement to come. If it was, hardly anyone would ever be there."

"I don't know," she said, realizing she'd once again fallen into her favorite answer.

"I actually haven't finished this month's book," Emmalyn said. "So you wouldn't be the only one who hasn't read it, Ava. You should come. Lexie will be there, too. And a couple of other women from the building. Have you met Paige? She's a single mom with an adorable six-year-old boy, Henry."

"No. I didn't realize there were any kids in the building." She turned her head, hearing a sudden commotion across the room. She was shocked to see John Peterman staggering toward Maggie's table, looking almost as drunk as he had yesterday.

"So this is where you are," John said in a loud, accusing voice, as if he'd just found Maggie in the middle of an affair.

"What are you doing here, John?" Maggie asked in shock. "Are you drunk?"

"Are you?" he countered. "Is Frank the reason you won't call me back?"

Frank stood up. "I think you should go, John."

"And I think you should mind your own business," John said, jabbing his finger into Frank's chest.

Frank, to his credit, didn't react, but he also didn't back down. "This isn't the time or the place."

"Don't tell me what to do, you wife-stealer."

A hush fell over the room as John's voice rang through the crowd.

"Don't call him that," Maggie said as she stood up. "Frank has nothing to do with you and me."

"Then why are you here with him?"

"Please, just go, John," she begged.

"You should go," Josie said, rising to her feet, the three of them facing John down.

But John didn't seem inclined to go until Liam came around the bar and stepped between John and the three of them.

"Let's go, John," he said, attempting to grab the older man's arm.

John shoved his arm away from him. "Get out of my way, Liam."

"Not going to happen," Liam said firmly. "If you want to talk to Maggie, you'll do it when you're sober, and when she wants to speak to you."

"You don't want to piss me off," John warned. "I hold your future in my hands."

Liam ignored that. "Let's go."

"I'll come outside," Maggie said. "Anything to end this now."

At her words, John turned toward the door. Liam and Maggie followed him outside.

When Liam didn't come back right away, Ava wondered if he was staying to referee. Probably. He'd want to protect Maggie, and he'd probably also want to protect John from himself. But he might have made a bad move, acting against the man whose business he wanted to buy. The fact that he was willing to do that said a lot about his character.

And, damn it, she had just found another reason to like him.

CHAPTER FOURTEEN

"You can go, Liam," John said.

"I think I'll stay." He sent Maggie a questioning look. "Unless you want me to go?"

She didn't answer. She didn't seem to care whether he stayed or not. There was a fire burning in her eyes as she turned to John. "What on earth were you thinking?" she demanded. "Getting drunk, saying those horrible things to me, accusing Frank of stealing me. That's crazy. You and I split up months ago. Our separation has nothing to do with Frank."

"He's putting ideas in your head. He's working against me."

"Against you? We've been drifting apart for years. You know that."

As their conversation turned more personal, he thought about slipping away, but he wasn't sure how aggressive John would be toward Maggie, so instead of leaving, he took a few steps back, still close enough to help, but not standing right in the middle of their conversation.

"It's been ten years since we had any fun, a real conversation, a shared joy of anything," Maggie continued.

"That's not true. We've had fun."

"No, we haven't," she said. "And I don't see anything in our future that would suggest that's going to change. All you want to do is go to Michigan and be near your family. You don't care that I don't want to go, that my life is here."

"It's too damned expensive."

"We've been in California for forty years; I know what it costs," she snapped. "And I'm not saying it has to all be on you. I've got some money from my mom that I could use to help out."

"That money is for our daughter. I'm not touching it. We both agreed."

"You can't have everything your way," she said in frustration. "And I already talked to Tori about the money. She doesn't need it. Kyle makes great money, and so does she."

"It's not my way; it's your way," John argued. "You're the one who left our marriage."

"Only physically. You left it a long time ago, and you know that."

Liam felt more and more uncomfortable. John didn't seem as aggressive as he'd been earlier. Maybe it was time for him to leave. But then John took a step forward and grabbed Maggie's arm.

"What are you doing?" she asked, trying to shake her arm loose.

Liam stepped closer to them. "Let her go, John."

"What are you—her bodyguard?" John demanded. "I'm not hurting her. I just want her to listen."

"I'm right here. I'm listening," Maggie said. "What do you want to say?"

"You're my wife. We should be together. If you move to Michigan with me, I'll take you on that cruise you want. In fact, I'll take you on a cruise once a year."

"This isn't about a cruise, John."

"You've been talking about it for years."

"Because I wanted to find a way for us to do something together. All you want to do is talk to your surfing buddies and watch TV. I want more for the rest of my life. I don't want to be with someone who just needs me to cook him dinner and do his laundry. Someone who barely answers me when I speak to him because he's too busy getting riled up by some cable news program about things that are far less important than our marriage. I've told you this many times. If you want another chance with me, it has to happen here."

John let go of her arm. "Would it happen here if I agree to stay? Would you come back to me?"

His questions hung in the air, and Liam held his breath, knowing that her answer could affect his life, too.

"Well?" John pressed when she didn't answer. "What if I don't sell the store? Or I wait for a bigger offer? Are you going to come home in the meantime?"

"Will things be different?" she countered. "Are you coming to trivia nights with me, planning vacations, going out dancing, seeing friends…"

"Dancing? We've never gone dancing, Maggie."

"Because you wouldn't. But I want to. I want to have a life. I know everyone else would say we're old and we're done, but I don't feel old or done. Our daughter is grown. Our grandkids are in school and busy. I don't want to just dance; I want to ride bikes, go to movies, read books and talk about them. I want to have friends over for dinner. I want to socialize. And I'm willing to do that by myself because I'm not sure you want to change. I think you're just scared to be alone. That's why you're here. And that's not a good enough reason for us to stay together. I deserve more. And so do you, John. If you don't want the life I want, then you should find what you want and do that."

There was so much passion and intensity in her words that Liam found himself changing sides with every other sentence. The more Maggie spoke, the more he wanted to tell her she should keep going down the path she was on, and it wasn't because her leaving John would free up the store for him; it was because she sounded like she really needed to have the life she wanted before it was too late to get it.

"I don't know what you want from me," John said.

Liam inwardly groaned. Considering what Maggie had just told him, John should absolutely know what she wanted. Was he just too drunk to pay attention or did he never listen to her?

"I just told you," Maggie said in frustration. "Why do you even want me back?"

"You're my wife."

"You know what a better answer would have been?" she challenged. "I love you. That's what you should have said."

"Well, you already know that," he muttered angrily. "It's Frank that has you confused."

"That's enough." She held up her hand. "If you want to talk to me again, do it when you're sober, and when you actually know what you want to say, because this conversation is over."

She turned and walked back into the bar.

As she left, John let out a shaky breath. "I knew talking to her was a bad idea."

"Talking wasn't a bad idea," he replied. "Not listening was the problem. She told you she wanted your attention, John. Didn't you hear that?"

"I don't want to do all that stuff she wants to do. I don't dance. I don't read books. She's got girlfriends to talk about books with."

"In Michigan? Because it sounds like her friends are here."

"So, I should just let her go and sell the store to you? That's what you want, right?"

"This isn't about the store."

"Good. Because I don't think I want to sell to someone who keeps getting in my business. This is my life. Stay the hell away from it." With that proclamation, John staggered out of the parking lot. Fortunately, he didn't head toward a car, so he'd probably walked from the Beach Shack or his house, which he knew was somewhere in the nearby vicinity.

As he turned back toward the bar, he saw Ava standing just outside the door, a concerned look on her face.

She walked toward him. "That didn't go well, did it?"

"No. I think I just made myself John's least favorite person."

"I think Frank has you beat for that position. I only heard the last bit. But Maggie looked pissed when she blew past me."

"Maggie told John what she wanted, and he didn't respond. I'm not sure he even heard her. I think they're done." He let out a sigh. "I might be done, too."

"He probably won't remember what he said to you, Liam."

He shrugged. "We'll see. I better get back to the bar before I lose the only other way I have to make money right now."

She put a hand on his arm.

He gave her a questioning look. "What?"

"I just want to say, you did good, Liam. You stood up for Maggie, at your own expense."

Her admiration shocked him. He didn't think he'd done much good at all, but she seemed to feel differently, and the electricity sizzled between them once more. He was about to kiss her again when the front door opened, and a chorus of female voices rang out.

Ava immediately stepped back, dropping her hand from his arm as Emmalyn and Kaia came toward them.

"Everything okay?" Kaia asked, giving them both a sharp look.

"Yes," Ava said quickly. "John has left."

"Well, that's good. I've never seen him so angry or jealous," Kaia commented. "But Maggie didn't look too beaten down when she came back inside. She appeared almost triumphant, like she'd gotten something off her chest."

"I think she did exactly that," Liam said. "I need to get back to work. I'll see you all later."

"Are you ready to go, Ava?" Emmalyn asked.

"Yes. I'll see you at home, Liam."

"At home," he echoed, thinking how oddly ironic it was that the apartment they were both watching over temporarily felt more like home than any place he'd lived.

Maybe Josie was right about Ocean Shores weaving magic around its tenants. Because if it wasn't magic, then the only other possibility was one very prickly blonde, who he really wanted to kiss again.

———————

Liam got up at seven on Wednesday morning. Ava's door had been closed when he'd gotten home from the bar, and he hadn't had a chance to confirm that she'd join him for a surfing lesson this morning, but he became more hopeful when he smelled coffee. When he entered the kitchen, he found Ava standing at the counter, wearing shorts and a tank top, with flip-flops on her feet, not running shoes. The straps of her bathing suit showed under her shirt, too. He took all that as a good sign.

"Are we doing it?" he asked as he filled a mug. "Surfing," he added hastily as his mind, and maybe hers, too, seemed to have flashed on an entirely different scenario.

She sipped her coffee, then gave him a different answer than she usually did. "Yes."

Excitement ran through him. "That's great."

"Unless you think the waves or the weather aren't good enough."

He smiled at the worried look in her blue eyes. "It's a beautiful day and the waves will be small swells, not great for the experienced surfers but perfect for us."

"You mean perfect for me."

"Correct. It will be fun, Ava, I promise."

"I don't have a wetsuit."

"I have one you can use."

She raised a brow. "You do? Am I going to fit into your wetsuit?"

"I have a smaller size."

"Interesting. For who?" she asked.

"For whoever needs it," he said vaguely, not really wanting to get into who had used that wetsuit last. He took another sip of coffee and then set down his mug. "I'll get the wetsuit and our boards in the car, and then we can go. You can change into the wetsuit at the beach. It's not comfortable to travel in."

"Okay. You have two surfboards as well?"

"Yes. I've got you covered. Any more questions?"

"I'm kind of wondering about sharks."

Her muttered comment made him smile. "Of course you're wondering about sharks. We'll be fine."

"Have you ever seen a shark?"

"A couple of times, but not around here, and we'll be close to shore. Trust me, Ava. I'm not going to let anything happen to you."

"You can't guarantee that, Liam. The ocean is unpredictable."

He understood that for Ava to put her trust in anyone, especially when it came to something as unpredictable as the ocean, was a very big deal. He decided to be completely honest. "You're right. I can't guarantee anything, but I'll make my best effort. How's that?"

She seemed to appreciate that he wasn't trying to brush over her concerns. "That's good. Let's go before I change my mind."

———

After arriving at the beach, they donned their wetsuits and took their boards to the water's edge. Before wading into the ocean, he went through some basic instructions, showing Ava how she would sit on the board, how she would paddle, and how she would stand up and balance. She had a million questions, which he answered as patiently as he could. He was beginning to realize that Ava dealt with anxiety by arming herself with a lot of information and preparing for any possible outcome.

It took almost forty-five minutes for her to run out of questions, but he wanted to give her as much time as she needed. If he pushed too hard too fast, she'd probably bolt. Although, she did have a determined expression on her face. Even with her fear, she'd made a commitment to the lesson, and she was going through with it.

Finally, they entered the water. She squealed a little as the cold hit her feet.

"You'll get used to it," he told her. "And your wetsuit will keep you warm."

"I feel like a stuffed sausage in this thing," she said.

"You don't look like one," he said, his gaze moving over her beautiful form. The wetsuit fit her like a glove, a very pretty glove. "Are you ready?"

"I don't know," she said as the breeze whipped her blonde ponytail around her face, and trepidation filled her gaze. The waves were very mild, but to her they probably looked like monsters.

"You don't have to do this if you don't want to. You don't have to prove anything to me."

"I know. But maybe I need to prove something to myself. I never take risks. I always say no. I'm starting to think that isn't the best way to live. So…" She drew in a breath and let it out. "I'm not ready, but let's do it anyway."

"Okay. We're going to paddle out to the waves. Follow me."

"Don't worry. I am not letting you out of my sight."

True to her word, she followed close behind him. It only took a few minutes to get closer to the shallow breaking waves, and he took his time, wanting her to get used to the ocean and the feel of the board. He'd never actually given a lesson to someone so reluctant to participate, and he had second thoughts the deeper they got. She wasn't in danger. He knew that. But he also didn't want to let her down. He wanted to make this experience the best it could be.

And he would do that, he told himself. He was one of the best surfers in the world, and these gentle swells could be ridden by an eight-year-old. In fact, that's how old he'd been when he'd entered his first junior competition. He'd never been afraid of the sea. It had been his playground for as long as he could remember. It had brought him some of the best days of his life. That's what he wanted this day to be for Ava. Maybe not the best day of her life, but in the top ten.

As they drew closer to the breaking waves, she gave him a nervous smile that sent a tingle through his body. He didn't see her smile that often, but when she did, it was potent. He suddenly wanted to make her smile as often as possible. He sat up, straddling his board, and she did the same.

"What now?" she asked, her gaze growing a little more concerned. "We're pretty far from shore, aren't we? It didn't look that far when we were on the beach."

"You seem comfortable in the water. You're a good swimmer, aren't you?"

"Not a good ocean swimmer."

She was already starting to overthink things and he didn't want that. He paddled closer to her so that their boards were almost touching. "I got you, Ava."

She met his gaze. "I'm nervous, Liam."

"I know. But isn't that when life is the most interesting?"

"It's usually when I'm about to throw up."

He laughed. "You're not going to throw up."

"You better hope not." She drew in a breath. "So, what do I do?"

"First of all, you want to look for a wave that's just starting to form, not one that's already breaking. When you see the right one, you start paddling to match its speed. When the wave catches you, you'll feel the wave lifting you up, and that's when you stand up. You'll balance as best you can, the way we practiced on the beach. And then you just enjoy the ride for as long as it lasts."

"That's kind of your motto in life, isn't it?"

He tipped his head in acknowledgment. "True. It's a good motto. Do you want to give it a try?"

"What if I fall?"

"If you lose your balance, relax and let go of your board. Try to stay calm. When you surface, look for your board and keep an eye out for any other surfers. Since there's no one else out here but us, you'll be fine. Once you're in the clear, get back on your board and we'll do it again."

"Okay."

He stretched out on his board as she did the same. He watched the waves for a moment and then said, "Here we go."

"So fast?" she asked in alarm. "I thought we'd have to wait a while."

"Nope. This is it."

"I'm not ready," she protested.

"Yes, you are. Start paddling."

Ava didn't want to start paddling. She felt frozen in place, but Liam was shouting, "Come on," and she didn't want to be left alone in the middle of the ocean. As she paddled behind him toward a rising wave that suddenly felt huge, she was quite sure this would be a disaster. She just hoped she didn't drown. If she died, who would take care of Serena?

It was a thought that always came into her head. But now she realized she didn't have to think that way. Her sister was married. Brad would take care of her. She didn't have to be the only one who worried about Serena, the one who had to be careful because her sister depended on her. The realization felt suddenly freeing.

And then there was no more time for thinking.

The swell caught her, and she tried to remember what Liam had said, which wasn't that difficult since he was yelling instructions at her to shift her weight and use her arms for balance as she got to her feet.

His voice was filled with encouragement and confidence. "You're doing it, Ava!"

She was shocked that she was on her feet, that she was actually doing it. She was gliding along the wave, and feeling fairly triumphant until she lost her balance and tumbled into the water.

As her head submerged, she felt a rush of panic. She told herself to shake it off. She knew how to hold her breath and how to swim.

It took only a few seconds to come back to the surface. And when she popped up, Liam was right next to her. He pulled her onto his surfboard.

"Okay?" he asked, a concerned light in his eyes.

She nodded, looking around. Her surfboard was floating a few feet away from them. She brushed wet strands of hair from across her face.

"That was really good," he told her.

"I got to my feet," she said proudly.

"I saw. I wish I'd taken a photo. You did great for your first time."

"I think so," she agreed.

"Was it fun?" he asked.

"More fun than I expected."

Relief ran through his expression. "Thank goodness."

"I want to try it again. I think I can do it better."

He laughed. "I knew you were competitive. I also knew you'd like it."

As their gazes met, she realized he was beginning to know her quite well, maybe even better than she knew herself. She didn't really understand how that was possible, but it was.

"Thank you," she said, leaning forward to give him a kiss. He tasted like the sea, salty and a bit chilled, but the heat of their kiss quickly took the cold away.

"You're welcome," he said, a darker light of passion in his eyes, one that made her more nervous than the sea.

"I better get my board," she said quickly. "Should I swim for it?"

"I'll get you over there," he replied as he quickly paddled a few dozen feet to her floating board.

She crawled onto her board and said, "Let's do it again, Liam."

"Anything you want."

She liked the sound of that. She was just afraid that she might want more from Liam than a surfing lesson.

CHAPTER FIFTEEN

AVA HAD TAKEN to surfing far more easily than he'd imagined. They'd spent over an hour riding the small waves, and she had become more and more comfortable as time passed. In fact, she'd looked disappointed when she'd realized it was after nine and she needed to get back for a work call.

Now, they were home. He'd showered and dressed while she'd done the same in her room before jumping on a work call.

He wanted to be at work, too. He wanted to be moving forward on his business deal, but he wasn't, and he felt restless and frustrated. He needed to speak to John, but he had no idea what he should say. He also didn't know if John would be sober or still drunk from last night and whether or not John would remember what had happened at Maverick's.

He still also hadn't had a chance to sit down with Ava and go over her notes. He probably should have put that before the surfing lesson. But he had no regrets. It had been fun to watch her blossom out of her comfort zone. He was glad he'd pushed her, and she'd seemed pretty happy about it, too.

As he paced aimlessly around the living room, he realized her notepad was on the coffee table, along with John's ledgers.

Maybe she'd worked on them in the living room last night while he was at the bar. He sat down and picked up her pad.

What she'd called notes he quickly realized were detailed questions and then thoughtful analyses of those questions. She really was an intelligent woman, and some of her comments he'd never considered before. He'd thought he'd done his due diligence, but he hadn't gone as far or as deep as she had.

After reviewing her notes, he looked through John's ledgers himself. Two hours later, he had his own set of notes. As he sat back on the couch, he considered his options with a clearer mind than he'd had previously. That surprised him because he had believed he'd always had a clear mind. But he'd definitely gotten caught up in his intense desire to have a business of his own and he'd overlooked some things.

He heard the bedroom door open around one, and Ava walked into the living room. She'd changed into more work-appropriate clothes, a light-blue cardigan sweater over a pair of dark jeans.

Her gaze swept the coffee table in front of him. "You found my notes," she said. "I've been meaning to type them up for you."

"Not necessary. I read them, and then I looked at John's books."

She sat down on the couch next to him and gave him an expectant look. "What did you think?"

"That I didn't do my homework as well as you did. I'm guessing you were an A plus student."

"Guilty. And you weren't?"

"Mostly Bs."

"Too busy surfing to do homework?"

"And moving around. Starting over in new schools, I was often behind. But none of that matters now. I also didn't see some of what you saw because I had blinders on. I was so focused on what I could do with the building, the business, and the property that I didn't ask enough questions. The Beach Shack isn't as profitable as John implied."

"No, it's not," she said quietly. "But it could be. I have ideas on how to improve the bottom line."

"You still think I should buy it?"

"What do you think?" she countered.

He thought for a moment. "I still want it. I know I don't want to pay more than our agreed-upon price, and probably that price is too high."

"You could try to renegotiate."

"Frankly, I don't even know if John would sell it to me now, no matter what I offered. He didn't like that I kicked him out of the bar or got in the middle of his conversation with Maggie."

"He was drunk. He may not remember."

"I need to return his records to him and discuss next steps, but I wanted to have a better vision of everything. Thanks to you, I do now. You're very smart, Ava. You wouldn't advise your company to invest in this business based on what you saw, would you?"

"No. But getting investors to spend their money is a different proposition than an individual buying a business for themselves. When you have an investor, you have to make sure they're profitable, which means a much bigger margin is required. While some businesses can be very lucrative for a single owner or a smaller group, they don't make sense for an investor."

"That makes sense. But I'm still trying to get your opinion on what I should do."

She gave him a knowing smile. "Since I met you, Liam, you have always known exactly what you should do. You don't need my opinion."

"I know what I should do, but it's not what I want to do," he said in frustration.

"I suspected that was the problem. Talk to John and then go with your gut."

"Sounds simple."

"It does. And I usually complicate things, but I think that's all you can do at the moment."

"Fair enough. How's your day going?"

She shrugged. "Same old, same old."

"You don't sound excited about your work," he commented, thinking that she spent a lot of time on video calls and at her computer, which did not seem interesting to him in the slightest. But then he'd never worked in an office or for a company like hers, so he had no real idea what it was about.

"I've been at this job for seven years," she said. "Ever since I graduated from college. I worked my way up from entry-level to a lower mid-level position, which I'm sure doesn't sound very exciting. Because when I say it out loud, it doesn't impress me, either. I've told myself it's all good and I will get to a more important position at some point. I just have to pay my dues and continue to do good work, but I'm starting to wonder if that's true."

He'd never believed in waiting for someone to give him something. But she'd been helpful to him, and he knew security was important to her, so who was he to judge her choices.

"Anyway," she said. "I have another call in like fifteen minutes, so I'm just going to grab a water and get back to it."

"Do you have this many meetings every day?"

"Yes. And most of them are pointless. I'm just updating my boss on what I'm doing or explaining things to him so he can pretend he knows what he's talking about when he speaks with his boss. I'd like to get to the point where I have people reporting to me."

"Are you close to that point?"

"Sometimes it seems that way, and sometimes it feels like I've made very little progress in that direction. You don't want to hear about my problems."

"It's a nice chance of pace from mine," he said.

"What are you doing for the rest of the day?"

"I'm going to track John down. And then I'll head to Maver-ick's around five for my shift."

"Do you think you could help me with Miss Daisy's medicine before you go to work tonight?"

"Absolutely."

"Thanks." She paused. "You looked like you were having fun behind the bar last night. Did you enjoy it?"

"It was fine. Lots of interesting people to talk to, but it's not what I want."

"You just described my job, somewhat interesting, but not really what I want to be doing." She got to her feet. "After this morning, I can see why you liked being a professional surfer. It must have been great to have the ocean as your office. All that fresh air and sunshine. Friendly people to hang out with. Are you sure you won't miss it, Liam?"

"I plan to continue surfing, just not traveling all over the world to enter competitions. I'll still be a part of that world, but my world will be bigger and more rooted. I like that idea."

"You don't think staying in one place will be boring after the life you've led? Looking at the same view, the same beach? It's one thing to imagine it and another to live it."

"I'll never find out if I don't give staying in one place a try."

"But what if you spend everything you have and then find out you don't like it?"

"Then I'll figure out what to do next."

"It's a big risk. I know those are the only kind you like, but you could lose a lot, Liam. You might be overpaying for a busi-ness that you can't resell for the same price. Not every buyer will have your level of passion for the store."

"I'm aware of the risks, but I want to take them. My gut has never steered me wrong."

"Then I hope your lucky streak continues."

"Me, too." He paused as a knock came at the door.

"I'm up. I'll get it," she said.

As she opened the door, a familiar voice brought him to his feet.

He walked over to the door to find a very blond, very tan guy on the landing. "Nate, what are you doing here?"

"Looking for you," Nate replied as they exchanged a quick hug and slap on the back. "I thought you had become a retail store owner, but here you are loafing around as usual."

"Hardly," he said. "Come on in. This is Ava Campbell."

Nate gave Ava an appreciative look. "Nice to meet you. I'm Nate Walker."

"Hello," she said.

"Nate is an old friend of mine," Liam said. "We met when we were about eighteen, I think."

"I was seventeen, old man," Nate joked. "Let's not forget that."

"I'll let you two catch up," Ava said.

"You don't have to run off," he told her.

"I have a work call. I'm just going to grab a water from the kitchen and then I'll be out of your way."

"Can I get a water, too?" Nate asked. "Or do you have a beer?"

"I do," he replied, as they made their way into the kitchen. Ava grabbed a bottle from the fridge, flashed them a smile, and then left.

Nate gave him a questioning glance. "So, who's the pretty blonde?"

"My temporary roommate." He handed Nate a beer and then grabbed one for himself. "I'm apartment sitting for Brad, who just married Ava's sister, Serena. She's taking care of Serena's cat."

"Sounds cozy," Nate said with a grin as he sat down at the kitchen table.

He took the chair across from him. "What are you doing here?"

"I took a late entry into the San Diego event on Saturday," he said, mentioning a surfing event several miles down the road. "Are you in it?"

He shook his head. "No. Although, I might rethink it now that my deal has been delayed."

"It's delayed?" Nate raised a questioning brow. "What happened?"

"Owner is having second thoughts about selling."

"That sucks."

"I'm still working on it."

"I'm not surprised. I wouldn't think you would quit until you were forced to." Nate tipped his beer bottle to his mouth and took a long swig.

"Are you staying in San Diego?" he asked.

"No. I'm at the Crescent motel down the street for a few nights. Thought we could hang out before the competition."

"Allie isn't with you?"

"No," Nate said with a sigh. "Allie and I are having problems. We might be breaking up."

He was shocked to hear that. Nate and Allie had been together for five years. "Why? What happened?"

Nate shrugged. "She wants to have a baby."

"Oh." He was surprised to hear that. "Well, you've been together a long time. Have you talked about having kids?"

"Never. It just came out of the blue, a couple of weeks ago. She had a bad fall at the Baker's Beach Invitational. She knocked herself out and bruised one of her ribs on a rock. She was banged up pretty good, and after that she said she wanted to quit competing. She wanted to get married and have a baby. She wanted to buy a house near her parents. It was like she turned into a complete stranger. That bump on her head changed everything."

He smiled at Nate's disgruntled expression. "But you love her, don't you?"

"I love the girl I've been with all these years, the one who likes to travel and surf. I know we're not getting any younger, but we're only thirty. There's time to do that other stuff."

"Did you tell her that?"

"Yeah, but she doesn't believe me. She thinks I'll be saying the same thing when I'm forty, and then it will be too late for her to have kids."

"Could she be right?" he challenged.

Nate frowned. "I have no idea. I don't think that far ahead. I know I like our lives the way they are now. I know it won't last forever, but we still have time." He paused. "I thought you liked the life, too, Liam, but you're giving it up. Britt walked away from it a while ago. I remember when the four of us were jetting all over the world, having the time of our lives. We were a good crew. And then you and Britt ended. Now, I feel like Allie and I are on the way out, too. What made everyone want to change? Help me out here, Liam. Make me understand. What am I not seeing that everyone else does?"

"Your choices aren't wrong if they're right for you, Nate. But I was in that life longer than you. I was with my dad when he was competing. I'm tired of living out of a suitcase or a temporary apartment or sleeping on someone's couch."

"Isn't that what you're doing here?" Nate asked dryly.

He tipped his head. "Fair point, but I am planning to rent my own place as soon as my deal goes through. The bottom line is that I want to build something that's mine, that will last. And I think I've found the perfect way to blend my surfing experience with a different kind of adventure. It's not like I'm giving up surfing. I was on the ocean this morning. I just don't want it to be my whole life."

"You'll get tired of looking at just one beach," Nate said, once again echoing Ava's earlier words.

Now he was wondering what everyone else was seeing that he wasn't. But they weren't in his shoes. They hadn't lived his life. They weren't in his head. He'd been restless for a very long time, far longer than anyone else knew. "Maybe I will, maybe I won't, but I want to find out."

"Britt called me yesterday. She said you haven't been returning her calls."

Britt was the last person he wanted to talk about or to. "We don't have anything left to say."

"I told her you barely return my calls, so she's not that special."

"I call you back, but you're busy, and I'm busy. Once I'm set up here, you'll always know where to find me. And if you ever get bored, you can come work for me."

"Me? Work in a store? I don't think so. I need to be outside. I can't be confined."

He laughed at Nate's passionate words. "You could run my surfing school."

"Well, that's a bit more interesting, but I'm not ready to stay in one place."

"I get that."

"So, what do I do about Allie?" Nate asked.

"Talk to her. No, don't talk, listen." He realized he was giving Nate the same advice he'd given John, and who the hell was he to think he could straighten out anyone's relationship? Running a hand through his hair, he added, "Or don't talk to her. It's up to you. I don't know why anyone would want relationship advice from me."

"That's true. What was I thinking?"

"I have no idea," he said in response to Nate's teasing comment.

"Are you going to call Britt back?"

"No. I have a lot to think about right now, and I can't deal with whatever drama she's planning to bring into my life."

"She does like the drama." Nate paused. "Do you want to do something tonight, or do you and your hot roommate have plans?"

"I'm working at Maverick's tonight. Bartending."

"Why?"

"Cash," he said with a shrug.

"If you need cash, why aren't you competing on Saturday?"

"I thought I'd have my deal wrapped up by then."

"It's a weak field, Liam. You could probably take the whole thing, and first place for our division is ten thousand dollars."

He slowly rose. "I'm sure entries are closed."

"They're not. The Barry brothers just pulled out. One is injured and the other is sick. Although, I don't know why I'm pressing you to compete. You'll probably beat me. Anyway, give Kent a call. I'm sure he'd love to have you in the event. You have a lot of fans, Liam. And I wouldn't mind competing against you one more time. I always like to go against the best."

"So do I, Nate, and you've won your share of events."

"Not as many as you, but I still have time."

He'd thought he was done competing, but maybe one last event was worth another payday. "I'll give Kent a call."

"Great. I'll stop by the bar later, and you can buy me a drink."

"You're on," he said as he walked Nate out of the apartment.

When his friend was gone, he took out his phone and called Kent Robbins, the organizer of the San Diego event he'd won three times already. Maybe he had one more good run in him.

Kent didn't answer so he left him a message. Then he decided to get back to resolving his real business. Grabbing his keys, he headed out the door.

CHAPTER SIXTEEN

THE BEACH SHACK was closed when Liam arrived at two thirty. As he peered through the front door, trying to see if John might be in the store, he heard a voice behind him. "Man, is he still gone?"

He turned his head to see a sunburned, lanky teen behind him. "The store is closed."

"I thought he'd be open by now. I came by this morning, and it was closed then, too. I'm supposed to pick up my surfboard today. Do you know where the owner is?"

"I don't. Sorry."

"I gotta go," the kid muttered, heading back to his car.

His gut churned with worry about John. He could be on a bender somewhere, and that wouldn't be good. He knew John didn't live far from the store, because he'd mentioned walking to work, but he didn't have his address. But there was one person who would have that.

He walked quickly back to Ocean Shores and headed straight for the apartment where Maggie was staying.

Josie answered his knock with a wary smile. "Hello, Liam. What can I do for you?"

"Is Maggie home?"

"No. But she's on her way home from the market. She should be here in a few minutes. Why don't you come in?"

"Thanks." As he entered the apartment, he was immediately struck by how much stuff she had. It wasn't messy, but every inch of wall space was covered by a photo or a movie poster. Her comfortable furniture was an eclectic mix of colors, and there were plants everywhere with a subtle smell of weed in the air, which wasn't surprising. It was a poorly kept secret that Josie grew weed in the garden and often smoked it.

"Have a seat." She waved him toward the couch.

As he sat down on the sofa, he picked up a framed photo from the side table. It was a picture of Josie as a much younger woman. She had been truly stunning, with platinum-blonde hair and piercing brown eyes. She was holding an award. His eyes widened. "Did you win an Oscar?"

She nodded, a small smile playing around her lips, the same small, almost sly smile she wore in her photograph. "Yes. For supporting actress in *Heart of the Wolf.*"

"That's amazing. I saw that movie when I was a kid. I don't remember exactly what it was about, except that there was a pack of wolves running around. What part did you play?"

"I played a single mom with a child who adopted a wolf he thought was a dog."

"Oh, right. You were great."

"Thank you. I'm surprised you saw the movie. It was released before you were born."

"My parents rented a lot of movies when I was young." He set the photo down. "I knew you were an actress, but I had no idea you had won an Oscar. Why did you quit acting? It sounds like you were at the top of your game."

"I had a lot of reasons for leaving Hollywood, none of which I'm sure you came here to talk about. So, tell me why you want to see Maggie."

He was actually surprised she didn't want to talk about her career, because he was interested in her story. But he did have more pressing concerns. "I'm worried about John. I just went by the store, and it's closed. I don't think he's been there all day. After what happened last night, I'm concerned."

"I am as well. I've known John a long time, and I have never seen him get that drunk or that angry. Maggie said he's changed in the last few years, and I'm beginning to see what she means. He's become a very unhappy man. By the way, I appreciate you looking out for Maggie last night. I had to stop Frank from going out there. I didn't think his presence would help."

"No. It wouldn't have helped. John blames Frank for stealing Maggie away from him."

"That's absurd. They're friends."

"They looked like they were enjoying each other's company last night."

"Maybe something will happen in the future; maybe it won't. But even if it does, Maggie and John are separated."

"Legally? Because John acts like Maggie is just staying with a friend temporarily."

"Legally, they are married. Maggie told John she was talking to a divorce attorney, but I'm not sure he heard her. At any rate, I have not been encouraging Maggie and Frank to get together. I wouldn't do that. But time gets shorter when you get to our age, and I think Maggie has become very aware of that." She paused, giving him a speculative look. "You have a vested interest in Maggie and John's relationship, don't you?"

"My business deal with John has ended up in the middle of their relationship. But putting that aside, I am still worried about John. I think he's in crisis. I want to know he's okay. I need his address."

"272 Fairview Road," she replied. "Let me know if he needs more help than you can give him so I can let Maggie know. She cares about him a great deal, even if he doesn't believe that. I would go check on him myself, but he's angry with me for inviting Maggie to stay here. He thinks I fill her head with ideas, which is part of the problem. He doesn't realize that his wife of thirty-eight years has plenty of her own ideas."

"I don't disagree," he said. "Thanks. I will let you know if he needs more help."

"On another note," she said, as she walked him to the door. "I heard you might be looking for an apartment, and I have an open two-bedroom on the second floor. I think you'd fit in really well here."

"I'm interested, but I can't make a decision on where I'm going to live until I know if I'm buying the Beach Shack."

"If it doesn't go through, what will you do?"

"That's a good question. I wish I had an answer."

After leaving Josie's, he headed to John's house, which was a one-story bungalow a half mile away. The grass was long, the flowers were overrun by weeds, and it looked like the house could use a coat of paint. He wondered if the neglect had come after Maggie moved out or if things had been going downhill before that.

There was a car in the drive, so, hopefully, John was home. He went up to the porch and rang the bell.

John took his time opening the door. When he appeared, he looked like hell, with red eyes, greasy, tangled gray hair, and a sallow tone to his skin. He seemed to have aged ten years overnight.

John let out a long, weary sigh as their gazes met. "Why am I not surprised it's you?" he said in a raspy voice that sounded exhausted but not drunk.

"I went to the store, and it was closed. I wanted to return your financial records." He held up the books in his hands.

"You want out of the deal?" John asked.

"Do you?" he countered.

It seemed to take forever for John to answer. "I think I've lost Maggie," he said, his lips drawing into a tight line.

He didn't know what to say to that.

John squared his shoulders. "But that's not your problem."

It felt like it was very much his problem. "Can I come in? Can we talk?"

"Sure. Why not?" He stepped back and motioned him inside.

The living room felt as messy and neglected as the outside of the house. There were junk food wrappers on the coffee table as well as a variety of dirty dishes and tangled blankets.

"I'm not much of a housekeeper," John said with a shrug, taking in his gaze. "That was Maggie's job." He grabbed the blanket off the couch and tossed it over the armchair. "I've been sleeping out here. Too hard to be in our bed alone." He paused. "You can sit."

He took a seat on the sofa while John sat in the armchair next to him. He set down the ledgers on the crowded coffee table and for a moment, they sat in silence. Neither one of them really knew what to say. But someone had to start.

"Ava and I went through your financial records," he said. "I can't pay more than our agreed-upon number, which, in light of what I learned, is probably too high. But I want the Beach Shack, and I made a deal with you that I'm willing to honor. It's my fault for not looking at things as closely as I should have." He paused. "Your turn."

"I know I've been drinking too much, acting like an asshole."

"I can't argue with you. Do you remember last night?"

"Parts of it, and those I'd like to forget." He took a breath. "I need a couple of days to figure things out. I realize that's not fair to you, Liam, but it's what I need. You can't pay more, but I might be able to get a better price from someone else. There's a sporting goods chain that's interested in the space."

He sat up straighter. "You never said that before."

"The rep called me yesterday, asked me if it was a done deal. I said not yet."

"John, if some corporation looks through your books, they're going to see what I saw, what Ava saw. They're not going to offer you what you think."

"I gotta find out," he said stubbornly. "I'm going to talk to them tomorrow."

"We had a verbal agreement. Doesn't that mean anything to you?"

"I feel badly, but my marriage, my life is at stake here. You don't know what it's like to work your whole life, love one woman, and then have it all disappear. I need to see all my options, Liam. I'm sorry. I didn't know that Maggie was going to be so obstinate. I thought she'd be back home by now. Give me until Saturday to figure it out."

"A sporting goods chain won't keep the Beach Shack the way it is. It won't be your legacy. But I would incorporate the past with the future. We come from the same background. We were both surfers. Doesn't that mean something to you?"

"It does. I just don't know if keeping my legacy is alive is worth giving up my wife."

He felt a shocking jolt of disappointment as his dream slowly died right in front of him.

He told himself it might not be completely dead. Maybe the chain wouldn't make an offer once they saw the books, or that offer would be lower than his. But it was a risk. The chain might see the potential of the store and the location and cut him out of a deal he'd been working on for almost a year.

"At least give me the courtesy of matching the offer," he said.

John stared back at him. "You just said you couldn't and shouldn't pay more."

That was true. He felt torn between logic and emotion. Even though he knew emotion had no place in a business deal, he couldn't seem to shut it down. "Will you give me a chance to their offer?" he repeated.

"I guess I can do that," John said.

"Okay, good." He paused. "Are you going to be all right, John?"

"Why would you care? I just bailed on our agreement."

He shouldn't care, but he did. "You need help, John. You need to stop drinking. You should speak to someone who can help you navigate what's happening in your life."

"I've made it to seventy-one without needing a shrink. The only person who can help me is Maggie."

"You're wrong, John. Maggie isn't the only one who can help you. You can help yourself." He got to his feet. "I'll see myself out. By the way, some kid was at your store hoping to pick up his surfboard."

"Damn," John muttered. "I forgot all about that. I'll call him now."

As he left John's house, he felt overwhelmed with frustration. He'd never been a patient man, and he didn't want to wait until Saturday to find out if some corporation was going to buy the Beach Shack out from under him. But he didn't have any other choice.

———

"It was your choice to work remote, Ava," Jeff said.

Ava stared at her computer screen, at the smug, cocky look on the face of her coworker. "I've been out of the office since Friday. It's Wednesday. That's three business days. I can't believe you rescheduled my pitch meeting for Calyx. You had no right to do that, Jeff."

"Dave asked me to move it up to tomorrow at nine. He's going to be out of town on your original date."

"I could probably drive in and get there in time for the meeting," she said.

"That won't work. I spoke to the team at Calyx an hour ago. We already went over the pitch. I'm handling it."

"I've done all the research on Calyx," she protested, knowing her words wouldn't make a difference.

"And you'll get credit for that," he assured her. "Dave knows how valuable you are."

Dave should know how valuable she was, but Jeff was probably undercutting her work behind her back, claiming he'd done more of it than he had.

"Relax, Ava," he continued. "I've got this meeting. Just enjoy your time away."

"I'm not on vacation. I'm working remote, Jeff."

"You know what I meant."

She did know what he meant. Jeff was going to use her time out of the office to do everything he could to get ahead of her.

The pitch with Calyx was supposed to be her opportunity, but he'd stolen it out from under her, with apparently Dave's blessing. She probably should have made a better effort to get closer to Dave as Jeff had done, but she'd never been one to play the political game at work. She'd always believed her work would speak for itself, but maybe that wasn't enough. Perhaps she needed to get better at personal relationships, at putting herself into more social situations even at work.

A knock came at her bedroom door. "Come in."

"I need to take off soon," Liam said as he poked his head into her room. "Do you want to do Miss Daisy's medicine now?"

"Yes." She got up from her chair and followed him into the kitchen. Miss Daisy was pacing around by her empty food bowl. She'd definitely gotten more used to them being in the apartment.

Liam grabbed the cat while she got the medicine, and as usual Miss Daisy started to purr in his arms, making it easy for her to get the medicine into her mouth. Then she jumped down and ran away.

"I'll give her a minute and then put her food out," she said as Liam nodded.

His eyes were a little dull, his mood definitely toned down. She was used to his sunny personality, his optimistic, cheerful smile, both of which were missing. "What's wrong, Liam?"

He shrugged. "Nothing. I have to get to Maverick's."

"Wait. Something is clearly off with you. Just tell me."

"I spoke to John earlier. He has a potential buyer with deeper pockets than mine. He wants to entertain an offer from that company. It's a sporting goods chain. I didn't get the details."

"I don't understand. You have an agreement."

"A verbal one."

"That can be binding."

"I can't afford to fight it. I told John after looking at his records, I couldn't justify raising my offer and that, in fact, I thought I was overpaying, but I would stick by our deal. He didn't disagree. He knows there are holes in his records."

"Which this other company will find, especially if it's a corporation with a staff of lawyers and financial analysts. He won't get a better deal."

"I hope not. I asked him to give me an opportunity to match their offer. He said he would, and he should have more information by Saturday."

"Do you think there really is another buyer, or is he just using the thought of it to get you to come up in money?"

He stared back at her, his mouth tightening. "I'd hate to think he was playing that game, but you could be right. Whatever it is—my life is on hold until Saturday."

She could hear the frustration in his voice and could totally relate. He was so close and yet so far away. "I'm sorry."

"Thanks. What are you doing tonight?"

"Probably just working."

"You've been doing that all day. Is there a big project going on or something?"

"No. Just the usual workload."

"Well, you can always come down to Maverick's for a drink if you want a break."

"Thanks, but I'm going to stick close to home tonight. I was thinking that it might be fun to go surfing again tomorrow morning, unless you're busy."

The heaviness surrounding him seemed to lift with her words.

"Seriously?" he asked. "You want to go out again?"

"Only if you want to take me."

A smile slowly spread across his lips. "You've caught the fever, Ava."

"I wouldn't go that far, but I would like another shot at doing it better."

He laughed. "You are so competitive. You pretend you're not, but you are."

"I don't pretend anything. And I didn't say I wasn't competitive, but it's more with myself than anyone else. I like to be good at things."

"I get that. And I would love to go surfing with you tomorrow. Seven thirty?"

"I'll meet you here," she said. "First one up gets the coffee going."

"Deal. You're turning out to be a better roommate than I expected, Ava." He gave her a smile. "Now, you say the same."

"Go to work," she said instead.

"You are one tough lady. But I know you like me. Maybe more than you want."

Definitely more than she wanted, she thought, as he left the kitchen, leaving her feeling both relieved and disappointed that he was gone, which seemed to be two emotions that were becoming very familiar when it came to Liam.

Miss Daisy came back into the kitchen with an accusatory meow. "Sorry," she said. "I know you want your food." As the cat meowed again, she added, "And you probably already miss Liam, don't you?"

Miss Daisy's third meow definitely felt like an agreement.

She smiled to herself as she fed the cat. Who was she kidding? She was the one already missing Liam, which was ridiculous. She'd seen more of him in the last five days than she'd seen any of her friends in the past year.

But Liam wasn't a friend. She didn't know what he was.

And deep down inside, she kind of wanted to find out.

CHAPTER SEVENTEEN

THE WAVES WERE BIGGER Thursday morning than they'd been the day before, but Ava was determined not to let fear scare her away from the challenge in front of her. If Liam was willing to take her out, she had to trust him. And strangely enough, she did. That surprised her because she couldn't remember when she'd trusted anyone except herself.

Not even Serena had earned her trust, because her sister often had crazy ideas that led to trouble. Usually those ideas came from a good place or a naïveté that was pure Serena. But she'd always worried about her sister's choices.

Liam was different. He'd earned her respect—at least in this area.

As she paddled out to the breaking waves, she tried to just enjoy the moment. It was sunny. It was relatively warm. And she was with Liam, a man who was quickly making every day an exciting new adventure. When they reached the spot they'd been at yesterday, Liam turned to her. "Do you need a refresher course?"

"No. I remember what you told me."

"I'm not surprised."

"I just hope I can execute."

"You will."

She thought through the instructions he'd given her the day before, going over each step in her mind. Unfortunately, she was thinking so hard she missed the first wave by starting out too late. With the second one, she made it to her feet and then promptly lost her balance, but this time she bounced right back to the surface and grabbed her board again. The third time was another disaster.

"Maybe I'm not going to be better at this today after all," she told Liam as she took a minute to catch her breath.

"You will," he said confidently. "You're learning something every time you fall."

"Haven't I learned enough already?" she complained.

He laughed. "I still haven't learned enough, and I've been doing this for years. You're going to get it."

"That might take all day, and I only have an hour."

"There's always tomorrow."

She didn't know if she could face another day of disappointment, but Liam's encouraging gaze buoyed her spirits. "I'll keep trying."

"Good. I believe in you, Ava. You just have to believe, too. You can do this. And when you do, you'll feel amazing. Bet on yourself, Ava. You can't lose."

His words touched an emotional nerve, maybe because she hadn't heard anyone say they believed in her in a very long time.

"Hey, you're not going to cry, are you?" he asked in alarm.

"No. I just have water in my eyes," she lied. "From the ocean."

He gave her a disbelieving look. "What did I say?"

"Something very sweet. Thank you."

"You're welcome. Now, let me see you kick some wave's ass."

She laughed. "I'll give it my best shot."

Forty-five minutes later, and a dozen more attempts, and she finally stayed upright on the board, riding a wave all the way to the end, with Liam cheering her on with his endless encouragement and support.

Deciding she'd had enough, she paddled toward shore with Liam behind her. When they reached the sand, she dropped the board and turned toward him with a triumphant smile. "I did it."

"I never had a doubt."

"You were so great out there, Liam. You never let me give up."

"That was easy. You never really wanted to give up. And I knew you could do it."

"I don't know how you know me better than I know myself, but I just want to say thanks again." Before she could think twice, she threw her arms around his neck and gave him a kiss of gratitude and appreciation that quickly changed into something more.

Kissing Liam made her feel like she was back on another slippery wave, trying to stay on her feet, trying not to fall…because this kind of fall would be a lot worse than just sliding off a surfboard.

Normally, the fears and worries popping up in her head would instantly make her stop what she was doing. But there was too much temptation in the other direction, too much desire to just stay in this passionate moment as long as she could. She wouldn't have this man for long, but she had him now, and she didn't want to let him go.

And then a rush of cold water hit her feet, an unexpectedly high-breaking wave. They pulled apart with a laugh.

"The ocean wants you back," Liam said with a smile that twisted her heart into a needy knot. He caught her by the hand. "But I might want you more."

A shiver ran down her spine at the look of desire in his eyes.

"Does that scare you?" he asked.

"A lot of things scare me," she said.

"But you push past the fear."

"Sometimes. Not always."

"You did today."

"Because you were there. I knew I wasn't in danger."

"I'm still here."

"But this danger is different," she said. "I'm leaving in a couple of days, Liam. There's no time to start something."

"A lot can happen in a couple of days."

"But then what?"

"Who knows?"

"Exactly," she said with a helpless shrug. "I don't know. And that kind of situation doesn't work for me."

"Maybe you don't know it will work because you've never taken the risk."

"I can't take it now," she said softly. "I'm sorry."

His lips tightened with regret. "Me, too."

She dropped his hand as a trio of teenage surfers ran past them, effectively ending their private moment, which was probably good. "We should go back. I have some calls."

"Okay, but this isn't over, Ava."

"Since neither of us knows what *this* is, maybe it is over."

"Or maybe we'll find out what it is," he returned. "We still have time."

They did have time. She just wasn't sure what to do with it.

Ava spent the rest of Thursday in a swirl of emotional turmoil that came back every time she finished a work call and her mind flashed on Liam and the kisses they'd shared on the beach. Not knowing what she wanted to do about her unexpectedly strong feelings for him had made her stay in her room all day, not even leaving for lunch.

Around five, she got a text from Liam that he'd given Miss Daisy her medicine because he didn't want to interrupt her, and he needed to get to Maverick's.

She wasn't surprised he was able to do the medication

himself. Miss Daisy was shockingly docile when it came to Liam. Although, maybe not that shocking, since she also couldn't seem to avoid ending up in Liam's arms. He was like a magnet. She couldn't seem to resist him.

She smiled at that thought. And then she texted him a thanks with a smiley face. That felt kind of stupid after she sent it. But it was too late to take it back. She really was awkward when it came to texting with men. Serena would have said something flirty and far more interesting.

But that was her sister, and this was her.

She set down her phone and decided she was done with work. She hadn't heard what happened at Jeff's pitch with her client. Apparently, the meeting time had been moved back to four, and she hadn't spoken to either Jeff or Dave since early in the morning. Jeff had definitely gotten one up on her. But it was one meeting, and surely that didn't negate all the work she'd put in the last seven years.

At least, she hoped it didn't.

She closed her computer and got up to change. Tonight was the girls' night gathering at Kaia's apartment, and she could use a distraction.

An hour later, she made her way downstairs. When she neared Kaia's apartment, she could hear laughter and that seemed like a good sign. She knocked on the door, and Kaia answered a moment later, holding a bottle of wine in each hand.

"You came," she said with a genuine smile. "I'm so glad. Come on in… I think you know most everyone."

She followed Kaia into her apartment, which was a similar version to the one she was staying in but was a one-bedroom. Kaia's style was modern and clean, with white and gray furniture and accent décor that added a touch of color.

Kaia introduced her to Skye Davis, a stunning woman with curly black hair and eyes, wearing white jeans ripped at the knees and a tank top. Skye was the manager of the local coffee shop, Tidal Brews, and lived on the second floor with a male roommate named Kevin.

She was also introduced to Paige Kendry, a curvy dark-blonde with brown eyes and a friendly smile. Paige was mom to a son, Henry, who was six years old and apparently staying with a friend for the evening. Paige was a nurse at the hospital, which was where Kaia had originally met her and had encouraged her to move into a second-floor unit at Ocean Shores a few months earlier.

After a flurry of additional warm greetings from Lexie and Emmalyn, she settled in one of the armchairs across from the couch where Paige, Skye, and Emmalyn were seated, while Lexie was in the other armchair. Kaia brought her a glass of wine and then pulled an ottoman away from the wall and moved it next to her, taking a seat.

"That doesn't look very comfortable," she said. "I can trade you."

Kaia waved the suggestion away. "This is fine. So, who read the book?" she asked the group.

There were a lot of guilty smiles. "I read the first three chapters," Paige said.

"I got halfway through," Emmalyn replied.

"I didn't start it," Lexie admitted. "I got really busy this week."

"Well, it's good you're busy," Kaia said. "That must mean your photography business is taking off."

"I'm getting a lot of bookings for kids' parties and family portraits, but it's not that exciting," Lexie replied with a small sigh. "I love taking photographs, but dealing with people at parties is a hassle."

"That's not the kind of photography you want to do, is it?" Emmalyn asked.

"No, but it pays the bills." Lexie took a sip of wine. "And I can't quit another job. I can't be the woman who quits everything."

"There aren't any rules as to how many times you can change a career," Kaia said.

"Says the girl who has been a paramedic her entire life," Lexie returned.

"Well, I found what was right for me. I got lucky."

"You did. And it's not just that I can't quit for pride's sake," Lexie added. "When I decided to leave the law, my father turned over my student loans to me. He was so disappointed I gave up the law, and I wouldn't follow in his footsteps. I am a huge disappointment to my family. They are all overachievers and horrified by my new career plan, so I can't fail being a photographer, too."

"It sucks not to have family support," Paige interjected. "I have an unsupportive father, too. When I divorced my ex, my dad said, 'Well, don't expect me to take care of you.' As if I should just stay married so someone would take care of me. Oh, and by the way, my father never took care of me. I'm the one who paid for all my college loans. Anyway, sorry, didn't mean to jump on your story, Lexie," she added hastily.

"No problem," Lexie said. "We can toast to unsupportive families."

"I can't toast to that," Kaia said, shaking her head. "I had a very supportive dad, so I can't join this particular session of whining. But if anyone wants to talk about bad dates...I'm there."

"Me, too," Skye said. "On dates. I had the worst one in the world last Friday night."

"What happened?" Ava asked curiously.

"Well, the guy was waiting in the bar when I got there, and he'd ordered a really expensive bottle of champagne. I was immediately impressed. He followed up with an array of appetizers and some decent conversation. He'd traveled a lot and had some good stories to tell. I thought we were vibing, and then he went to the restroom."

"I think I know where this is going," she said, sending Skye a sympathetic smile.

"He didn't come back," Skye said. "He left me with a huge check to pay, and I never heard from him again. He was clearly just scamming for dates to get food and drinks."

"I can't believe that," Emmalyn said, shaking her head. "It's so slimy."

"That's a good word for it—slimy," Skye agreed. "What happened on your last bad date, Kaia?"

"He spent most of the hour we were together on the phone, and every time another woman walked by, his gaze followed her ass across the room," Kaia replied. "It was disgusting. After we finished one round of drinks, he suggested we have sex to see if we were compatible for taking things further." She shook her head. "It's rough out there, ladies."

"I'll drink to that," Lexie said, raising her glass.

As all the women leaned forward to clink their glasses, she belatedly jumped in.

"That was a little slow," Kaia commented. "No bad dates in your history, Ava?"

"Are you kidding?" she replied. "I've mostly done online dating the past five years, with terrible results. Most men don't even get past the texting stage, but when I have met them in person, it's been universally boring, with awkward conversation and no chemistry. Every so often, I delete the apps and say I'm never going back, but then some time passes, and I get bored and take another look."

"It's like an addiction," Lexie agreed. "I wasn't dating much when I was an attorney because I had zero time. After I moved here, I thought it would be a good way to meet people. It turned out, I was just meeting the wrong people."

"I don't like online dating. It feels too risky to meet a stranger. I'd rather meet someone organically," Emmalyn said.

"We all would," Kaia agreed. "But where are they?"

"Some are living right here," Skye put in. "Is no one trying to date Max or Gabe?"

"Max told me he doesn't want to date anyone in the building," Lexie said. "He thinks it would be awkward, especially since we have so many Ocean Shores events."

"That's a fair point," Kaia agreed. "Dating in-house has its challenges. Although there is one hot guy currently here, who may not be staying in this building permanently." Her gaze moved to Ava's. "Unless he's off the table?"

She took a sip of her wine. "If you're talking about Liam, he's definitely not off the table." Despite her words, she found herself feeling a little unhappy about the idea of any of these lovely women going after Liam, which was ridiculous. They'd kissed a few times. They'd never gone on a real date. And she would be leaving soon.

"Aunt Josie said Liam is interested in renting an apartment here once Brad and Serena get back," Lexie put in. "I think he would be a great fit."

"I agree," Kaia said. "Speaking of new men in the building, has anyone talked to Captain Hunter Kane yet?"

"I ran into him in the laundry room," Skye said. "He was not friendly, but he was hobbling around and looked like he was in pain, so I didn't want to bother him. He is very handsome in a dark, angry, brooding kind of way."

"He lost some friends in the crash that injured him," Lexie said somberly. "He needs some time to recover. Maybe once he's further away from that incident, he'll open up a little."

"Who needs more wine?" Kaia asked as she got to her feet. At the chorus of replies, Kaia laughed and said, "Okay, it's going to take me a minute."

"I'll help," she said, following Kaia into the kitchen.

"Are you having fun, Ava?" Kaia asked.

"I am. I don't have many girlfriends. I work with a lot of men, and while there are a couple of women I hang out with at work, we aren't close outside of the job."

"It's important to make time for girlfriends. Living here at Ocean Shores has changed my thinking about that. I was a little like you when I first got here, kind of standoffish, not really sure how close I wanted to get with my neighbors, especially the women. I grew up with two brothers and a dad, so I was a tomboy all my life. I never really had a female crew until I moved here. I like it a lot."

"Serena told me this place changed her life. I thought she was just referring to Brad, but I can see now that she meant everyone changed her life."

"Maybe you should think about moving here permanently," Kaia suggested.

"My job is in LA."

"They wouldn't let you work remote?"

"No. They don't believe in that. Even if they did, the odds of getting promoted would suffer if I wasn't in the office. Just coming here for the week has already inspired one of my coworkers to get me off an account."

"That's terrible."

"It's why I never take a vacation."

"Well, that's terrible, too, for a different reason."

"How do you like your job?"

"I love the combination of action and medicine and being able to help people in their worst moment."

"That sounds so much more important than my job."

"I suspect I get paid a lot less," Kaia said with a laugh.

"Probably. But you have other rewards. You save lives."

"I do. And while I wish I never had to save anyone's life, I'm really glad when I can." She handed her the open bottle of red wine. "Can you take this, while I bring the white?"

"Of course. Thanks for pushing me to come. This is fun."

"I'm glad you're enjoying yourself. Serena was worried you weren't going to like apartment sitting for her, but I told her we'd make sure you had fun. Of course, I didn't know at the time that you'd have Liam for a roommate."

"He was a surprise to me, too."

"Liam was great at the bar the other night, defusing that whole situation with John and Maggie. He's a good guy. You could do worse, Ava."

"I'm not doing anything," she said, even though she was beginning to wish that wasn't true.

CHAPTER EIGHTEEN

WHEN AVA GOT HOME Thursday night, it was almost eleven. Liam was sitting on the couch, looking at his phone, with music playing across the speakers in the apartment.

"Hey," he said, lowering the volume of the music as she kicked off her shoes and sat down on the couch. "Did you have fun with the girls?"

"Maybe a little too much," she said, feeling buzzed from the two glasses of wine she'd consumed.

The heady feeling increased when she looked at Liam's handsome face, his amused smile, his sparkling green eyes. She actually felt a pit in her stomach, a hunger for this man that she hadn't felt in…forever.

But she couldn't do anything about it. She'd already played with fire just by kissing him a few times. Anything more wouldn't work. He was staying. She was leaving. And there were a million other reasons why taking things further was a bad idea.

"Ava?" he said, giving her a thoughtful look. "What's on your mind?"

At his direct question, she found herself hesitating, unable to express what she was thinking, feeling, or needing. She wasn't good at asking for things. She tried to find an answer that would save her from making a total fool of herself.

"I—I was thinking I should go to bed," she said finally.

Disappointment ran through his gaze. "Now? It's not that late."

"I have to work tomorrow." Despite her words, she didn't make a move from the couch. She wasn't quite ready to stop talking to him. "How was your night?"

"It was fine. Maverick's wasn't too crowded."

"That's good."

"Not really. Slow night means low tips."

"Are you sorry you agreed to pick up extra shifts while you're waiting on John?"

"No. Money is always good. And I know how to do the job. When my mom wasn't waitressing, she was bartending, so I learned how to make drinks at an early age."

"Your parents are so fascinating." She settled more comfortably onto the couch. "Tell me more about them."

"What do you want to know?"

"Were they in love?"

"Absolutely. They were crazy about each other. They met when they were sixteen, and they knew instantly that the other person was the one."

"They were teenagers. They probably would have thought anyone was the one."

"Well, they're still together, and it will be thirty-five years this summer. They're going to spend their anniversary in Bali."

"Bali sounds exotic and wonderful. Have you been there?"

He nodded. "It's exactly what you said. Very romantic."

"Bungalows over the water?"

"Yes."

She let out a little sigh. "I can't even imagine."

"You don't have to imagine; you could go."

"Go to Bali, just like that?"

"Just like that," he said, meeting her gaze. "I have a feeling you have a little nest egg saved up."

"For emergencies, not trips to Bali."

"Make it a mental health emergency," he said with a smile.

She couldn't help but smile back at him. "You always have a good answer, Liam."

"You work hard, Ava. You should treat yourself once in a while. Why don't you?"

"That's a complicated question."

"Uncomplicate it for me."

She thought for a moment. "Well, when my parents died, my aunt and uncle were forced to take us in, and money seemed to be tight. I learned later that my parents hadn't had much in the way of savings or investments. We were both told that college would be on us, and when my aunt and uncle left the country and Serena moved in with me, I had to be so careful with money. My aunt and uncle gave us a chunk of money to cover rent until Serena was eighteen, but there was no cash for anything extra, so both Serena and I had to get part-time jobs. She was only fifteen, so she didn't bring in much, and what she did bring in, she wanted to immediately spend. I had to be the gatekeeper and the accountant. I didn't want Serena to suffer, so I usually put any extra money I had toward something she wanted, like a prom dress or highlights in her hair. I wanted her to have a good high school experience." She paused. "I might have spoiled her a little. But she deserved to be spoiled. She didn't have our parents as long as I did. She was three years younger than me when they died. It wasn't fair."

"You were very generous, Ava."

"Serena is my sister. I love her. And it was just us." She took a breath. "Until she moved here and met Brad. I was a little jealous when she started raving about him to me. She was overwhelmed by her feelings. And I wasn't just worried for them; I was worried for myself, for my relationship with Serena. So don't give me too much credit for being generous. I can be selfish, too."

"What you are is too hard on yourself. Of course you wouldn't want to lose Serena. It was just the two of you for a long time. It makes sense how worried you were about her quick decision. I still think Serena and Brad will be okay, but I understand why you're concerned."

"I've been trying to let my worries go. Meeting everyone at Ocean Shores has helped. The people are so nice and genuine, and I love that. I can see why Serena feels at home here."

"You seem pretty at home, too. Maybe you should think about moving here. You could be closer to your sister."

She could be closer to him, too, and that thought had crossed her mind. But it was too wild to consider. "My career opportunities are in LA."

"You couldn't find something closer—in San Diego, perhaps?"

"I don't know. I haven't thought about moving. I've been focused on working my way up in my company, staying the course, eye on the prize."

"Not a bad philosophy."

"Maybe too narrow?" she queried.

"Maybe. If you never look away from the road, you might miss some interesting turnoffs."

"I bet you always look for interesting turnoffs."

"I like getting off the beaten path," he admitted. "You never know what you're going to see."

"You could end up in a dangerous situation."

"Or a beautiful one."

"We see life very differently." She told herself to cling to that perspective, because it might provide a much-needed barrier between them.

"We do," Liam agreed. "But maybe we rub off on each other in a good way."

She licked her lips, feeling like she was getting into the danger zone she had just mentioned, because she was going way off her usual beaten path. She tried to focus on something else, but it felt like her whole world was Liam. His voice, his breath, his scent surrounded her. All she could think about was him. Every sense in her body was firing, her nerves tingling.

"I like this song," he suddenly said, catching her off guard.

"What?" she asked in confusion.

"This song." He picked up his phone and increased the volume. "I like it. What about you?"

"It's nice," she said, listening for a moment. "It reminds me of the music my parents used to play when they'd dance after dinner."

"I love that image of your parents dancing around the house. It's nice to see parents doing things other than nagging at each other or cooking dinner, doing laundry, all that boring stuff."

"Did your parents actually do boring stuff?" she challenged.

"Some of the time. But I liked the moments when I saw their love right in front of me, the way he'd take her hand, the way she'd look into his eyes. I never doubted their love for each other because even when they were arguing, they were still in love."

"My parents were in love, too. Serena and I would sometimes sneak down the hall after we were supposed to be in bed and spy on them. When they weren't dancing, they were playing cards or reading together. They enjoyed each other's company so much. They were always smiling, laughing at some inside, intimate joke. I think that's one thing I've never really found with anyone—that shared intimacy and the ability to just sit quietly and feel completely comfortable together." She stopped abruptly, realizing she was feeling exactly that way with Liam, and now that made her tense. "I have no idea why I just told you that. I need to stop talking."

"No, you don't. But let's do something else."

Her heart skipped a beat as he got up and held out his hand.

"What?" she asked warily.

"Don't worry. I'm not asking you to risk anything. I just want to dance with you."

"I don't dance."

"Well, I do. Come on."

It was impossible to ignore his outstretched hand or the determined look in his eyes. "You really like pushing me out of my comfort zone, don't you?"

"It's just a dance, Ava."

She slipped her hand into his, feeling a jolt of electricity that told her this would be much more than a dance, just like his kiss had been much more than a kiss.

Warning bells screamed in her head, but they were drowned out by the loud beating of her heart. And then she was on her feet and in his arms.

He broke the tension by giving her a spin and another heart-stopping smile that she couldn't help but return.

"I thought we were going to just rock back and forth," she said breathlessly.

"We can do that, too." He pulled her up against his chest, gazing into her eyes. "Is this better?"

"So much better," she breathed. "And so much worse. I don't know what to do about you, Liam."

"What do you want to do?"

She really shouldn't answer that question, but the word slipped out before she could stop it. "Everything," she whispered.

His arms tightened around her. "That's exactly what I want to do. We're in perfect sync."

She wanted to be in perfect sync with him. And the force of that desire was overriding her brain, her normal extreme sense of caution. Maybe it was the wine. Maybe it was him. Maybe she was just tired of playing it safe.

She didn't want to think anymore. She also didn't want to talk.

She wrapped her arms around his neck and pulled his head down for a kiss. As their mouths came together, the spark between them burst into fire, reminding her how badly she could get burned. That would be a worry for later.

Liam deepened the kiss between them, his hands running

down her back, then up and through her hair, holding her prisoner to the needy exploration of his mouth, the sweep of his tongue against hers. She couldn't get enough. And neither could he.

"I want you, Ava," he whispered against her mouth.

Her heart sped up at the urgency of his words, to know that his desire matched hers. Wherever they were going, they were going together, and she was done questioning it.

She pulled away and grabbed his hand. "My room," she said.

"Wait. I need one second."

She felt a little cold when he moved away from her, but he was back a second later with condoms, and she realized that her practical brain should have been the one to consider protection before him, but she wasn't thinking anymore. Thankfully, he was.

They walked into her room, and as she closed the door, he pressed her back against it and gave her another kiss, this one more demanding than the last. She could feel his body hardening against hers, and she slid her hands under his shirt, savoring the hot heat.

Her touch drew goose bumps along his skin. And then he let go of her and pulled off his shirt. She did the same, needing to touch him, needing him to touch her.

As soon as their clothes hit the floor, that's exactly what happened.

His hands ran along her curves with a thrilling look of appreciation in his eyes. And she explored his body with the same excited curiosity. She didn't want to turn off the lights. She wanted to see everything. She wanted to feel everything.

They hastily moved toward the bed, and she pulled him down to the mattress, needing to feel every inch of his body against hers.

He was happy to comply, touching her just the way she wanted, the way she'd imagined, only it was far better than any dream she'd had. Her nerves turned to fire. She felt wild and reckless and passionate, completely unlike herself. And damn if it didn't feel amazing to let go of the tight control she'd always had, to live in the moment, to trust herself and this really amazing man who had turned her life completely upside down.

Ava was a quiet sleeper, Liam thought, as he studied the beautiful woman beside him, the light from the windows putting a golden shine on her hair and turning her cheeks pink. She looked so much different now than the first night he'd met her. She was much softer, more vulnerable, and at this moment, completely relaxed and unguarded.

His body still tingled with memories of the night they'd spent together. He'd liked the way she'd let go of her usual rigid control and just focused on pleasure. And there had been a lot of pleasure for both of them.

He hadn't met anyone like her before. Most of the women he'd dated had been part of his surfing world or adjacent to it. They'd been free spirits, casual, and easy. They'd generally had fairly low expectations when it came to a relationship, mostly because they were also traveling and living moment to moment, the way he was. He'd thought that was the kind of woman he wanted, someone who lived his life. But the women he'd been involved with had never worked out. Maybe they'd been too alike.

Ava was nothing like him. But he'd found softness, creativity, and genuine kindness behind her sharp-edged, rigid exterior. She was a woman who loved her sister deeply, who'd given up her own life for her sister in so many ways. She was also driven to succeed and had a big need for security.

He shared some of those traits. He was also driven to succeed, and he was fiercely loyal to people he loved, but he had never had a need for security. He wasn't afraid of new things; he relished them. The bigger the challenge, the more he felt engaged in life. That's partly why he surfed. He needed that thrill, that huge obstacle to get over, and Mother Nature could be aggressive and often victorious. Who better to go up against?

But over time, he'd lost interest in attending an endless number of surfing championships. He'd been there and done that. And he was tired of always being on the move. He wanted a new challenge, and he'd found one in the Beach Shack. But that challenge might be out of his hands, and it was frustrating not to have control over that.

Maybe he and Ava were a little more alike than he thought when it came to being in control. As his gaze drifted back to her, he couldn't help thinking that they'd had a very good time sharing that control last night.

Her eyes suddenly flew open, and in one second, she went from sleepy, soft, lazy Ava to an alert and hyperaware woman. She definitely did not wake up slowly.

"Good morning," he said.

She sat up, pulling the sheet over her breasts and then tucking her hair behind her ears. "Morning," she said, not quite meeting his eyes. "When did you wake up?"

"About five minutes ago."

"You should have woken me." Her gaze moved to the clock. "I have to work this morning."

"It's not late," he said. "Only seven thirty."

"That's true." She paused. "So, uh, I'm not very good at morning-after conversation. I don't actually do this a lot."

"I'm glad," he said, his words finally bringing her gaze to his. "I hope you don't have any regrets."

"How could I?" she asked with a helpless shrug and a small smile. "I'm sure you know you're very good at…well, you know what I mean."

He laughed. "You really aren't good with words the morning after. But I'll take that as a compliment. And last night I was very appreciative of your desire to be the best you can be at anything you do."

"I was enjoying the moment."

"So was I. Is the moment over?"

"I have a call at nine, and I need to shower and prepare for it."

"Okay."

"But…" she began. "Maybe there could be another moment."

"There definitely should be," he said, happy to hear she wasn't ready to end everything immediately.

As she sat there, looking a little unsure of what to do next, he realized she probably didn't want to walk around naked in front of him, which he found endearingly sweet.

"I'm going to head to my room and take a shower," he said, not at all worried about getting out of bed in front of her. In fact, he very much liked the way she looked at him now. He gave her a questioning look. "Rethinking how much time you have before your work call?"

"Yes," she admitted. "You are really attractive, Liam."

"So are you, Ava."

"But I don't have all that sculpted muscle stuff going on," she said, waving her hand at him.

He laughed. "No, you have very soft curves, and I'd like to explore them again."

"Go take your shower," she said, a slightly desperate note in her voice. "I can't miss my call. It's with my boss and the coworker who's trying to get ahead of me."

"I'm going," he said as he moved quickly toward the door. He needed a shower, and after the way she'd looked at him with naked hunger in her eyes, it needed to be a cold one.

—————

Ava's shower was filled with heated thoughts about Liam and the night they'd spent together. At times, she found herself smiling for absolutely no reason at all, except she felt happy, maybe happier than she'd been in a very long time. Even exchanging awkward morning-after conversation had been easier because it was him. Liam didn't judge her. He didn't set unreasonable expectations. He didn't question her choices. He just accepted her, and that was so unexpected, as was the gathering of emotional tears in her eyes now.

What on earth was wrong with her? She never cried. She'd learned a long time ago that crying wouldn't make any difference. She'd just end up with red eyes and a stuffy nose. Plus, people would ask her how she was. Some of them would have pity in their eyes and that would make everything worse. So, she'd gotten good at putting on a mask. It made everyone more comfortable, including herself.

But the time for introspection and happy memories was coming to an end. She needed to focus on the upcoming meeting with Dave and Jeff. They were going to update her on what had happened at the Calyx pitch, and Dave also wanted information on another company she'd just started working on. She needed to have her head together before she got online with them.

After finishing her shower, she dried her hair, put on her makeup, and a long-sleeve, button-down top over a pair of white jeans, which they wouldn't see on the video screen.

Then she headed into the kitchen to feed Miss Daisy and make some coffee. As she reached the living room, she could hear Liam in the kitchen, grinding the beans she'd brought, and she smiled to herself. He had clearly taken a faster shower than she had, and he was making coffee. The man really did have a lot of good traits.

The ring of the doorbell took her by surprise, and she whirled around. She wasn't expecting anyone. On the other hand, this was Ocean Shores. It was probably one of her new friends or neighbors dropping by.

Liam poked his head out of the kitchen. "Someone here?" he asked.

"I've got it." She opened the door to a stunningly pretty brunette, who was tall and thin, with hair that reached her waist.

She had a perfect face, too, with the whitest teeth she'd ever seen.

"I'm looking for Liam Nash," the woman said. "I heard he was here."

"Yes. He's here," she said slowly.

"Good. Can I come in?" the woman asked.

"Who are you?" she returned, not sure why she'd uttered the question, because Liam was in the apartment and, clearly, this woman knew him.

"I'm his fiancée, Britt Shelby."

Her stomach dropped. "What?"

Before the woman could reply, Liam stepped up beside her.

"Britt! What are you doing here?" he asked.

"Looking for you. You haven't been returning my calls."

"No, I haven't. So, why are you here?"

"She's your fiancée?" she asked Liam, interrupting their conversation. "You don't think you should have told me you're engaged?" Rage suddenly ran through her. She'd let this guy past her defenses. What a fool she'd been.

"Wait, Ava," Liam said as she moved past him.

But she couldn't wait. She had to get away from him before she completely lost it.

CHAPTER NINETEEN

LIAM RAN toward the bedroom door Ava had just slammed in his face. He tried the handle, but it was locked. "Ava, I need to talk to you."

"Go away, Liam."

"It's not what you think. She's not my fiancée."

"That's not exactly true," Britt said, coming up behind him.

He looked at her in anger and confusion. "Of course, it's true. We broke up almost a year ago." He turned back to the door, knocking again. "Ava, please."

"I have a call I can't miss. Please move away from the door."

He swore in frustration, then stepped back. He would make her hear him later, but she had a work call, and he needed to deal with Britt. He walked into the living room and then the kitchen, so whatever yelling was about to occur wouldn't interrupt Ava's call.

"Okay, what's this all about?" he demanded.

Britt smiled. "You look good, Liam."

He ignored that. "Why are you here? Why are you calling yourself my fiancée?"

"We were engaged."

"And then we weren't," he said pointedly.

"Maybe we should be again."

"Why?" he asked in astonishment. "Why would we get involved with each other again after everything that happened?"

"Nate told me your deal with the Beach Shack is in jeopardy, that you're bartending at Maverick's to get more cash, and that you might continue competing for the same reason."

He had no idea why Nate would have related everything they'd spoken about yesterday to his ex-fiancée. "You seem to know a lot. I can't imagine why you would be interested in what I'm doing."

"We were a popular couple, Liam. Everyone loved us. Photographers always wanted to take our photo. Sponsors wanted to do joint deals with us. We had a fairy tale romance."

"That turned into a nightmare."

"No one knows what happened between us. There's always been a romantic mystery about our breakup."

"I have no idea what you're talking about, Britt."

She gave him a calculating look, then said, "There's a producer who believes a show starring the two of us getting back together would be a phenomenal hit and bring in a lot of money for all of us."

He couldn't believe what he was hearing. "Are you out of your mind?"

"No, I'm quite sane. This could be a great deal for both of us. It's a reality TV show. All we have to do is be engaged again. For three months of filming, we'll get a house somewhere that we'll call home. We'll go out on the surfing tour, but only a few times for filming purposes. The rest of the show will focus on our daily lives—my journey to being a successful actress and your life running a cute little store on the beach where you sell surfboards and teach lost little kids how to fill their empty lives with a surfing lesson."

Despite his anger, he had to admit he was impressed with how well she'd just created that story. Although, it had probably been brewing for a while, so she'd had time to practice her pitch.

He couldn't believe she'd had the guts to come to him with such a ridiculous proposition.

But why couldn't he believe it?

It had become clear to him that while he and Britt had once had a fun, romantic relationship, she'd only gotten engaged to him because it had gotten her more media attention. Planning their wedding had given her fodder for her social media accounts, and his fan base had become hers. They'd been the golden couple of the surfing world, until he'd realized just how much she was using him and how far she would go to get what she wanted.

"I'm not interested," he told her. "You can go."

She frowned. "I knew you were going to say that, but there's a lot of money on the line, Liam. Nate said you might have to up your offer to get the Beach Shack, but you could be tapped out."

"You and Nate had a long conversation. I can't believe he's involved in this." He was surprised and angry Nate would give so much information to Britt.

"Well, actually Nate told Allie, and Allie told me," Britt admitted. "I called her yesterday to ask her how you were doing and where I could find you. She said Nate and her were having problems, and Nate had gone to see you in Oceanside. After you talked to Nate, he got on the phone with Allie to try to work things out with her. She didn't believe she was spilling secrets when she talked to me, Liam. And it's not like I've never heard about your plans to buy the Beach Shack. You were talking about that right before we broke up."

"Fine, whatever. It doesn't matter. I don't want to be involved in your scheme, so you wasted your time coming here."

"Don't answer so quickly. Think about this logically, not emotionally. You need money. And I need to be on TV. The filming will take three months at the max. Maybe we can whittle it down to two months. You only have to fake it for a short time. Then we both get everything we want."

"Two or three months pretending to be your fiancé sounds like a life sentence to me," he said grimly.

She sent him a dark look. "Well, that's kind of mean, Liam. And it's not like you to be so hateful."

"The answer is no, Britt."

"Don't just say no because you're mad at me. Think about it. I'll be at the Viceroy Hotel. Call me or come by."

"Not going to happen, Britt. You're wasting your time."

"At least let me show you the numbers. This is a fantastic opportunity, and it's an adventure. You love adventure." She paused. "You used to love me, too. Would it really be that difficult?"

Considering he barely recognized the woman standing in front of him anymore, he knew it wouldn't just be difficult, it would be impossible.

"Yes," he said. "Not to the deal. To your question as to whether it would be difficult."

"Because you still have feelings for me?"

He had to smile at that. "Because I don't have any. And I won't pretend I do."

She gave him a hurt look that was still pretty, which was why she'd make a perfect actress but a horrible fiancée. She opened her designer bag, took out a folder and put it on the kitchen table. "Look at the proposal, at how much money you will make for a very short period of your life—the blink of an eye. I think you'll change your mind." She walked to the door, then paused, giving him a thoughtful look. "Is the real problem the woman who ran into the bedroom? Because you can tell her it's fake. In fact, I might be able to carve out a cash flow for her to play along."

"You're unbelievable."

"I know what I want, and I go after it. Same as you, Liam. We're not that different. And this is a win-win for both of us."

He didn't say anything, and after a moment, she turned and

walked out of the apartment, slamming the front door behind her.

The apartment shook for the second time in less than fifteen minutes.

He walked out of the kitchen and back to Ava's bedroom door, pausing before he knocked. He could hear voices. She was already on her call. He needed to wait. And then he needed to tell her that Britt was not his fiancée and never would be again.

Ava couldn't concentrate on her team meeting. Fortunately, so far, the only person talking was Palmer Daniels about internal company policies, which made it easier to drift away, especially when there were too many thoughts clashing in her head.

She didn't know if Liam was engaged or not, but he'd never even mentioned having had a fiancée in the past, which seemed odd. But was it? They'd known each other for less than a week. Which was probably why she shouldn't have slept with him, why she should have listened to the alarm bells going off in her head, instead of ignoring them.

And Britt Shelby was ridiculously attractive, a perfect ten, with hair that could be in a shampoo commercial, teeth in a toothpaste commercial, and a supermodel runway body. Britt probably surfed, too. Ava could picture Britt running down the beach in some skimpy string bikini with all eyes on her. Of course Liam would have been involved with someone like that.

"So, Ava, we need to talk about Calyx."

At Dave's words, she refocused.

"You've done a great job on Calyx, and I know this might not be the outcome you were hoping for," Dave continued. "But now that Calyx is moving onto our books, they need a full-time manager, and Jeff will take that role."

"What?" she asked in shock. "I've been working with Calyx since the beginning."

"And you've done a fantastic job. You are great at assessing the early stages of development, which is why I need to move you onto three other start-up accounts that we're looking into. Lisa will send you the details. I know you'll do a great job developing those portfolios."

"I can do that and still work with Calyx," she said, aware of the suddenly rising discomfort of everyone else on the call, with the exception of Jeff, who looked very smug.

"The decision has been made," Dave said. "We can talk further when you get back. Now, let's move on."

Having effectively shut her down, she had no choice but to sit back and seethe as the meeting continued on to other topics. She hated having to look at Jeff's sly smile. Even worse, she hated that he'd won. He'd used her physical absence from the office to ingratiate himself with their manager and her client, one she had worked with for almost a year.

She was happy that Calyx would get the investment they wanted, because she believed in them. But it was very discouraging to see how easily she'd been replaced, not only by her manager and coworker, but also by Calyx. Why hadn't Ron said he wanted to continue working with her? She'd thought she had a good relationship with the CEO. Although, that relationship had always been formal and mostly through emails. Jeff didn't operate that way with his clients. He got them on the phone. He took them to dinner. He asked them to play golf.

She probably needed to learn how to play golf.

She probably needed to do a lot of things differently.

For the next half hour, she completely zoned out. She had always been the person listening, the one paying the most attention, working the hardest, going the extra mile, and for what? So she could get shoved back to some small start-up accounts while Jeff got to move ahead of her? She was smarter than him. She did a more thorough job, but she was still in second—the first loser.

Liam's words ringing through her head unfortunately also brought him back to mind. She couldn't let herself go too far down the anger track when it came to Liam. They hadn't known each other long. There were things she didn't know about him, things he didn't know about her.

She'd jumped into bed with him because she wanted to be with him. She wasn't going to have regrets about that. They'd had an amazing night together. She'd just felt blindsided when Britt had shown up.

In retrospect, Liam hadn't looked happy to see Britt, either. And he had tried to talk to her. Maybe Britt had lied about them still being engaged.

Did it matter? What was she even doing with Liam?

Whatever this was couldn't be more than a fling. She didn't live in this town, and she didn't even know if in another few weeks Liam would still be living here. They'd had a fun night. That was all it was.

That thought made her even more depressed and it was all she could do not to let her feelings show on her face, although Lisa kept sending her sad and angry emojis in a side chat, so she had a feeling she wasn't hiding her emotions very well. Although Lisa didn't know about Liam and his unexpected fiancée. Her hugs were all about Jeff stealing her account.

She was feeling annoyed with all men at the moment.

Finally, the meeting was over. She shut down her video screen and let out a breath. She didn't have another call for a few hours. And she needed to talk to Liam. She just wasn't sure what she wanted to say.

As she got up from her chair, her gaze caught on the bed, on the tangled covers, and a rush of memories ran through her. She told herself to be happy that the memories were great, to not have regrets, because she had chosen to live in the moment and moments didn't last forever.

She forced herself out of the bedroom to find Liam sitting on the couch with Miss Daisy on his lap. He hastily put the cat aside and got to his feet, which did not make Miss Daisy happy. She gave a hiss and then jumped off the couch and ran into the bedroom.

"I guess that's another female I've pissed off," Liam said soberly. "Britt isn't my fiancée, Ava. We broke up almost a year ago. I had no idea she was coming here."

"What did she want?"

"She had a ridiculously crazy business proposition for me."

"Business proposition?" she queried, not expecting that answer.

"Do you have time to sit down and talk about it?"

"Yes," she said as she sat down on the couch with him.

"Let me start at the beginning. Britt and I met on the beach when we were in our early twenties. She was a decent surfer but not great. She was, however, good at wearing the bikinis made by many of the sponsors."

"I bet," she muttered.

"Britt began modeling and became an influencer on social media for all kinds of beach, summer, and surfing-related products."

"She has the looks for it."

"Yes. She's very pretty," he said without a trace of emotion in his voice that she found a little surprising. "But it doesn't go deep. I found out that a lot of our relationship was just a way for her to get more attention. I had my own fan base, my own social media buzz going, and I was getting endorsements because I was winning surfing competitions."

"You're also a very attractive Australian surfer. Who wouldn't want you touting their goods?"

"I can't say I hated the money, but I didn't surf to get endorsements. It was just part of it. And I didn't get engaged to Britt because I thought we were some golden couple, who could rake in more money if we exchanged rings. Britt, however, was not on the same page. It's a long story, but eventually I saw her for who she really was, and we split up. That was a year ago."

"And what's happening now?"

"Her agent got an offer from a reality show producer who is a big surfing fan and remembered our love story. This producer wants to create a show where Britt and I get back together. I spend time on the tour while I build my business at the Beach Shack, and she models and goes for auditions for film roles."

"I can sort of see that as a show," she admitted.

"A network said the same thing. Britt gave me a proposal." He tipped his head toward the folder and loosely spread papers on the coffee table. "There's a lot of money on the line for both of us. We just have to pretend to be engaged and live together for three months while they film and then keep the pretense up for at least six months after that until the show can air. We don't have to continue living together, but neither of us can be seen dating anyone else, and they'll be feeding stories to the media about us when they get ready to launch the show."

"That's quite a deal."

"I said no. I told her there was no way I would do it."

She thought about that. "But you read the proposal after she left."

"Yes, while I was waiting for you to get off your call. I know you think I lied to you—"

"I don't," she said, cutting him off. "You didn't lie. You had no reason to tell me."

He gave her a guarded look. "Really? You seemed pretty angry before."

"I felt blindsided, but I thought about it, and we barely know each other. We had a night together. If I'd wanted your life story before that happened, I should have asked for it."

He ran a hand through his hair as he looked at her with a mix of emotions in his eyes. "Britt hasn't been a part of my life for a long time, so I didn't think to mention her."

"Really? Because I remember having a conversation where you told me about all the girls you loved starting with when you were nine, and Britt didn't come up."

"You didn't let me go that far. You said you'd heard enough," he reminded her. "You didn't need my life story."

"Still, I think you probably could have mentioned being engaged. Why didn't you?"

"To be honest, I put Britt out of my mind when our relationship ended. It was a stupid and embarrassing part of my life, that I don't like to think about. I got taken by someone I cared about, and I'd like to forget it."

"That makes sense."

"Anyway, I'm not interested in this deal."

"Are you sure? You do want to buy the Beach Shack, and it sounds like you might be able to get enough money to compete with that sporting goods chain." She paused. "Is that why you looked through the proposal?"

"It was curiosity, nothing else. There were a lot of dollar signs, but they didn't change my mind, Ava. I'm willing to do a lot to get what I want, but I'm not willing to sell my soul and pretend to be engaged for a fake television show just to get cash."

"Will Britt take no for an answer?"

"She hasn't so far. She's staying at a hotel in town, and she will try to change my mind. Britt is stubborn and determined when she wants something. And she wants this."

"Did she ask you who I was?"

"She didn't ask, but she did tell me that if you were going to be a problem, she could carve out an income for you, too."

Her eyes widened in surprise. "Seriously? She would pay me off?"

"To be quiet about the fact that it's all a sham—yes. She would definitely do that."

"It's amazing what some people are willing to do to get ahead." She wasn't just thinking about Britt. She was also thinking about Jeff and how easily he'd gotten her demoted just because she'd taken a few remote working days.

"It's unbelievable," he agreed. Pausing, he added, "Do you

really believe I would have spent the night with you if I was engaged?"

She hesitated. "I don't know."

Disappointment ran through his gaze. "I thought you knew me better than that."

"It's been a little less than a week, Liam."

"We've spent a lot of time together. We've talked a lot, Ava."

Now she felt like she was in the wrong. "But in all that talking, you never mentioned Britt. Is it really that surprising that I'm not completely sure who you are? I don't think you know who I really am, either."

He shook his head. "Don't do that."

"Do what?"

"Start rewriting our history."

"We don't have a history. We have six days."

"That's a history. And I do know who you are—at least the important things. And one thing I know is that when you get scared, you run, you hide, and you pretend you don't care and that something doesn't matter. And I don't want you to do that now—not with us."

His words hit their target because he had nailed her defense mechanisms so accurately. And that made her more scared. How on earth had she let him get to know her so well?

"I should go back to work," she said.

"Or you could not run away, and we could keep talking."

She hated that she was about to prove him right, but her instinct for self-preservation was just too strong. "I have responsibilities. I'll talk to you later." She returned to her bedroom and closed the door.

As she sat down at her desk and stared at her dark screen, she felt an intense wave of anger. It wasn't toward him; it was toward herself. She had run. She was hiding out, and she was going to pretend that she didn't care enough about their relationship to keep talking about it.

But they didn't have a relationship. They'd had a night. And, yes, maybe a great week of getting to know each other. She had done more with him in a few days than she'd done with other people in six months. And she couldn't imagine what it would feel like not to see him every day.

But she was soon going to find out. Because whatever was going on between them had always had an expiration date. Maybe that date had just been moved up, but it had always been there.

"Damn," she muttered aloud. Why was she so good at rationalizing and running away, and so bad at taking risks and going after what she wanted? Why couldn't she be as brave and fearless as Liam? Hell, why couldn't she be as ballsy as Britt, who was willing to ask the guy who broke up with her to get engaged again so she could be on TV? Britt certainly hadn't let fear stop her.

She suddenly got to her feet. She needed to stop hiding. Before she could think more about it, she opened the door and left her bedroom. "Liam," she called.

There was no answer, and the silence in the apartment was deafening. She had a feeling she'd missed her chance.

But her chance to do what? Talk to him again? Or did she want more?

Of course she wanted more, but not even her newly found courage would allow her to declare exactly what she wanted a chance to do. That felt like too big of a risk, because the logical part of her brain told her there was no good ending in sight. And it was just as well he was gone. Better to be a little unhappy now than a lot unhappy later.

Wasn't that what she always told herself? But today it didn't make her feel better at all.

CHAPTER TWENTY

LIAM DID what he always did when his life was filled with turmoil. He took his stress to the beach. He was an hour into surfing, or he should say paddleboarding, because the waves were barely there, when he saw a familiar figure paddling toward him.

"On a scale of one to ten, with ten being the highest," Nate said, as he drew close to him, "how much do you want to punch me in the face right now?"

"Fifty-seven," he replied.

Nate sat up on his board. "I didn't tell Britt where you were, but I did tell Allie. I called her after we spoke yesterday, and we hashed things out. During our conversation, she asked about you and your business plans. I didn't know she was going to tell Britt any of it. But Allie gets kind of flustered around Britt. She has this weird admiration, idolization thing going with Britt."

"It's fine. I don't really care. But you might have given me a heads-up."

"Allie didn't tell me until about an hour ago. I've been calling you."

"I've been here."

"I figured. What did Britt want?"

"Allie didn't tell you?"

"Allie didn't know. Britt said it was a secret for now, but she needed to talk to you as soon as possible, and that you would want to hear what she had to say."

"Well, I didn't want to hear it. She wants me to pretend to be her fiancé for a reality TV show. It's a crazy idea, but apparently a lucrative one."

"That is wild. I can't imagine a person less able to pretend to be something he's not than you. And I mean that in a good way. What did you tell her?"

"I said no, but she left me the proposal to look at, which I did, out of curiosity."

"And…"

"The answer is still no."

"Just playing devil's advocate for a second. How lucrative are we talking? Would it allow you to raise your offer for the Beach Shack?"

"Yes. But I'd rather lose that deal than get involved with Britt again."

"You hate her that much?"

"I don't hate her. I don't feel anything."

Nate stared back at him. "Okay then."

"What happened with you and Allie? Are you still breaking up?"

"Not at the moment. She admitted that she jumped off the cliff ahead of me in terms of marriage and babies, but that it was something she wanted. I need to figure out if there will be a point in my life where I'll want the same. If there's no possibility, then she doesn't want to be in a relationship with me."

"Is there a possibility you'll want to settle down and marry her and have kids?" he asked, thinking that was a stretch for someone like Nate, who really loved being free.

"It gives me hives to think about taking all that on," Nate admitted.

"You and Allie have been together for a long time. Will anything really change?"

"It feels like everything will change. We're good right now. I like the way we are. But marriage and kids...my parents couldn't get through all that. They divorced when I was six, and my siblings and I were put through hell for years, going back and forth, having to pick sides, trying to make the other one feel like they were the best parent. I wouldn't want to put my kids through that."

"You're not even married, much less getting a divorce, and you don't have any kids. You are looking too far down the road, Nate."

"Do you ever look down that road, Liam?" Nate challenged.

"I did when I got engaged to Britt. Since then, no."

"Britt did a number on your head."

"Maybe when it first happened. But she's not in my head or my heart anymore."

"Glad to hear that. So, there's no one you're interested now?" Nate asked. "Not even your hot roommate?"

"I don't want to talk about Ava." His feelings about her were too confusing and too unsettling to discuss. He liked her—a lot. But time was running out on them, and he didn't know what to do about that.

Late Friday afternoon, Ava heard the doorbell ring. Liam still wasn't back, so she headed to the door with some trepidation. It turned out that foreboding feeling was right on the money, as she once again stared into the beautiful face of Britt Shelby.

"Hello again," Britt said. "Is Liam here?"

"No. And I don't know when he'll be back. Try his phone. I'm sure you have the number."

As she started to close the door, Britt stuck her foot out. "Wait. We got off to a bad start this morning."

"I don't think we got off to anything," she said curtly.

"I shouldn't have said I was Liam's fiancée. I'm not."

"He said you broke up almost a year ago."

"That's true. Did he tell you about the reality show project I brought to him?"

"He mentioned it."

"Can I come in and talk to you? Just for a few minutes," Britt said, throwing another dazzling smile in her direction.

She had a feeling that what Britt wanted, Britt got. And while she felt absolutely no compunction to have a conversation with her, she was slightly curious about what she might have to say. "Fine. Come in."

Britt walked into the apartment with a confident smile, as if she'd already won something, although Ava couldn't imagine what that would be.

Britt took the armchair, so Ava sat on the edge of the couch, feeling wary and uncomfortable. She didn't know why she had to be involved in any of this, but, somehow, she was.

"So, you and Liam?" Britt began.

Ava couldn't begin to answer that question, so instead, she said, "What do you want?"

"I want you to understand this project wouldn't affect your relationship with Liam."

"How is that possible? He'd be on television, pretending to be your fiancé."

"That would just be for the cameras. You would have to keep your relationship private, but it wouldn't be forever, and it would be very lucrative for Liam and also for you."

"This deal is between you and him. I don't need to be involved."

"He cares about you; I can tell. And if you're good with it, I think he will be, too."

"You're giving me too much credit. I don't have any influence over Liam."

Britt stared back at her for a moment, then said, "Liam is a really good man. We started out as friends before it turned into more. But I hurt him, and I feel badly about that."

"Is there a point to this?" she interrupted. "Because I don't need to know your story."

"The point is that I didn't treat Liam well, and I want to make it up to him. I know how much he wants to own the Beach Shack and he needs cash. I have a proposition that will get him that money. It's just a fun reality show. No one takes those seriously, and I'll really be the focus, so Liam doesn't have to do much. He just has to be around, and we have to pretend to be engaged. That's it."

"He already told you no. I don't know what you want me to say."

"He said no because he doesn't want to mess up whatever he has going with you."

"I don't believe I'm a factor in his decision," she countered. "He doesn't want to pretend to be someone's fiancé. He doesn't want to go on TV and put forward a fake story. He's not that kind of man. You must know that. You were engaged to him."

"He can be too ethical," Britt said. "But this isn't like lying; it's just acting, putting on a show and making a lot of money. What's three months when you consider the return? I have talked to the producer, and they'd be willing to pay you a fee for going along with the pretense."

"That's not necessary. Liam and I are not a couple. He can do whatever he wants."

"I saw the way he looked at you."

"You mistook whatever you think you saw. But you should talk to Liam about all this, not me. I don't want to be involved." She got to her feet. "If there's nothing else…"

Britt slowly rose, then said, "You keep saying there's nothing between you, but when you mention his name, your voice catches a little."

"You have a big imagination. Liam doesn't look at me a

certain way and my voice does not catch when I talk about him," she argued.

"I'm not imagining anything. But I will talk to Liam, and if you're truly not going to be a problem, then I hope you'll let him know."

"That won't matter. Liam makes up his own mind." She walked to the door and opened it.

Britt moved toward her, pausing once more. "I think owning the Beach Shack would make Liam happy. Seems like you might want him to be happy, too."

"You never stop pushing, do you?" She was truly amazed by how persistent Britt was.

"How else will I get what I want?" Britt asked.

"Why don't you just do the show yourself if you're going to be the star anyway?"

"Because the executive producer has a crush on Liam, and she says romantic couples always sell better."

Did everyone in the world have a crush on Liam? It certainly felt that way. "Well, good luck."

"I don't need luck; I need your help. At least encourage Liam to think about it. He can be so stubborn and narrow-minded sometimes. There's a bigger picture that could work for all of us."

"But you most of all," she said pointedly.

Britt shrugged unapologetically. "Well, I'm doing the work, so I deserve the extra time and cash. We'll talk soon."

"I don't think so." She gently pushed Britt onto the landing.

After closing the door, she leaned against it, thinking about their conversation. Britt was bigger than life—beautiful, athletic, vibrant, and confident. She was so sure of herself. She would never let anyone get one up on her. And she'd never stop asking for what she wanted.

She felt like a pale shadow next to Britt. They were certainly nothing alike. Opposites in every way. And yet Liam had obviously been attracted to both of them. She didn't know what to make of that.

Did it even matter? She wasn't in a relationship with Liam. And Britt was probably just trying to manipulate her by suggesting she could read something in Liam's eyes and her voice. That was just silly.

The door suddenly opened, and she stumbled forward as Liam came into the room, giving her a questioning look.

"Were you leaning on the door?" he asked.

"Yes."

"Why?"

"Because your ex-fiancée just left, and I was getting my bearings."

"Oh. I didn't see Britt. But I understand the getting your bearings part," he said dryly. "She can be a lot. What did she want?"

"She wanted me to convince you to do the show. She made it clear how much you'll both benefit from it. She's not giving up, Liam."

"She can do it by herself. I just went to her hotel to tell her that. I left her proposal at the front desk with a note saying I was not interested."

"I doubt that will stop her from coming back for another conversation. She's very determined. She also said her producer has a crush on you, so she definitely wants you in the show."

"Whatever. I said no, and that won't change. What are you doing tonight?"

"I—I don't know," she said, surprised by the sudden change in topic.

"I ran into my friend, Nate, at the beach. He's going to bring over some pizza. I'd really like you to join us, Ava."

"You don't need me to join in. You should spend time with him on your own."

"We've spent enough time together. He'd like to get to know you."

"Why?" The word burst through her lips before she could stop it.

Liam stared back at her. "Because I like you, Ava, and because Nate is my friend."

"Isn't he also Britt's friend?"

"He is, or he was, but we won't be talking about Britt."

"Britt is beautiful and very bold. I can see why you fell for her."

"She's not pretty at all to me anymore," he said.

"How can that be?" she asked doubtfully.

"I don't see her looks; I see who she is, and there's no beauty on the inside. I don't want to waste time talking about her. Will you please join me and Nate for pizza? I really want you to."

She felt helpless under the direct onslaught of his smile and the look of desire in his eyes. "Okay. I'll join you."

"Good." He stepped forward, putting his hands on her shoulders. "I'm sorry our morning after went the way it did, because I didn't have a chance to tell you how much I enjoyed last night."

"I enjoyed it, too," she murmured. "But…"

He groaned. "No *buts*."

"We can't do it again, Liam. I'm leaving next week, and our lives will be in different cities, going in different directions."

"We have time together now. Why waste it because there's an end in sight?"

Before she could answer, there was a knock at the door, followed by a loud, booming voice.

"Pizza delivery," Nate said.

Liam let go of her hands. "I'm going to ask that question again later."

He could ask the question again, but hopefully she wouldn't change her answer, because it would be smarter and far less risky to stop fooling around with him and just go back to being roommates.

The pizza and conversation with Nate were more fun than she'd imagined. Nate was a fun-loving guy with a million stories about Liam, all of which were entertaining. Having met as teenagers, they'd lived wild lives growing up on surfboards and traveling the world.

They'd snuck into bars, slept on beaches, and probably made out with a million girls. Nate shared that Liam had been a superstar surfer all his life, and that it was usually Nate who came in second, not Liam. Watching the banter fly back and forth between them brought a wave of jealousy at their long friendship, and a wistfulness for friends she'd let go a long time ago.

After her parents had passed away, she and Serena had had to leave their home and their friends to start over in a new city. She hadn't wanted to open herself up, to get close to people, to share her feelings. So, her friendships were fun but surface-level. With her work friends, she talked about work. With friends she'd made while running or working out, she talked about exercise and fitness. She'd told herself what she had was enough, but since coming to Ocean Shores, she'd begun to question that.

The women she'd met here were all friendly and interested in her. And the guys were as well, especially Liam, who had gotten her to open up to him in ways that still scared her.

But she would be returning back to her life soon, and she was starting to wonder if that life would be enough. Work wasn't going well, and her apartment building was filled with strangers.

What was she doing with her life? Why hadn't she realized before now she needed more than just her sister in her life?

"I think Ava has heard enough of our stories," Liam said, interrupting her thoughts. "Sorry to bore you."

"I haven't been bored," she said quickly. "You two have had amazing experiences. I'm jealous."

"We've had some good times," Liam agreed.

"I should probably go," Nate said. "I need to be on my game to beat you tomorrow, Liam. It's been some time since we went head-to-head. I'm looking forward to it. I'm glad you decided to enter."

She started at Nate's words. "You're competing tomorrow, Liam?" she asked in surprise. "I thought you were done with that."

"There was a last-minute opening in the field, and I decided to take it," he replied. "While I'm waiting for John to make up his mind, I might as well see if I can make some cash."

"You should come, Ava," Nate said. "See this guy in action. Unfortunately, for me, my shot at the top prize went down as soon as he entered. But it will still be fun to go against each other."

"It will be," Liam agreed. "And probably for the last time."

"We'll see," Nate said with a knowing smile. "I'm not sure you'll ever want to give it all the way up. You're too good."

She wasn't sure of that, either.

"I hope to see you tomorrow, Ava," Nate continued. "If not, it was great to meet you."

"You, too." She got to her feet as Liam walked Nate to the door.

When Nate was gone, Liam turned to her with a hot gleam in his eyes.

"You should probably get some rest if you don't want to lose to Nate tomorrow," she said hastily.

He walked toward her. "I'm not tired. Are you?"

She wasn't, but she really should say she was. "It's not a good idea, Liam."

"I disagree. Being together with you is a great idea."

"Isn't there some rule about not having sex before a competition?"

He laughed. "On the surfing tour, absolutely not. What else have you got?"

"It's complicated." She desperately searched for a good reason to say no.

"I want to be with you, Ava. Do you want to be with me?"

"It's not that simple. I can't just keep living in the moment, Liam. It's not who I am."

"Maybe it is who you are now, just not who you used to be." He leaned in and gave her a slow, gentle, exploring kiss that gave her plenty of opportunity to pull away, to say no, to go to her room, but she wanted to do none of those things. She just wanted to savor the taste of his mouth. And if it all went bad in the morning or three days from now, at least she'd have one more night.

"Okay," she said. "But if you fall off your surfboard tomorrow because you're too tired, don't blame me."

He smiled. "If that's why I fall, it will be totally worth it."

CHAPTER TWENTY-ONE

AVA DROVE herself to the surfing competition in San Diego around eight since Liam had gotten up at seven to head down there, and she wasn't entirely sure she should go. In the end, she couldn't stay away. She wanted to see him in action. Although, she didn't know how well he was going to compete, because they hadn't gotten a lot of sleep last night. But he'd seemed in good spirits when he'd kissed her goodbye and said he hoped to see her there.

She'd been noncommittal about attending, which he'd taken in stride, apparently getting used to her saying "I don't know" when invited to do something. She really did need to break that bad habit.

When she got to the beach, all the parking lots were jammed, so she had to park about a half mile away and walk back.

There was a festive atmosphere and energy on the wide sandy beach, with a platform set up for the judges, and a registration table for competitors, as well as several tents and booths selling food, drinks, apparel, and surfboards.

It seemed like the kind of place a business like the Beach Shack should be at, she thought, as she moved through the crowd. That was probably something Liam would do if he was able to get the business. Maybe today would bring good news on two fronts: a win here, and a win with John Peterman.

She took off her sweater as the sun hit her face. It was already warm for half past eight, with the sun bright in the blue sky, shimmering off very sizable waves that made the waves she'd surfed look like swells in a bathtub.

There were already surfers out in the water. She wondered if Liam was one of them.

"Hey, Ava," a woman said.

She turned to see Lexie moving toward her, camera in hand, a smile on her face, her brown hair pulled up in a ponytail. "Hi," she said, happy to see a friendly face. "Are you photographing the event?"

"Not officially, but I thought it would be good to shoot photos and build my portfolio. Are you here to see Liam?"

"Yes. But I'm not sure where he is, or if he's already in the ocean. Have they started the competition yet?"

"The first heat starts in five minutes. Each heat gets twenty minutes to perform. Liam is going out later, I think. I just saw him with his friend, Nate." Lexie turned her head. "Oh, there he is."

As Lexie pointed to Liam who was standing in a group with Nate and a female surfer—who wasn't Britt, thank goodness—he turned around and saw them. His gaze instantly fixed on hers, a smile spreading across his face as he walked toward her. Lexie was saying something to her, but all she could see was him.

He was so damned attractive, she thought, especially seeing him bare-chested, wearing only a pair of board shorts that rode his narrow hips. He was fit and tan and powerful, and her stomach clenched as she remembered tracing all those muscles with her fingers, feeling all that power inside of her. Heat ran through her, and she felt a little sweaty as he joined them.

"You came," he said.

"I did," she replied, feeling her cheeks warming as they looked at each other.

"Why don't I get a photo of the two of you?" Lexie stepped back to take a quick snap. "Get a little closer."

"Happily," Liam muttered as he put his arm around her and pulled her closer to him. "I'd like to kiss you right now."

"That will get the gossip flying at Ocean Shores."

"Who cares? Never mind, I know," he said with a teasing smile as he let go of her. "You care."

Maybe she did or maybe she didn't. She was tired of caring so much about so many things that probably didn't matter.

"I'm going to take some more shots," Lexie said. "I'll catch up with you, Ava, when Liam goes out."

"Sounds good." After Lexie left, she turned to him. "So, when is it your turn?"

"Nate and I are in the second heat. It starts in twenty minutes."

"How do they decide who wins?" she asked.

"There's a complicated scoring system based on the length of the ride, the size of the wave, and the maneuvers made."

"What kind of maneuvers?"

"Cutbacks, aerials, barrels."

She looked at him in confusion. "Aerials—you're airborne?"

He smiled. "Yep."

"As if riding a monster wave isn't enough."

"It's not enough if I want to win," he said with a smile.

"Well, you better win, because I didn't come all the way down here to see you be the first loser."

"There's some motivation." He looked around, then stole a quick kiss. "I'm glad you're here."

"I wanted to see you in your element, doing your thing."

"It might be the last time."

"Really?" She waved her hand around the beach. "There's a lot of excitement here. I can feel it, and I don't even surf. It must get you going, too."

"The ocean gets me going more than all this, but it is fun."

"Do you surf more than one heat?"

"Yes. My division has three heats. The top two surfers in each heat then compete in the finals." He paused, his gaze narrowing.

She turned her head to see what had put the frown on his face and saw Britt making her way across the beach like a queen pausing every now and then to talk to her royal subjects.

"She does know how to make an entrance," she said, watching a group of teenage girls in bikinis run up to her to pose for a photo, which Britt happily obliged.

"Excuse me," someone said. She turned her head to see a young boy with a hat and a pen, looking up at Liam with adoration in his eyes. "Could you autograph this for me?" he asked.

"Sure." Liam squatted down. "Who's it to?"

"Joshua. My dad says you're the best surfer of all time."

"Well, thanks," Liam said as he signed the hat. "Is your dad here?"

The little boy pointed to a stocky man standing a few feet away. "I got it, Dad," he said proudly.

His father gave him a thumbs-up. Liam waved to the dad, who seemed a bit shocked to have gotten any recognition at all. And then the little boy ran back to his father to show off his hat.

"The best of all time, huh?" she said. "I think you've downplayed your career to me."

"That was an exaggeration. But I am good, Ava."

She laughed at his words. "I'm sure you are. You don't lack confidence, that's for sure."

"I am confident about surfing, not necessarily about everything else, but don't tell anyone. It would ruin my image."

She liked that he could make himself somewhat vulnerable to her, because she'd certainly done the same for him.

"Get ready, Ava," Liam said, his smile vanishing.

"For...?" She didn't have to finish her sentence because Britt was right there.

"Hello," Britt said, shocking Ava with a hug that she hadn't expected. And then Britt turned to Liam, who suffered an awkward hug as photographers snapped photos of them.

Britt really was smart, Ava thought, hugging her first to make it look like they were all friends, but making sure to get a photo with Liam. Although, his irritated expression probably wasn't helping Britt's cause.

"Don't do that again," he told her. "Don't set me up."

"It was just a hug and a picture. No big deal. Good luck today." She paused. "Oh, sorry, I forgot how much you hate thinking there's any luck involved. So, I'll say, do your best. I think it's about time for you to hit the water. I'll keep Ava company."

"Actually," she said, "I have a friend here, so I'll see you both later." Irritated with the way Britt was trying to control every-thing, she impulsively walked over to Liam and gave him a kiss, gossip be damned. She felt a little foolish after she did it. She didn't know why she'd felt the need to stake a claim, because she certainly didn't have a claim on him, but it was nice to stick it to Britt. Unfortunately, it didn't matter, because Britt had already walked away, and the photographers had followed her.

"I expect a bigger kiss when I win," Liam told her.

"We'll see," she said.

He laughed. "Well, that's a nice change from I don't know, even though it means the same thing. I liked that you stuck it to Britt."

"I don't know why I did. It was silly."

"Whatever your reason, I liked it."

And she liked him. "I want to say good luck, but I guess that's taboo."

"No, it's not. Not from you."

"Well, just to be safe, I'll say I hope you win. And be careful." She felt stupid for adding those words on, because the last thing Liam was going to do out there was to be careful.

"I'll see you soon." He kissed her again and then jogged down the beach.

She saw Britt watching her as she held court a few feet away, a thoughtful and possibly worried expression on her face. Maybe she was finally starting to realize that when Liam had said no, he meant it.

For the next twenty minutes, she wandered around the event, perusing cute bathing suits, tote bags, and sunglasses. But when she heard the announcer call Liam's heat, she walked over to the makeshift stands and climbed to the top row to get the best view she could.

All the surfers were in wet suits now, and from her distance, she couldn't quite make out which one was Liam. But then the announcers called off their names in order, and she kept her gaze focused on him. There wasn't a lot of action at first. Everyone seemed to be waiting, and then finally someone took off. That person started out strong, then spun off the board in the middle of a turn and landed in the water.

"That wasn't good," Lexie said as she sat down next to her.

"It wasn't Liam."

"I know. He's too good for that. At least, that's what I've heard. Brad and Tyler have raved about his surfing skills many times."

"He's going now," she said, her nerves jumping as Liam chose the next wave. "That's a big one."

"That will get him more points," Lexie said. "The higher the difficulty, the better the score."

"And the better chance of getting hurt," she muttered, silently hoping it would all go well.

"He's doing a great job," Lexie put in.

She had no idea what the moves he was making were called, but his form did seem good, and he rode the wave all the way to the end.

"That's going to be a good score," Lexie predicted.

She turned toward the scoring table to see Liam's score posted on the digital board. It was high enough to put him in first place. "He's ahead," she said with delight.

Lexie smiled, a new gleam in her brown eyes. "You like him, don't you?"

"Yes," she admitted, tired of pretending otherwise. "But I'll be leaving soon."

"Do you have to? Are you sure you can't talk your boss into letting you work remote permanently?"

"I'm absolutely positive I can't do that."

"Too bad. I don't know Liam that well, but what I know is impressive. When I first met him, I thought he'd be cocky, but he's really not."

"No, he's not," she agreed. "He's really down-to-earth."

"I hope he gets the Beach Shack. Would he leave town if he doesn't get it?"

"I don't know."

"Maybe he'd go to LA," Lexie suggested.

"I don't think so," she said quickly.

"You never know."

"Well, I don't want to wish for that because he really wants that store, and he's worked hard to get it. I hope it happens for him." She didn't know why she felt so emotional at the end of her sentence. Maybe because this conversation was making her very aware of how little time they had left. But she had to stay in the moment, just enjoy where she was. She turned her gaze back to the ocean. "Are the waves getting bigger?"

"I think so," Lexie said as they both watched a monster wave rise out of the sea and come crashing down. No one in the current heat, including Liam, had chosen to ride that wave, and Ava was happy about that. But she was less happy about the next wave beginning to build. "Do they ever bring the surfers in if it gets too rough?"

"I don't know. I haven't been to that many competitions," Lexie said. "I'm sure Liam will be fine. He knows what to do out there."

"Right. Of course he does." But she couldn't help thinking that Liam had a lot of motivation to stay out there. There was prize money on the line, maybe enough cash to help him buy the Beach Shack if John raised the price. Not that she thought it was worth more, but there was always an intangible value when the buyer was extremely motivated to go all in.

Over the next ten minutes, she saw surfers charge the intensifying waves, most of them crashing out at some point, but Liam and one other guy were able to complete a second ride.

"How long do they stay out there?" she muttered, wanting Liam out of that crashing white water as soon as possible. She'd enjoyed going surfing with him. She'd loved the challenge and being in the water, but this competition felt like it had turned into a death-defying challenge and the thought of Liam getting hurt filled her with a dread she couldn't shake.

"I think they have five more minutes," Lexie said. "He's done well with two good rides."

"But he's in second. He hates second place. He'll go again."

"Well, that is what this is about," Lexie said with a sympathetic smile. "I'm sure he's fine, Ava."

"You must think I'm silly to be worried. I just don't want anything to happen to him."

"I'd probably be worried, too, if it was my boyfriend out there."

"He's not my boyfriend," she said, not sure why she felt the need to argue that point.

The announcer came over the loudspeaker to let the surfers know they had two more minutes.

"Oh, God," she murmured as probably the biggest wave of the day began to gather force and she saw Liam was going to take it on. She hoped it would all come together: his timing, his balance, his strength and power. But this was the ocean—unpredictable, ferocious, unforgiving. She felt suddenly sick to her stomach. She wanted to look away, but she couldn't.

Miraculously, Liam was on his feet, riding the wave, but sometimes barely visible as the rolling break almost covered him.

"He's doing it," Lexie said excitedly. "I think he's going to make it."

She bit down on her lip so hard she tasted blood. He was almost there. So close. She held her breath as he finished the ride to a crescendo of cheers from the crowd.

And then the heat was over.

Liam's score was huge, and he was in first place. She wanted to feel happy, but all she felt was sick to her stomach, the fear of losing him drowning out every other feeling. Because she knew there would be a final heat. He wasn't done. He would go back out there and do it all again.

"Let's congratulate him," Lexie said, jumping to her feet.

"I'll be right there," she said tightly.

"Are you okay, Ava?"

"Yes. I'm fine. I just need a second."

"Okay. Do you want me to wait?"

"No. Get a photo of him coming in. I'd love to see that."

"I will."

As Lexie left, she drew in a few deep breaths and let them out. The fear she'd just lived through had reminded her of all the terrifying days she'd had since her parents died. After their shocking and unexpected crash, she'd foretold numerous tragedies happening to her or to her sister, worrying about one of them ending up alone, without anyone.

And now she was worrying about a man who made his living in a fight to the finish with Mother Nature, and she couldn't handle it.

She got up and moved down the stands and then started walking away. She didn't want to ruin his moment, his victory, but she couldn't face him right now. And she couldn't watch him do it all again. She moved faster until she was out of the parking lot and on the sidewalk.

And then she heard a shout behind her and saw Liam coming after her.

For a moment, she considered running so he couldn't catch her. But he probably would catch her, and the two of them would look ridiculous. With all the photographers around, the last thing she wanted was a scene.

"Where are you going?" Liam asked when he caught up to her. "There's still another heat to go."

"I—I—" She shook her head, unable to find the words. "I just have to go. Congratulations. You did great." She gave him a tight smile. "First place."

"So far. What's wrong, Ava?" he asked, his gaze searching hers.

"Nothing. I'm happy for you. I just have to go."

"Why?"

"Please just go and get ready for your next heat." She felt desperate to get away from him.

"Not until you tell me why you're upset. Did Britt bother you again?"

"No. It was the ocean. Those waves were huge. You could have died," she bit out. "That monster wave could have crushed you."

"It didn't. I'm okay. I knew what I was doing."

"Knowing what you're doing and being able to fight the ocean are two different things. You're not a superhero. You're not stronger than the sea."

"It was a risk, but that's what this competition is about. Frankly, I've ridden bigger waves."

"Right, of course you have. That makes me feel so much better. I'll see you later."

He grabbed her arm. "You were that worried about me?"

"How could I not be?" she asked. "I know this is what you do, and you love it, and it's exciting and all that. But I didn't realize until just now how dangerous it really is. I could have..." She couldn't let herself finish that sentence.

"You could have what?" he pressed.

"You know I have a lot of fears and one of them is tied to death, to tragic accidents, to losing people I care about. They aren't rational fears, but that doesn't stop me from feeling them, and I can't do this. I can't watch you risk your life. I'm sorry. I have to go, Liam."

"I won't go out again. I'll go home with you."

She shook her head. "No. This is your life. And I don't want to stop you from winning that prize. I just can't watch it. Please, just let me go."

He looked like he wanted to argue, but then he said, "Okay. We'll talk later."

She nodded in relief. Her emotions were all over the map, and he probably thought she was a lunatic. Maybe it was good they'd both finally realized how different they were. It would make it easier to say goodbye.

Or maybe they'd just done that.

CHAPTER TWENTY-TWO

LIAM COULD BARELY CONCENTRATE on the competition, his mind swirling with thoughts about Ava. He'd been surprised by the level of worry in her eyes, the desperation in her voice. She'd practically been shaking from fear at the thought of him being crushed by a wave. It was an extreme reaction but one he probably should have seen coming, because she was definitely riddled with anxiety when it came to losing people in her life. He just hadn't realized he meant that much to her.

Or maybe that wasn't even true. Maybe she'd have been that worried about anyone she knew, because her fears were never far away.

He'd wanted to take her in his arms and reassure her, make her feel less scared, less alone, but she hadn't wanted that. She'd just wanted to leave. He was quite sure by the time he saw her again, she'd be acting like it was not a big deal. But he'd seen the truth. And they were going to talk about it.

First, he had to make all of this worthwhile. Since he'd stayed, he was going to try to win. He just had to get his head in the game and focus.

Nate had also made it into the final heat and as they paddled out, Nate gave him a questioning thumbs-up. Nate had tried to talk to him when he'd returned to the beach, but he'd brushed him off. He hadn't wanted to get into it then, and he didn't want to get into it now. He sent him back a thumbs-up. He was okay, and he was going to win.

An hour later, he'd made good on that promise with a first-place finish and a check for ten thousand dollars in his hand. It took him another thirty minutes to make his way through the crowd, accepting congratulations from competitors and bystanders before finally getting to the parking lot.

After he put his board into the back of his rented SUV, he let out a breath and took another look at the ocean, at the event that was still going on with the juniors now in action.

This had been his life for so long, and today was a good day. He'd done what he came to do. He'd won the cash prize. He should feel good. And he did, but not the way he used to. These competitions were never going to fill the hole inside of him, and today was just confirmation of that. He needed more.

He needed his business deal to go through. And he needed to talk to a woman he couldn't stop thinking about.

"Liam."

Britt's voice made him groan. He hadn't seen her in a while and was hoping she'd left, but obviously she had not. When he turned around, he was surprised to see she was alone, no photographers in her wake. There was also an uncertainty in her eyes that reminded him of the girl he'd first met, the one who was pretty and sweet and a little lonely, because her divorced parents didn't care much about what she was doing. But that girl had disappeared a long time ago, replaced by a cunning, ruthless, determined woman who would use anyone to get ahead. And he couldn't let himself forget that.

"How many more times do I have to say no?" he asked wearily.

"Zero," she replied.

He raised a brow. "You finally accept my answer?"

"I have to. You're in love with someone else."

He stiffened at her words. "I don't know if I'd call it that."

"Oh, come on, Liam. I know what you look like when you love someone, because you used to love me until I ruined it."

He couldn't deny that she had ruined it, so he didn't even try.

She waited a few more seconds, then added, "I didn't realize there was anyone else in the picture, someone you wouldn't want to hurt with a fake engagement. All I could see was a way for both of us to get what we wanted. I really did believe there was enough for you in this deal to make it worthwhile."

"Even if there was no one else in the picture, I would have still said no. I don't want to pretend, Britt, especially not with you. It's still hard to accept how very unreal our relationship actually was."

"It wasn't all fake, Liam. You know I cared about you. I just wanted more. Ever since I was a little girl, I wanted to be somebody. I wanted attention. I wanted to matter."

He knew where those needs came from, but he still didn't approve of the steps she'd taken to fill those needs. "Well, I hope you get what you want, but leave me out of it."

"I just wish you didn't hate me."

"I don't hate you. I don't feel anything."

She paled at his words, pretty little tears gathering in her eyes that meant absolutely nothing to him, because they were as fake as she was. He felt like the luckiest man alive for never having married her.

"That was harsh," she said.

"Goodbye, Britt."

He walked around his vehicle, opened the door, and got behind the wheel. Britt was still standing nearby when he pulled out of the parking lot, but he didn't look at her, and he was barely a block away when he stopped thinking about her. There was only one woman he wanted to look at, talk to, and think about. And that was Ava.

Liam got back to Ocean Shores around two o'clock, and the apartment was ridiculously quiet. He knew immediately that Ava was gone, and when he walked into her bedroom, that thought was quickly confirmed. The suitcase she'd had next to the closet was gone. The workstation she'd set up on the desk had been dismantled. The bed was neatly made. It was almost as if she'd never been there, they'd never made love in this room, and all that had happened between them had just been erased.

His gut clenched as he returned to the living room, seeing Miss Daisy giving him a curious gaze as he reentered the room.

"Why didn't you stop her, Miss Daisy?"

The cat lowered her head and went back to sleep. He knew why the cat hadn't stopped her from leaving, because he'd already proved he could take care of Miss Daisy on his own. He probably shouldn't have done that. He'd made it easier for her to leave.

But he was pissed that she'd left without saying a word. Why did she have to run? He hadn't hurt her. He hadn't used her. He'd just ridden a big wave, and her reaction was too much.

Realistically, he knew it wasn't just the wave that had scared her; it was Ava realizing how much she cared about him and wanting to protect herself. She probably wished they'd never started anything, but he didn't wish that, because he liked her. He liked her a lot. And maybe Britt hadn't been all wrong in suggesting he might even love Ava.

That thought made his heart race. After what had happened with Britt, he wasn't sure he could ever trust that emotion again. But Ava wouldn't use him, not the way Britt had. Ava wasn't fake. She was very real and when she let down her huge guard walls, she was sweet and vulnerable and passionate. She was also super intelligent, and he liked that about her, too.

What he didn't like was that she was gone.

Pacing around the apartment, he made his way into the kitchen, his heart skipping a beat when he saw the note pinned to the refrigerator door with a magnet, his name scrawled across the front.

He took the note down and slowly unfolded the piece of paper. He didn't want to read her words, but he knew he had to. He also knew they were probably going to sting.

Liam—I'm sorry, but I had to leave. We only had a few days left anyway. I need to get back to my life and to my job. I had a really good time with you. You're an amazing person, and I hope you get the Beach Shack. I know you'll make it a huge success. I owe you a lot. You changed my life in a few short days. I experienced more with you this past week than I have in a long time. I'll never forget my surfing lessons, the way you encouraged me to believe in myself and to take a risk. But we're going in different directions, and I need to say goodbye now. I wish you the best. I really do. Ava

He sat down at the table as he read the letter a few more times, wishing for a different outcome. It was a nice blow-off, probably one of the nicest he'd ever gotten. And how typical of Ava to write it down instead of sending a text or an email. This felt more personal, even though it still felt bad.

On the other hand, maybe she'd written the note because he couldn't respond to it like he would have been able to do with a text or an email.

Not that he still couldn't send her a message. He took out his phone and opened the app. He stared at it for a couple of long minutes and then put it down.

What could he say? *Come back for three more days and then we'll say goodbye again?*

How would that work? Their lives were in different cities, at least for now. Who knew what was going to happen with the Beach Shack? He might have lost Ava and the deal.

He jumped as his phone suddenly vibrated on the table, and John Peterman's name ran across the screen. It looked like he was about to find out if he'd lost the deal or not.

"John," he said as he took the call.

"Hello, Liam."

"Do you have an update?"

"Yes, I do," John said. "I'll sell you the store if you can come up ten thousand dollars."

The exact amount of money he'd just won. He wondered if John didn't know that.

"What about the other buyer?"

"I'd rather sell to you. My attorney can meet us at two o'clock on Monday to sign the papers. What do you say?"

"Yes. I say yes," he said, pushing all of his misgivings out of his head. "I'll meet you at two."

A mix of emotions ran through him as he set down the phone. He should be happy. He'd won the competition, which gave him the money to pay more. He'd made the deal.

But Ava was gone.

And buying the Beach Shack meant setting up his life here, two hours away from hers. She wasn't going to move, and he wouldn't be able to move.

The reality hit him hard.

He could have everything he'd wanted and been working toward for the past year, but he couldn't have her, too, and that sucked.

CHAPTER TWENTY-THREE

MONDAY MORNING AVA was back in her office, and it felt like nothing had changed. Her desk was the same. Her cubicle was the same. She had picked up the same matcha latte on her way into work, said hello to Lisa, and then settled in at her computer. After a long, restless Sunday, hoping and dreading she'd get a text or a call from Liam, which had never come, she'd been looking forward to starting her work week, but now that it was here, she didn't feel any better than she had yesterday.

It was difficult to concentrate on research or meetings, and even running out to grab a sandwich at lunchtime in the bright sunshine hadn't lifted her spirits. Now it was almost two, and she still had a few hours of work to get through before she could go home and probably feel even more depressed.

She'd said goodbye to Liam in her note and she hadn't wanted him to get in touch, but a small part of her had wondered if he would argue that they still had time. Maybe he would have even suggested coming to LA for a few days until his life got settled in Oceanside.

She should be happy he hadn't reached out. Any contact would only be temporary, and she needed to get used to being alone again: no apartment building filled with new friends, no cozy bar where she'd find someone she knew whenever she stopped in, no hot surfer challenging her in so many ways to open her eyes, open up her life.

"Ava?" Lisa said as she came over to her cubicle.

Lisa was a dark-eyed brunette with a quiet personality and a strong work ethic, much like herself.

"Am I interrupting?" Lisa asked.

"No. I could use a break. How are you?"

"Honestly, last week was awful without you here. I had to watch Jeff ingratiate himself into Dave's life, and it was sickening. The way they took Calyx away from you made me so angry. How are you feeling about it all?"

She should be feeling angrier than she was, but instead she just couldn't seem to find the will to care. "It's done. There's nothing I can do about it."

"I guess not, but I hate to see Jeff win."

"He'll have a lot more work now, so it's not a total win. I definitely won't be helping him."

Lisa gave her an uncertain look. "I wouldn't be so sure about that. I think Jeff might be angling to get you on his team as a support person."

"That's below my level. We have plenty of support people."

"You know the company better than he does."

"I don't think Dave would go for that. He gave me some new companies to look at."

"All small start-ups," Lisa pointed out.

"Well, one of them might hit it big," she said, trying to be positive. "I'll have another chance to prove myself, to get promoted."

"It should have happened already. You're one of the smartest people here, Ava, but you don't play the game as well as some others."

"Because I don't play games. I do the work, and it should speak for itself."

"I would like to believe that, but I don't know," Lisa said. "Anyway, I'm glad you're back. Should we do lunch tomorrow?"

"That sounds good."

Lisa turned to leave, then paused. "Why did you come back early? You weren't supposed to return until Thursday."

"Someone else was able to take care of my sister's cat, and I didn't like what was going on here."

"That was smart. Taking that week remote set you back. Who knows what other damage could have happened in the next three days?"

Lisa's words ran through her head after she'd left her cubicle. She should have been able to take a remote week without losing her biggest client and without having to worry about her job getting taken away. She'd been a loyal employee. She never took time off. She always did what was asked and beyond, and she never complained.

Now it felt like none of that had mattered or would matter going forward. She was someone they could count on but not someone they wanted to promote. Maybe it was time she faced that fact. Perhaps there was nowhere else to go at the company.

Moving on was a risk. She'd lose all her seniority, all the time put in. But if that seniority and time didn't matter, what was she hanging on to?

Being at Ocean Shores, surrounded by people who were chasing their dreams had made her see her life differently. And it wasn't just Liam attempting to change his life; it was Lexie who had given up the law to be a photographer, and Max who tended bar while he wrote screenplays on the side, and Gabe who had opened a food truck until he could get his own restaurant.

Her sister might not have found a career awakening in Oceanside, but she had found a man she loved and adored, and she'd made it to Paris for her honeymoon. Everyone else was taking risks, but she was still playing it safe.

As she sat back in her chair, she thought about her two surfing lessons, about how Liam had told her that choosing the right wave was about preparation and insight but then also about the guts to follow your instincts, to bet on yourself.

She'd never bet on herself. But she had bet on other people. Maybe it was time to stop being a spectator and start surfing her own life. She smiled at the thought. Liam had rubbed off on her in so many good ways. She couldn't regret the time they'd spent together. She'd never forget him. He was an amazing man. And she wanted to be as amazing as he was.

Her watch vibrated with a reminder for her meeting with Dave. She got up with a new resolve in her heart. Maybe she would just tell Dave how she was feeling and see if she could get anything changed.

Unfortunately, when she entered Dave's office, her resolve faltered when she saw Jeff.

"Come in," Dave said as she hesitated.

"I can wait if you want to finish up with Jeff," she told him.

"No. Sit down. I have some news for you."

Judging by the smug look on Jeff's face, she had a feeling she was not going to like that news. "What's going on?"

"I'd like to move you to Jeff's new team," Dave said. "You'll be able to work together on Calyx, which I know you would like to do, so this should work out well. Lisa will also be on the team, but I haven't had a chance to speak to her yet."

She stared at him in disbelief. So many emotions were running through her head, she could barely keep up with them. Her stomach was churning, her pulse was racing, and she felt like she was going to blow up. This was the time when she always talked herself down, told herself to be patient, that her time would come, that this was just a setback, and she should keep her eye on the long-term goal of stability and a secure future.

Screw that!

"No," she said.

"No?" Dave asked in surprise, raising a brow. "You don't want Lisa on the team?"

"I don't want to work for Jeff," she said flatly. "I've been here five years longer than him. I know Calyx better than he does, as well as just about every other company we've worked on the past two years."

"You're very good at your job," Dave said, taken aback by her words. "But Jeff came with experience from another company."

She didn't bother to look at Jeff. "I know exactly what his experience was and what his level of intelligence and capability are now. I also know he went behind my back to steal my account—"

"I didn't do that," Jeff interrupted. "You need to calm down, Ava."

She sent him a steely glare. "Don't tell me to calm down, Jeff. Don't speak to me again."

"Hey, that lack of respect is not going to fly on my team," Jeff said.

"I'm not going to be on your team." She drew in a breath, feeling like she was about to jump off a cliff, but she kept on going. Looking back at Dave, she said, "If Jeff is the one you want to be a manager and run a team, then I quit."

"I don't like ultimatums," Dave said, anger in his voice. "You should think about what you're saying, Ava."

"I don't have to think about it. I'm not going to work for Jeff."

"Then you won't work for this company," Dave said. "This is your last chance to take your words back, and I'm only giving it to you because you've been a good employee, and clearly you're upset."

She let his words stay in the air, mostly because the silence seemed to make them both uncomfortable, and that she could appreciate. "I am one of the best employees you have ever had. But you don't appreciate my work, so there's nothing more to say." She got to her feet.

"You can't just quit, Ava," Jeff said, probably realizing he was going to have a lot of work to do without her help. "Maybe you can get a money bump to make this feel more palatable."

"That's possible," Dave said slowly. "But I don't like to reward threats."

"It wasn't a threat, Dave," she said. "And we don't need to negotiate. I know my worth, and you don't."

"At least give us a month's notice," Jeff said. "You have information on Calyx that I need to get up to speed on."

"No." She shook her head. "You wanted the job, so do it. I'm leaving now." She walked out of the office with her head held high, but she was still shaking when she got to her cubicle. She grabbed the few personal items she had in her desk and put them in her bag. Then she headed for the elevator.

Lisa caught up with her there. "What's happening? Where are you going?" she asked.

"Dave wanted me to work for Jeff. So, I quit."

"You quit?" Lisa asked in shock. "But what about your long-term plans, your determination to work as long as it took to get what you wanted?"

"Out the window," she said with a shrug. As the elevator doors opened, she said, "We'll talk later this week. Give me a call."

"Are you going to be okay, Ava?"

She smiled, suddenly feeling a huge weight slipping off her shoulders. "I'm going to be amazing."

———

Liam stared at the papers in front of him as he sat in the conference room with John and his attorney. The original purchase price had been crossed out, with ten thousand dollars added on. He knew he was getting screwed. But was he willing to lose this deal for an extra ten thousand when he had the money in hand?

The question ran around in his head as he flashed back on Ava talking to him about being blinded by emotion, not seeing the true value of something, not having a backup plan or enough capital to operate. How he'd blown past every red flag because he wanted something too much.

Was he making the right decision to move forward now? Was he acting on emotion when he should be acting on logic?

"Why aren't you signing the contract?" John asked.

He lifted his gaze to John's. "Because this is wrong."

"It's not wrong. It's what we agreed to. I need to take Maggie on that cruise, and I know you have the money now."

"Because I won the competition on Saturday."

"Yes. You're getting what you want. And I'm getting what I want."

"Was there ever another buyer, John?"

"Of course there was," John sputtered. "And they're still out there. If you don't sign this, I'll go straight to them, and you'll lose out."

John looked nervous, although he did look better than the last time he'd seen him. He was clean shaven, his eyes were clear, and he had good color in his face. His clothes were clean and unwrinkled. And he was sober.

He had no idea what had happened with John and Maggie. He'd spent Sunday in the water or on the beach, trying to distract himself from thinking about Ava. He'd thought about contacting her a million times. But she'd made it clear she didn't want to hear from him.

And what would he even say? He was about to buy a business that would keep him in Oceanside, and Ava was committed to her career. She wasn't going to leave her job for a man she'd known for a week. That was not her personality. She was thoughtful. She was a planner, and she didn't deviate from her plans, at least not for long. He'd gotten her off the path for a few days, but as soon as she'd felt out of control, she'd taken off.

He wished they could have had more time. Even if they would have still ended up here, he would have liked to spend the days they had left together. They'd started out as hostile roommates, but they'd ended up as so much more, and he missed her.

John's lawyer cleared his throat. "Is there a problem?" he asked.

"Yes," he said, making a decision he should have made a long time ago. "I can't pay you the extra ten thousand dollars, John."

"I don't understand. You have the money."

"That's not the point. I'm already paying more than the store is worth. We both know that. And I'll need money to operate, to make improvements in the business."

"Well, I can't do the deal if you won't pay my price."

"Then we can't do the deal," he said, meeting John's gaze head-on. "We had an agreement. I'm willing to honor that. But I won't go higher."

"You're willing to lose the store for ten thousand dollars?"

"I am. So, I'm going to ask you the same question. Are you willing to lose the deal for that amount of money?"

Ava didn't know what to do with herself. After leaving the office, she'd gone home and dropped off her things. Then she'd taken a long walk and stopped to pick up groceries on the way home. After cooking herself a very expensive piece of halibut and making a salad to go with it, she'd opened a bottle of even more expensive champagne, a completely ridiculous purchase, but she'd wanted to celebrate her freedom.

She might have made a big mistake quitting her job without another, but she was trying not to think too far ahead. She'd been saving her money for years. She had a nest egg. She would be okay. She'd planned for just this kind of possibility.

Well, she hadn't planned for quitting, but she had planned for ending up without a job and needing to be able to survive on her savings. She'd be okay. She'd find another position.

And tonight, she would just enjoy an evening with no responsibilities, no work looming over her head.

No matter what happened down the road, she wouldn't regret walking away from her job. She'd worked too hard to just lay down and let them walk all over her. She'd known for far longer than she wanted to admit that she wasn't being valued, and she'd finally done something about it.

She didn't know if that would have happened if she hadn't gone to Ocean Shores, if she hadn't found a new perspective and met a man who'd seen through her defenses and challenged her to want more, to do more.

Her eyes filled with moisture as she thought about Liam. She told herself that every day she'd think about him less, but right now that seemed like an impossible feat.

As she wandered aimlessly around her apartment, she couldn't help thinking how different it was from Serena's place. It was bigger and some would say better, with its brick walls, industrial-style windows and thick wood beams. Her floors were hardwood. Her furniture dark-brown leather. Her space was always clean and organized. There was no cranky cat needing food or medicine. There were no nosy neighbors. She'd thought it was pretty close to perfect until she'd spent a week at Ocean Shores, until she'd realized than an orderly and safe life was not all that she wanted.

Her doorbell rang, and she practically jumped out of her skin. No one rang her bell unless she was getting a delivery, and she hadn't ordered anything in a long time. Maybe someone had hit the wrong buzzer, because nobody just dropped by.

She got up and moved toward the intercom. "Yes?"

"It's Liam."

Her breath caught in her chest. "What are you doing here?"

"Let me in, and I'll tell you."

She really wanted to let him in. She also wanted to make him go. Seeing him again would only make saying goodbye a second time that much more difficult.

"Ava, please," he said. "I'm not leaving. I'll stand here all night if I have to."

She released the front door lock and stepped back to check her appearance in the mirror. She'd thrown on leggings and a T-shirt when she'd gotten home, and she didn't look sexy at all. But there was no time to change. She ran her hand through her hair and then heard a knock at her door.

She tried to get herself ready to see him again. She would be cool and calm.

As soon as she opened the door, that resolve went out the window, and she instantly felt hot and bothered. He looked so good in dark jeans and a short-sleeve polo shirt. His face showed a bit of a sunburn. His green eyes were bright and purposeful. Whatever he'd come here to do, he was definitely going to do it.

She swallowed hard. "What do you want, Liam?"

"I needed to see you, Ava." He pushed past her and walked into her apartment. Then he turned to face her. "Why did you leave without saying goodbye?"

"I said goodbye in my note."

"You didn't give me a chance to say goodbye to you."

"I was afraid you'd try to talk to me into staying until Wednesday when Serena comes home." She suddenly started. "You left Miss Daisy to come here. What about her medicine?"

"I gave it to her before I left. The cat is fine."

"Okay. Did you really come all the way here to say goodbye?"

"I have a few more things to add," he replied. "John offered to sell me the store. I went to sign the papers today. The price was ten thousand dollars more than we agreed on, the exact amount I won on Saturday."

"Well, that's good, isn't it?" she asked, not seeing the joy in his eyes she would have expected.

"No, it wasn't good because he was taking advantage of me, and worse, I was letting him. I was blinded by my goal. I was overlooking red flags. I was operating without a backup plan, and the extra money would strip me of capital I would need to move forward. Someone really smart made me see that."

"But you were fine with all that before. You said a backup plan only stops people from taking risks."

"Well, I was wrong. You made me realize I was acting on emotion."

"Did you really turn him down?" she asked, shocked by that idea. "You wanted the store so much, and you had the money."

"I couldn't move forward, knowing it was wrong. I told him I'd buy the business at my original price, or he could move on."

"And?" she asked, unable to read from his expression exactly what had happened.

"He argued for a while, and then he said yes."

"Oh, my God! So, you got the store?" She paused, searching his gaze. "Why aren't you happier?"

"Because I realized I couldn't have the store and you at the same time."

Her heart turned over at his words.

"I don't want this to be over, Ava," he continued. "I came up with some ideas on the drive here, and I think you should hear me out. We can do long distance for a while. We can meet up every other weekend. I'll come here. You'll come there. It's only a two-hour drive. It's not impossible for us to get together. Once I get the store running, I'll hire an employee. I can turn my weekends into long weekends. We can make it work."

She was completely shocked by his plans. "All this from a guy who likes to live in the moment?"

"Yes, because I can't have the moments I want with you unless I plan for them. What do you think?" He gave her an expectant look that held more uneasy tension than she would have expected.

"I don't think any of that will work," she said.

His face fell. "Seriously? You're not willing to even try?"

"Your plans won't work because I don't think I'll be staying in LA. I quit my job today."

Now it was his turn to be surprised. "You quit your job? Why?"

"Because I'd had enough. I was getting screwed over, too. I told my boss and my slimy coworker off, and then I quit without giving any notice."

"How did that feel?"

"It felt great. Of course, after I left the office, I started to doubt myself, but I know I did the right thing. I've been playing it safe for too long. You pushed me to get out of my comfort zone, to believe in myself, and I finally did. I am currently unemployed, and a little terrified, but I feel freer than I have in a long time. And that's because of you, Liam."

"You always had it in you, Ava. I knew that."

"You knew it before I did. I want more time with you, too, even though I'm still scared."

"I don't have to compete anymore. You won't have to watch me take on monster waves, if you're worried about that."

"It wasn't just the waves that terrified me, Liam. It was how much I cared about you. I don't like people very fast, much less fall in love with them. When I thought you could die, I realized how much I care about you. It made me panic."

"I saw that."

"So, I did what I always do—I ran away and tried to hide somewhere safe, get my life back into its normal routine. But that didn't work. I've missed you like crazy, and it's only been two days."

"I've missed you, too."

"I don't want to just feel safe anymore. I want to feel all the other emotions. I want to focus on being alive instead of worrying about death overtaking me or someone I love. I am kind of messed up from what happened to my parents. I know that. I just have trouble getting past it. But I want to keep trying."

"I'm glad. And I want to feel all the feelings, too," he said. "Does this mean you might come back to Ocean Shores?"

"Definitely. And we don't have to jump into anything. We can just see where things go. I'm not asking you to make me any promises." She wanted to be clear about that.

"What if I want to jump? What if I suggest we get an apartment together at Ocean Shores? What do you think about that? And don't say 'I don't know,'" he warned.

She smiled. "I won't say that, because I do know. I want to jump, too. And we were pretty good roommates, so I think we have a shot at making it."

He grinned back at her. "More than a shot. I'm falling in love with you, too, Ava. And envisioning a future where I never got to see you again was scary for me as well."

"You don't get scared of anything."

"That spooked me," he said with heartfelt sincerity. "I wasn't looking for love. I wasn't even sure I could trust that emotion again."

"Because of what Britt did?"

"More because I didn't see it coming. That bothered me. I thought I knew her, but I didn't."

"I would never use you, Liam."

"I know that, Ava."

"Good," she said. "But we don't know each other that well. Maybe we're mistaking lust for love."

"I don't think that's true. While we do have great chemistry, I also like talking to you about life, business, everything. You are so smart. Your brain is like a calculator."

"That doesn't sound very sexy," she complained. "You just called me a calculator."

He laughed. "That came out wrong. I'm awed by your brain. I'm fascinated by your body, and I'm in love with the person who is so tough on the outside and so wonderfully warm and kind and caring on the inside. I'm smarter because I met you. How's that?"

Her eyes filled with moisture. "Much better. And I want you to know that I'm braver because I met you."

"We did rub off on each other."

"We did."

"And if you need a job, you could work for me at the Beach Shack. The pay is awful. In fact, it will be nonexistent, and the work will be boring, but I'd love to have you on my team."

"That I don't know about," she said with a laugh. "But everything else, yes. I'm ready to ride this wave wherever it takes us and see what happens."

"That was good, Ava."

"I know. I'm talking in surfing metaphors and feeling hopelessly romantic, which is not like me at all. My sister will think I lost my mind."

"No. She'll think the magic of Ocean Shores worked exactly the way she wanted."

"Probably," she admitted. "I'm sure she thought it would be fun to set us up."

"Maybe Brad thought the same thing. But no matter how it started, I like where we are now, and where we're going."

She smiled at him, filled with a joy that was so overwhelming she felt like she was bursting with happiness. "Me, too. By the way, what happened with John and Maggie?"

"He told me that they're still talking. But nothing has been decided."

"Well, it's good they're talking. Maybe they'll finally figure out what's best for both of them without the sale of the store being part of it."

"I hope so."

"So, when do you want to go back to Ocean Shores?" she asked.

"Josie said she'd feed Miss Daisy in the morning, so we don't have to get back until tomorrow night. I'm not in a hurry. Are you?"

"No. I suddenly feel like we have all the time in the world."

"That's exactly what we have," he said, his green eyes bright and sparkling. "I'd like to see more of your apartment, maybe starting with your bedroom."

She drew in a breath as excited tingles ran down her spine. "My bedroom might be too far away, because I am dying to kiss you right now."

"I feel the same way," he said, putting his hands on her hips as he drew her up against him. "And I don't plan on stopping any time soon."

"I'm going to hold you to that," she said as she threw her arms around his neck, and their mouths met in a passionate, promising kiss.

WHAT TO READ NEXT...

Are you excited to go back to Ocean Shores?

Don't miss the next book in the series, Summer Loving!

For a complete list of books, visit Barbara's website!

ABOUT THE AUTHOR

Barbara Freethy is a #1 New York Times Bestselling Author of 89 novels ranging from contemporary romance to romantic suspense and women's fiction. With over 13 million copies sold, thirty-three of Barbara's books have appeared on the New York Times and USA Today Bestseller Lists, including SUMMER SECRETS which hit #1 on the New York Times!

Known for her emotional and compelling stories of love, family, mystery and romance, Barbara enjoys writing about ordinary people caught up in extraordinary adventures. Library Journal says, "Freethy has a gift for creating unforgettable characters."

For additional information, please visit Barbara's website at www.barbarafreethy.com.

Made in United States
North Haven, CT
06 May 2024

52144385R00157